Praise for *When the Birds Stop Singing*

"When an author can bring you seamlessly to another time it is truly a gift to the reader. Dwain L. Herndon does just that in his book *When the Birds Stop Singing*. I read approximately 25 books a year and it is definitely in my top five for 2014. The story takes place in rural Kentucky during the age of Prohibition. When you read this book you get to face everything: young love, intrigue, racism, secrets, murder, small town politics, and northern views—southern views regarding how we saw each other then. The characters are very well developed and the area is so well described you can almost hear the whippoorwills. When I had to put the book down I was excited to return to it as the mystery unfolded. Best of all, I couldn't predict the outcome, and that's rare! Congratulations, Mr. Herndon, this one is a winner."

– Elbie Ancona, former New Yorker now living in Atlanta

"This book turned out to be most riveting. It's very good with meaningful, well-developed characters and a plot that makes you anxious to turn to the next page. I truly enjoyed the book. It's a good read. I recommend it to anyone who enjoys a good page turner."

– Patricia Gates, suburban Atlanta

"*When the Birds Stop Singing* is an appealing story set in rural Kentucky during Prohibition. Mr. Herndon has brought to life well-developed characters from another era. His protagonist, Nick Kincaid, defies his father and follows his dream to become a teacher by leaving Chicago and moving to Kentucky. This carefully crafted story keeps the reader turning pages. Who was the killer? Whose baby was found in the woodbin? Who is trying to take over the whiskey business? Does Nick ever get his girl? The characters are engaging and the plot keeps shifting with ever turn of a page. I truly enjoyed the book."

– Mary Bowman, Lilburn, Georgia

Praise for Dwain L. Herndon's previous book
Beyond the Next Hill

"*Beyond the Next Hill* is a remarkable story of redemption, love, and the desire for one man to put to rest the ghosts of his past. Tyler Bracken comes across as real, down-to-earth, the kind of man who has made too many mistakes and knows it. When given the chance to right some of those wrongs, it's riveting to watch the character make the choices he does, some wise, some not. That's what makes Tyler (along with the rest of the characters) so compelling to this reader.

"Written in a very readable prose with vivid descriptions of both the characters and the area of Kentucky where the story is set, you will find this story hard to put down. It's gritty and emotional, a truly excellent debut novel."

> – Jana Oliver, award-winning author of the
> *Time Rover Series* and the *Demon Trapper Series*

"If you've ever hoped for a second chance in life, this book is for you. Tyler Bracken, the hero in the story, is a little rough around the edges, a little crude, and swings more temper than a boxer with an attitude. But underneath it all is a caring heart that's just waiting for a reason to come out.

"Dwain L. Herndon paints the small Kentucky town with all the warmth and kick of Southern whiskey. You can't help but fall in love with the characters. Forthright Molly, rebellious Luke, warmhearted Lindy, and my personal favorite, the sheriff. But it's not all down home appeal as the story unfolds the elements of an unexpected crime and people wrongly accused. Get ready to curl up with the book and just keep reading. I loved this story!"

> – Nanette Littlestone, award-winning author and
> publisher of *F.A.I.T.H. – Finding Answers in the Heart*

"I could not put this book down! I loved every beautifully crafted word in *Beyond the Next Hill*. The author's ability to turn a catchy phrase put vivid pictures in my head and made my experience more like watching a film than read a book. His characters are both realistic and enduring. I was engaged from the first sentence to the last."

> – Colleen Walsh Fong, Ezine.com expert and
> author of the touchscreen *Easy Weekly Meals* series

When the Birds Stop Singing

Dwain L. Herndon

WORDS OF PASSION • ATLANTA

Published by Words of Passion, Duluth, GA 30097.

Editor: Nanette Littlestone
Cover: KV Herndon
Interior Design: Nanette Littlestone and Peter Hildebrandt

ISBN-10: 0996070915
ISBN-13: 978-0-9960709-1-1

To my wife, Yvonne, whose great grandparents, Ed and Annie McCoy, owned the grist mill and country store. The story goes that he was Baptist and she was Catholic. They resolved their differences by building a Methodist church, from which the community got its name.

Acknowledgments

The story and characters in *When the Birds Stop Singing* are fiction, with no intended resemblance to persons living or dead. But the setting for the story is real. During Prohibition, in 1926, a narrow strip of land between the Tennessee and Cumberland Rivers was home for a close-knit community, somewhat isolated because of its geography. Woodson Chapel consisted of a grist mill, grocery store, church, and school. I first visited there as a young teacher in 1959 and was to later meet a few warm, friendly, fun-loving families who related stories about how life was between the rivers during Prohibition. When I developed the storyline for *When the Birds Stop Singing*, I knew it had to take place at Woodson Chapel.

Special thanks go to my writing buddies: Nanette Littlestone with Words of Passion, Colleen Fong, Aarti Nayar, Jana Oliver, and Teresa Bueno, all published authors. One or more of these fine writers have critiqued each chapter in the book. I also have to mention someone very special, my daughter Kim, known professionally as KV Herndon, for the book cover design.

Prologue

A strange cry snapped Ella Peterson from a light sleep. She sat up and listened but heard nothing. It didn't sound like her husband snoring. Besides, an earlier poke in the ribs had ended that. It could have been an animal . . . maybe a young bobcat lost from its mama. Frank mentioned seeing tracks near the hen house.

Ella fell back on the pillow, glad that she'd fastened the chicken house door last night. Her husband rolled over and reached for her. She gently pushed his arm away and sat up.

"Honey, you know I don't do no messin' around in daylight."

"Damn, Ella, does it have to be planned like a hog killin'?"

She giggled and slipped off the bed into floppy shoes. Her once petite figure had taken on thirty pounds since her marriage twelve years before. She no longer allowed Frank to see her nude and went behind the door to change out of her gown. Another cry brought her head around the door with both arms cradling her breasts. "Frank, did you hear it that time?"

"I heard somethin'. Most likely it's the old mammy cat comin' in heat. I'd say a tom is tryin' to get at her."

1

He flung back the patchwork quilt, yawned and stretched his six-foot frame, muscular and fit from years of work at the sawmill. "Me and that old tom's got the same thing on our minds this mornin'."

Ella giggled. "Don't sound like the tom is gettin' his way either. Baby, you know I only like to do it in the dark anymore. You can come scratchin' around tonight."

"Why not now and tonight too?"

She laughed. "Then you'd have reason to start bragging about two times a day after all these years together." Ella emerged from behind the door and rolled a wad of frizzled brown hair into a bun and secured it with a rubber band. She peered out the window. No cats could be seen in the backyard or in the area down the hill near the stables. "What kind of animal sounds like a baby?"

Frank answered in the middle of a yawn. "A lot of them, I'd think."

Frank built the modest tin-roofed house on the hill with a clear view of the Cumberland River the year before their marriage. Morning fog hugged the river like down on a swan's back, and the pink sky above looked as soft as cotton candy. "The Lord has sent us a nice day," Ella said. On the way downstairs she walked by the bed and tickled Frank's foot. He laughed as both legs shot up in the air. "Stop that."

Ella giggled again. "We're havin' eggs, sausage, and biscuits for breakfast. No oats until Boyd gets some in at the store. He's plum out."

Loose treads on the stairs answered each step as Ella descended into the small kitchen. She placed a handful of fine kindling on top of two kerosene-soaked corncobs and tossed in a match. A flame sent shadows racing across the ceiling.

The strange sound came again and much louder. It didn't sound like wind, but she cracked the door and listened anyway. Leaves on the trees were barely moving, so it couldn't be the wind.

The kindling had caught and Ella went behind the stove for wood. Frank always placed a few sticks there each night even in good weather to help her out. He'd forgotten. She would tease him about that, she decided on her way out the back door.

Foxhounds in the pen by the smokehouse scampered forward and lined the fence, whining and begging for kitchen scraps. They were barking and carrying on like crazy a couple of hours ago. There would be no leftover gravy and biscuits today. The biscuits were going into a bread pudding for supper.

Ella raised the woodbin's top and saw movement inside. She dropped the lid and jumped back, thinking a varmint was trapped. She started to call Frank, but he'd tease her if a big opossum crawled out. She peeked inside again and screamed at the top of her voice.

Frank must have taken the steps two at a time by the way the house vibrated. He shot out the door wearing a faded union suit and carrying his rifle.

Ella pointed toward the woodbin. "It's . . . a baby."

Frank leaned the gun against the wall and opened the woodbin. He gently lifted the infant up in his arms. The baby whimpered as Ella pulled the blanket aside. "It's a girl baby." She took the child and looked up at Frank as tears gathered. "I've prayed for a baby. The Good Lord sent us one just like Moses in the Bible."

"Moses was a boy," Frank said.

"That don't matter. We've been blessed just the same."

3

Frank leaned close and peered at the child. He frowned. "Ella, we can't keep this baby."

"Sure we can. The person who left her don't want her. She's a gift from God to make up for all the babies I've lost."

"We don't need trouble. There's the law to think about."

"Nothin' is higher than God's law. He sent me this baby."

"Honey, we've got to report her."

"No, Frank, we ain't reportin' nothin'. We're keepin' her."

"Ella, I understand why you want to keep her. But how would we explain her?"

"Explain her? She's a baby. That explains her."

He threw his hands in the air and spun around. "For God's sake, are you blind? How can you even think about keepin' her?"

"We can tell people I had her. Tell Boyd and Loretta. You know my sister's mouth. Everybody will believe I had this baby. Look at my belly. I look like I've been carryin' a baby for years."

"Your sister will know better. Everybody will."

"Loretta is gonna know what we want her to know."

"Damn it, Ella, look at her hair, her lips."

"Oh, my Lord, Frank, lots of people have full lips."

"Ella, sweetheart, it's a colored baby."

"No, no, this baby's white, just like me."

"Damn it, woman, look at her. She's colored."

Ella pressed her cheek against the baby's head and hugged her close.

Frank waited. He finally whispered, "Ella, honey, come on. It won't work."

She looked up with teary eyes. "Maybe she's a little colored, but it's not enough to tell. Besides, a little white lie ain't gonna hurt nobody."

1

A passing L train jarred Nick awake. It was moving day and the anticipation of starting a new phase of his life brought him out of bed. In two hours he'd be on a train heading south with nothing but excitement and adventure in his future. He was finally going to become a teacher, something he'd dreamed about for years.

The walls of his room were stripped bare of all childhood memorabilia, including his Sox pennants. Some had been there since grade school, nearly as long as he'd had the old rickety bookcase that appeared ready to collapse now that it was empty. His mom had purchased it at a neighborhood rummage sale and the two brought it home balanced on a little red wagon. Giggles and laughter had echoed throughout the house as the two wrestled it up the narrow stairs to the bedroom shared with two older brothers. There was always laughter with his mother, but less so with his dad.

A familiar sadness settled in as his eyes rested on a four-inch-wide floor-to-ceiling board. His father had tacked it on the wall when Nick's oldest brother was born. A different colored marker recorded each brother's age and height on their birthdays. Between birthdays, awards and achievements in sports were noted. Damon stopped at six-feet-four inches and was considered the best overall athlete, with Melvin not far behind at six-three. Nick was given the title of runt by the family and stood five-feet two with only one sports award. He would have beaten both brothers hands down if his father had counted scholastic accomplishments.

His brothers and every other kid on the south side of Chicago had found humor in teasing and calling him runt, bookworm, and mama's boy—all terms that suggested he was different or less than the next fellow in every way.

Kincaid's footsteps on the stairs snapped Nick back to the present. Everyone called Nick's dad Kincaid, even his sons.

"We need to talk," Kincaid announced as he shot into the room without as much as a tap on the door. He dropped down on the edge of the bed, winded from the climb.

Nick suspected his father was there to make a last-minute effort to keep him from moving down South. Nick waited for him to speak.

"Couldn't sleep much last night," the old man muttered. He yawned and rubbed his shoulder. "My arm ached like hell."

"Maybe too much lifting at work," Nick offered.

"No, it's age in my bones." He glanced at Nick then folded hairy arms and cleared his throat. "All I could think about last night was you and my old man. Do you remember him?"

"Just a little."

"He got me a job with him when I married your mother. I was seventeen. It helped me put a lot of bad feelings toward him behind me. I did the same for your two brothers, and it felt like I was giving them a future. I thought I'd be doing the same for you. Even after college I was sure you and Liz—"

"That isn't going to happen, Kincaid."

"You did like her, didn't you? She was damn good looking."

"Yeah, I liked her, but it would never work with us."

"What was wrong with her?"

"Nothing, we just don't like the same things. Besides, I got tired looking up at her chin. She was a head taller than me."

"What's so damn funny?"

"It's really not funny. I just like to be as tall as the girl I date." He turned and climbed into his pants.

Kincaid cleared his throat. "Short or tall, who cares, but maybe being a teacher does. Guys down at the plant said teaching is a woman's job. It could give the wrong impression. You don't want that."

"Are you concerned about my manhood?"

"Damn it, why are you always trying to be funny? Your manhood had nothing to do with it. It just makes sense to stay here with family and find work instead of going down South where people don't know you. I've heard people are different down there. Besides, Liz's old man would give you a good paying job. Think about it, Nick, you and Liz. Her old man's got money."

"Oh, God, that's too much . . . to marry for money. Is that what you're asking?"

"What's wrong with me wanting the best for my boys?"

"Marrying Liz is not best for me. I wouldn't do right by her."

"What do you mean by that? You did like her."

"Not enough to marry her for money or any other reason. I'd cheat on her like my brothers do to their wives."

"I've never cheated on your mother in my life."

"Good for you, Kincaid. When I marry, I won't either."

"Your brothers love their wives."

"Maybe, but to me love suggests trust and loyalty, something they don't practice."

Kincaid released a rush of air. "I give up. You're just different. It's your mom's fault. She babied you . . . always had your head stuck in a book. It kept you from being like other boys."

"I'm not other boys. I've learned to be me. I'm short, love books, and want to teach school. That doesn't mean I'm queer."

Kincaid jumped to his feet. "I never said that. I never thought that."

"Yes, you did. You worried about me liking books and music."

"No, I never worried about you being that way. You've always been a man's man. Your proudest moment was when you won that state boxing championship for your weight class."

"No, Kincaid, I hated boxing. It makes no sense to beat a man to a pulp for no reason. I agreed to join the boxing team because runts are fair game to get their asses kicked. I needed to be in a position to protect mine. I'm going to Kentucky to be a teacher because that's what I want to do with my life. What's wrong with that?"

Kincaid stared, red-faced for a moment. He jumped up and hurried toward the door.

"Wait," Nick called. He crossed to the old man. "I don't want to fight with you before I leave." He reached to hug his father.

Kincaid broke loose and pulled away. "For God's sake, what are you doing?"

Nick turned away and grabbed his shirt. "Nothing, I guess," he muttered, feeling the brunt of the rejection.

Kincaid shot out the door.

Nick finished dressing and hurried downstairs. He slipped into a seat across the table from Kincaid who had his head buried in the sports section of the Tribune. His mother turned from the stove and smiled. A tall vase stood in the center of the small table with a single red rose cut from the backyard. Nick couldn't remember the table without a fresh flower when in season or an artificial one at other times. It said much about the gentle woman who'd mothered three sons and answered the bidding of a demanding husband.

Kathleen placed a mug of coffee in front of Nick and then gave him a peck on the cheek. "We're going to miss you."

"I'll be back to visit."

Kincaid lowered the paper and glanced at Nick. "You shouldn't be going."

"Let's leave that alone, Kincaid."

Kincaid leaned closer. "I didn't notice upstairs, but your eye is puffed. Did it get in the way of a fist at the bar last night?"

"Something like that. My brothers are a bad influence."

"Let me see your fists."

Nick reluctantly held up both hands, knowing Kincaid expected bruised knuckles.

"Hell, boy, no bruises. You must have been throwing girlie punches."

"Yeah, that's me, always into girlie things like books and music and my girlie friends."

11

Kincaid jumped to his feet and shouted, "College has made you a smart ass."

Kathleen moved in front of him, "Please, Kincaid—"

"You made him too damn soft with books and stuff. That's why he's different."

"Leave her out of this," Nick shouted as he came to his feet. He knocked the table and the vase fell over, water seeping into the tablecloth.

Kathleen cried, "For God's sake, stop it, both of you."

The room fell silent.

"Please, Kincaid, don't fight. He's leaving today."

Kincaid looked down at her for a moment, then without a word he grabbed a cap from a peg on the wall and left, slamming the door behind him.

For a moment the two stared at the door like actors who'd forgotten their lines. Kathleen turned back and continued wiping the stove with a wet cloth. Nick settled into the chair and righted the vase with the rose.

"I'm sorry, I didn't mean for that to happen," Nick said.

Kathleen continued to wipe the same spot over and over. He suspected she was crying. Nick finally spoke again. "Did you ever want to leave him?"

Kathleen's eyes were red as she turned and moved toward Nick. "Me leave him? You listen and listen good. That man has more love in his heart than a dozen men. He walks ankle deep in blood and animal waste six days a week at the packing plant without a complaint. He does it for his family. For thirty years, he's never expected time off and he won't have any until the day he dies."

Nick rose. "Forget what I said—"

"No, you sit. I'm not finished. When he complained and bossed you boys, it didn't mean he was right. It meant he cared. He tries to run your life because he's scared for you, Nick. And who wouldn't be if they'd walked in his boots. He loves you."

"I know, Mom. I love him too, but he won't let me in. He has no feelings."

"No feelings? He's filled to the brim with feelings . . . just don't know how to show them. When you were a baby and close to death, I found the big lug out back crying and praying for God to take him and spare you."

Nick dropped his head and sighed. "Sorry, Mom, I've really messed up. I should have kept my mouth shut."

"No, you're a man now, you have a right to speak, but Kincaid doesn't see you that way. To him you're still a little boy. Just remember that he's got more bark than bite." She wiped her eyes and chuckled. "Other than when his mother passed, there was one other time he cried."

"When was that?"

Kathleen smiled. "On the day I agreed to marry him."

"You're joking."

"No, the big bear cried like a baby and you're the only person I've ever told. And the only person I'll ever tell."

"I can't picture Kincaid crying. He's as tough as nails."

"Yes, he is, but even a tough man with a heart as big as Kincaid's can cry."

"You were on your way to becoming a teacher when you married Kincaid. Why did you decide to give that up?"

"It was more important to be with Kincaid than to teach, and don't you dare ask why. I was in love with Kincaid."

"What does that feel like, I mean really being in love with someone."

"The feeling is bigger than words."

"Do you understand why I can't marry Liz?"

"Oh, honey, yes I do. You two have little in common. You're a bit of a dreamer and see the world like you want it to be. And there is nothing wrong with that. Liz is a little like Kincaid. He's a realist who sees his world as it is, without giving any thought of changing it. Don't stop dreaming, but keep it real. I have known for a long time that Liz isn't right for you, but that was not my decision, nor should it be Kincaid's."

"Thanks, Mom, you're so wise."

"Just more years of living than you. I realize you're moving south because of the dreamer in you and because of Kincaid."

"No, Mom, it's not Kincaid, I want—

"Don't deny it, Nick, it's something you need to do for a lot of reasons. You've lived in your brothers' shadows for a long time. The measure of a man is not about height or muscle. It's about character and values. Don't ever forget that."

"I love you, Mom."

"And I love you, Nick."

2

Disappointment weighed heavy as Nick entered Illinois Central Station. He wanted his dad to see him off, for things to be right between them. The fight had dulled the excitement he'd felt, and as usual their conflicts always ended with Nick feeling guilty.

His mom had been right. The "teacher wanted" notice posted at school had offered a chance for adventure and a way to escape the constant conflict with Kincaid. The posting reminded Nick of his maternal grandfather's stories about his adventures as a young man living in Kentucky. He told of winding rivers and sweeping green hills, a place he described as paradise. Images had remained with Nick and inspired him to read Kentucky writers such as Fox and Buck. He especially liked Buck's *Call of the Cumberland*, the book he carried under his arm. He planned to read it again to reacquaint him with Kentucky.

Nick waved down a passing paper boy and dropped two pennies into the outstretched hand of the thin-faced kid. The Tribune's headline announced the death of movie actor Valentino, which explained weepy-eyed ladies with their heads buried in newspapers.

Aroma from a coffee vendor's station near the main restaurant drew Nick to the far end of the terminal. He sipped the blackness and smacked his lips with approval.

"Coffee wakes up one's mornin', I always say." The voice came from behind him.

Nick turned and faced a tall, dark-haired man dressed in black. He'd attempted to engage Nick in conversation earlier at the ticket booth. The funny-talking man had to be from the South.

"Yeah, good coffee will do that," Nick answered. He forced a quick smile and hurried away. The stranger wasn't foppish, but regular guys didn't wear three-piece zoot suits, fedora hats, and custom boots. He looked much like the actor pictured on today's front page.

Nick moved to the train's boarding platform beneath the arched sheds that sheltered arriving and departing trains. Stench from spent coal and the sound of hissing steam filled the air.

Departure time was fast approaching and Nick kept watching the terminal door, hoping Kincaid would burst through the crowd with Kathleen rushing to keep up.

His parents failed to show and Nick's mood slumped even more. And it didn't help that the clasp on his suitcase refused to stay closed. He'd snapped it shut dozens of times after arriving at the station. With patience gone, he gave up on the clasp and tossed the luggage in the train's overhead rack and dropped into a worn leather seat.

The train's rocking motion soon caused Nick to doze, only to be awakened at each of the frequent stops at small towns. At some point, he heard the suitcase clasp snap and opened his eyes. The stranger in black towered above him. Nick came up with his fists drawn.

"Hold on, Partner." The man threw up his hands and staggered backward. "I didn't aim to scare you, but your case was about to fall on you. " He displayed a wide smile under a well-trimmed mustache.

Nick relaxed his fists. He felt an instant dislike for the man and wasn't sure why. "Sorry. Thanks for warning me about the case."

"I was stretching my legs and noticed the case. I should of woke you. My apology, Little Partner. I ain't introduced myself. I'm Vale McKinney."

The Little Partner comment further confirmed his dislike for the man. Nick thanked him again and dropped back into the seat, assuming that ended their conversation.

"And your name is?"

Nick had no choice. He extended his hand. "I'm Nick Kincaid."

"Where you goin'?" Vale asked.

"Eddyville, Kentucky."

"Been there before?"

"No. First time."

"You'll find livin' at Woodson Chapel different from Chicago."

Nick rose, along with his suspicion of the man. "What's going on? I said Eddyville, you said Woodson Chapel."

The man's expression changed slightly. He chuckled. "It's simple, Little Partner, you mentioned your destination when we chatted at the terminal. Remember?"

"No, I'm sure I didn't. I'm also sure you wouldn't have asked where I'm going just now if I'd told you before."

Nick waited. Vale shifted.

"It could be because I was born in Woodson. You said Eddyville. I say Woodson when talkin' 'bout that part of the country. My sister and brother-in-law own the place where you'll be stayin'. I may have heard them talkin' about you boardin' there." He chuckled again.

Nick continued to stare.

Vale sighed. "Little Partner, it was an accident, us meetin' like this."

"Too many coincidences bother me," Nick said.

Vale flipped lint off the fedora with his middle finger and perched the hat on his head. "Well, Little Partner. I ain't got nothin' more to say. Lord knows I've tried to be neighborly by keepin' the case from fallin' on your head."

Nick watched him move into the next coach. The man could have heard his family mention that Nick was coming. He snapped the clasp closed and shoved the case back into the rack. No thief would take his scuffed up case with all the new ones that lined the racks.

Nick settled back into the seat, still troubled about the encounter. The stranger was overly friendly, but people down South were rumored to be that way. He closed his eyes and finally dozed toward the end of the trip, vaguely aware of stops and starts until a whack on the head brought him out of his seat.

"Sorry," said a female voice from the seat behind him. A young lady attempted to place a large cardboard box onto the rack beside Nick's case. He gave the box a hard push and then stared into large, blue-green eyes. The lady was petite. Nick might be taller, or at least just as tall. Her red lips widened into a smile and her eyes twinkled. "Thanks," she said. "The box nearly got away from me."

Nick smiled and pushed a wad of light brown hair back from his face. The yellow dress pulled tight under her breasts unleashed a sexual thought that brought a blush as obvious as a cloud's shadow moving across an Illinois cornfield. He dropped down onto his seat with her face floating around in the fantasy part of his brain. He hoped she was going to Eddyville. Just in case, why not get acquainted? Nick turned with a smile in place, but she had settled in with her head back and her eyes closed.

The train left Paducah and followed a snake's path alongside the Cumberland River. An overnight rainstorm had created ocher-colored eddies that swirled and clawed at vegetation along the river bank.

The town came into view. Businesses lined the street parallel to the river. Nick stared wide-eyed at the box-sized depot. The original color appeared to be some shade of yellow with brown trim, but that must have been several years ago based upon the way it had cracked and faded, a far cry from Illinois Central.

Three men in dark suits paced in front of the aging depot. They stood on tiptoes and peered into the train's windows. Their actions bordered on the bizarre in a town that appeared to be a throwback to another era. Gramps never described anything like this. He could hear Kincaid saying *I told you so.*

Water-filled ruts lined the narrow dirt street, perhaps several inches deep. A team of mules tied in front of the post office had mud stockings up to their knees.

Nick stood in the train's doorway and stared. Could this be right? He took a deep breath and stepped down onto the boarding platform just as the three dark-suited men pushed past to board. In trying to avoid them, Nick collided with a young colored man who hurried alongside the train. His old black suitcase held together with a brown belt flew out of his arms.

"I'm sorry," Nick said.

The young man grabbed the case and went on his way without a word. The ticket agent had seen the incident from the doorway. "His kind will run smack over you if you let 'em." He hooked his thumbs under suspenders and hiked his pants up, proving himself to be without an ass, though he appeared to be one.

"We bumped together, just an accident."

"Clumsy ape bastard," the agent muttered and disappeared inside.

If that was a sample of Eddyville's hospitality, Nick wanted none of it. He hoped the voice of reason existed here. All the people couldn't be like that one.

Nick was told that someone would meet him, but the only interest shown came from a short-haired black dog that seemed eager to be his friend. The animal crawled from under a bench beside the doorway and demanded a pat on the head.

"You son-of-a-bitch, get yo' hands off me," came an angry shout from inside the end coach. Nick recognized the accent as belonging to the man that called himself Vale. People waiting to board turned their attention toward the commotion, which continued until the trio of men appeared in the doorway and wrestled Vale down the steps. He protested his rights and threatened lawsuits while two men did a body search and the third pawed through his suitcase.

"Who are those men?" Nick asked a stranger who'd stopped nearby to watch the ruckus.

"Government men," he muttered.

"Is he wanted?" Nick asked.

"He's wanted, but they've got to have proof to arrest him."

A tall, robust lady rushed down the boardwalk in front of the general store waving an umbrella and calling Nick's name. She lifted an ankle-length dress and crossed the street on long narrow boards placed over mud-filled ruts. Her smile created deep furrows around her aging mouth. Breathless, she asked if he was Nick Kincaid.

He smiled and nodded.

"John Frank asked me to welcome you. I'm his wife, Anna Louise."

"Please call me Nick."

Another outburst from Vale drew Nick's attention toward the men still searching Vale's luggage. Anna Louise whispered, "Don't mind them. It's to do with illegal transportin'."

"Of what?"

"Moonshine. It's Prohibition, you know."

"He makes moonshine?"

She lowered her voice and cupped her mouth. "Accordin' to the Feds, Vale is up to his eyeballs in it. The handsome devil."

Vale didn't fit the image of a barefoot moonshiner wearing overalls. The man had taken an unusual interest in Nick. He wondered why more than ever.

Anna Louise added, "Nobody has proved that Vale makes it."

The young woman on the train came down the steps. Nick assumed Eddyville wasn't her final destination and had left her dozing. She was beautiful, like a lady in a perfect dream.

Anna Louise called to her, "Jenny, come here. I want you to meet Mr. Kincaid."

The young woman smiled as she came forward, her body in perfect rhythm with each step.

"Nick will be our new teacher over at Woodson Chapel." She turned to Nick. "Jenny works for the state. Appointed by the Governor. She's the only female to hold such a position. Her job is to keep kids livin' in this end of the state in school. She's a career woman like her famous aunt. Mr. Kincaid, you'll be workin' with Jenny."

"Who is your aunt?" Nick asked. It was the only thing that came to mind to get a conversation going. He wanted to see more of this girl.

"Rebecca Fulton." She smiled. "You've probably never heard of her."

"I have. The first woman appointed to the U.S. Senate. I'm impressed."

She laughed. "Don't be. She was seventy-seven when she was appointed to fill the vacancy left by her husband's death."

"You two sound like you know each other," Anna Louise said.

"We sort of met on the train. How is your head?"

"It's okay."

"The teacher didn't want to talk. It's lucky I woke up. He left me asleep on the train." She flashed what Nick decided was a teasing smile.

"I wanted to—"

"Jenny, darlin', I need somebody to rescue me," a familiar voice called out before Nick could say more. Vale came forward, straightening his coat and tie. The trio of federal agents stared with scowls on their faces. He smiled. "Nothin' like bein' welcomed home by government men. Anna Louise, did John Frank arrange this as my homecomin'?"

"I'm sure he knew nothin'."

"Our good sheriff knows everythin', my dear." He turned to Jenny. "I kept Saturday night open just like always."

She laughed. "I was afraid you'd forgotten and I'd be left home all alone."

Vale belly laughed.

It was Nick's bad luck to find a good looking girl near his height and then learn that she was taken.

"Well, Mr. Kincaid," Vale said, "we both wound up in Eddyville, neighbors you might say, 'cept you're gonna live over by Woodson."

Nick spoke with enough arrogance to satisfy. "Then I guess we're not quite neighbors."

"You could say that. To show I want to be a good neighbor, I'll accommodate by givin' you a ride over to Woodson."

Anna Louise spoke up. "Ducky is waitin' to take him over."

"Be more comfortable ridin' in a car instead of an old wagon."

"John Frank is expectin' to meet with him before he goes," Anna Louise added.

Vale shrugged and turned to Jenny. "Sweetheart, may I escort you across the river?"

"That would be nice. I'm parked on the far side. Don't like driving onto the ferry."

"See you later, Partner," Vale said with a wink.

Jenny's gaze connected with Nick's. "See you around, Teacher Man."

Nick listened to their bantering fade as they continued down the street to a Model-A parked near the ferry. She'd given Nick the eye, but there was little chance that he could take her away from Vale.

"Jenny is a real sweet girl," he heard Anna Louise say.

"He's a lucky guy."

"Oh, she's not his girl. She would never go out with Vale. She teases and flirts with him, that's all." She giggled. "I believe you're smitten with her. She's a sweetheart."

The gods had smiled another time today. He reached for the case.

"Leave it. Ducky will get it." Anna Louise waved to the colored man sitting in the wagon and pointed to the suitcase. The young colored man Nick had bumped into from the train sat beside the older gentleman. "John Frank will be back in a while to meet with you. You must be nearly starved on that smelly old train. We'll go down to Fanny's and have a bite while we wait."

Nick followed her and successfully balanced on the boards while crossing the street. What he saw was nothing like he'd visualized in the books he'd read, and Gramps's description of paradise never included him wading ass deep in mud. Except for the river and green hills, the town was like something out of a bad Western movie.

3

Claude McKinney's afternoon nap was interrupted by a nagging pain that traveled the length of his back. It'd been more than three years since the mattress was last stuffed with fresh straw and it did no good to try to beat the lumps out anymore.

Swollen feet crowded his shoes and his knees trembled as he stood. He no longer took the stairs and slept in the storage room among chin-high stacks of sugar there to accommodate local moonshiners.

Claude emerged from the storage room and heard his daughter's footsteps overhead. She'd be cooking supper.

His hickory cane tapped out each step as he shuffled across the blackened pine floor. He paused by a jar of peppermint candy beside the cash register. Bony fingers gathered a handful of crushed sweetness. All but one piece went into his bib pocket for later. Claude loved the candy's biting flavor and rolled the red and white lump around in his mouth to rid the dryness.

He reached the store's lean-to porch and let the screen door bang shut. It frightened the bird that nested in the open rafters overhead and its fluttering escape startled Claude.

"Damn bird," he muttered.

His thin lips curled into a smile when he saw the bird droppings on the table against the wall. It had belonged to his dead wife. He whacked it hard with his cane, pretending it was her.

He sank into the hickory rocker with a sigh. Getting from the bed to the rocker had taken most of his strength. He'd turn eighty his next birthday. Napping each afternoon started ten years ago when he was forced to move in with Loretta and Boyd. He would have preferred to live with his daughter, Ella, but Loretta wouldn't hear of it.

Claude gazed at the Cumberland. Dancing white caps glistened in the afternoon sun like fish scales on a carp's back. A door closing drew his eyes toward the gristmill less than fifty yards down the hill. Mae was cleaning the millhouse rooms for Woodson's first male teacher. It was a waste of time since moonshiners would run the fellow off. He would most likely be a revenue agent sent to sniff out whisky stills.

The sound of Loretta's floppy shoes reached Claude's ears. He looked out toward the river and ignored his daughter as she emerged carrying a tray.

"Oh, look at the bird poop on Mama's table," she gasped. After placing the tray across the rocker arms in front of Claude, she grabbed a broom from against the wall and swept the table clean. "I've got to remember to scrub it with lye soap, 'cause the teacher will be eatin' off it in pretty weather."

Loretta positioned herself in front of Claude so he could see her lips. She spoke slowly. "Poppa, I brought you a piece of buttermilk pie just out of the oven."

Loretta tightened the belt on her blue wraparound housecoat. "Had my bath and my hair is curlin' for choir practice." She pushed dangling rag strips used to hold the curls to the side and shouted, "Did you have a good nap?"

"The fool birds hollered too loud."

"Poppa, I didn't hear no birds, and besides, you can't hear nothin'."

Boyd came around the corner of the building and up the steps.

"Hi, Sugar," Loretta called. "I'm 'bout ready for choir practice except for finishin' my hair and gettin' dressed." She cupped her mouth. "Poppa's talkin' about hearin' birds again. I'm afraid he'll lose his mind without tellin' us about you-know-what."

Boyd shrugged. "Maybe there never was any gold coins. I'm gonna run down to the creek and wash off. Been sweatin' like a mule gettin' them rooms ready for the teacher. He'll be gettin' here later tonight."

"Hurry up. You know I don't let nobody see me with my hair curlin' and no lipstick."

"What time are you leavin' for choir pracice?"

"Same time as usual."

Claude smiled. Boyd diddled the yellow-haired widow woman that lived down the road every Wednesday evening while Loretta attended choir practice. He'd heard them carryin' on in the storage room once a week for nearly five years. He should tell Loretta, but he'd never forgiven her for hauling him from his own home against his will. She'd ransacked his house and took everything down to the

27

bare floor. He didn't care about the things, but he resented being forced to move at an age when he wanted to be by himself. One day when he failed to hear Loretta call him, she carried on about him losing his hearing. That gave him the idea to pretend deafness. Since then he'd listened to what was being said by everyone within earshot.

"Poppa, you ain't even tryin' to listen. Are you?"

Claude cupped his ear.

"I asked if you changed underwear this week. I don't remember washin' none."

"Ain't been wearin' none."

She rolled her eyes. "What if you was to have a stroke? You ain't even combed your hair after your nap." She pushed frizzy white hair away from his eyes until he jerked his head away.

"What does a stroke have to do with wearin' underwear or combin' my hair?"

Loretta shook her head, causing the dangling strips of fabric to flop about. She pushed them to the side, again. "Poppa, you know I love you more than Ella and Vale. He's your only son and he never even comes to see you, does he?"

"Don't want him comin'."

"You can thank the Good Lord that I take good care of you. I was just wonderin', is all your affairs in order if somethin' was to happen? Do you need to tell me anythin'?"

"Yeah, don't bury me next to your ugly old mama."

"Don't say that. Me and Mama loved you the most. I was meanin' your finances. Some people think you have some money tucked away somewhere." She giggled. "Even gold."

Loretta continued to chatter about the rumor that Claude's daddy stole gold from the Union Army. Claude closed his eyes and let her talk. His head slowly slumped forward, and then he gave a loud snort. Loretta's chattering stopped.

"Poppa, are you asleep?"

He snorted again. Loretta jumped up and spewed out the word "shit" just before the screen door banged shut behind her.

Claude was glad to be rid of her. He ate the pie and leaned his head back and closed his eyes. He wasn't sure how long he waited before The Bird rounded the bend in the river. It floated on air currents and its feathers shined like pearls thrown at the sun as light danced off its silver-gray wings.

The bird settled on Claude's shoulder with the lightness of the wind. He was transported back to the big spring where he saw himself rip open the colored girl's dress and grab her young breast. She cried out and slapped his face. His punch sent the girl backward into the water. She thrashed around and soon disappeared.

The weight of the Bird became intolerable. Claude slumped to one side. He would have fallen from the rocker without its arms to hold him.

"Mr. Claude, Mr. Claude, wake up."

Claude jerked awake. He was glad The Bird was gone. His other son-in-law, Frank, stood at the bottom of the steps.

"What is it, Frank?"

"Ella wanted me to bring you the news." He came halfway up the steps and shouted, "Ella had a baby girl."

Claude sensed Frank was hiding something. Before he could question, Loretta charged onto the porch and demanded to know if she'd heard him right.

"Yes, ma'am, Ella had a baby girl."

Loretta's mouth went slack. She blinked and took a moment. "Frank, have you started drinkin' again?"

"No, I quit a long time ago."

Loretta's mouth quivered. "I don't know what to say. Ella wouldn't do that without tellin'me. She really had a baby?"

"Sure did, a girl."

"Poppa, are you hearin'? I can't believe she didn't tell me, her own sister." Her brow went up. "I know what's going on. Ella is jealous 'cause Poppa loves me best. That's why she kept the baby a secret, ain't it, Frank?"

"What are you talkin' about?"

"That's it," she cried. "Ella has tried to get pregnant for years. So she finally did it. Well, she's fat enough to carry two babies and nobody would know."

"That ain't a nice thing to say about your sister."

"It ain't nice backstabbin' me out of jealousy. I'm family." Loretta rushed over to Claude and shouted, "Poppa, you didn't know Ella was expectin', did you?"

"I knowed about the baby. The Bird told me."

"I'm gonna lose my mind over you and that damn bird." She whirled to face Frank. "I've got it figured. Ella shared the secret with Poppa to get on his good side because of his gold coins. That's how he knew. She's not gettin' away with it. You can tell her that for me."

"What are you talkin' about? I told Ella you wouldn't be happy."

"You tell Ella I'm happy," Claude said. He watched Frank walk away. Why would Ella not tell him about a grandchild coming?

Loretta sniffed. "I've got to talk to Boyd." She went down the hill calling for Boyd. He emerged from the mill and rushed to meet her. Claude couldn't understand what was said, but Boyd would have to do some fast talkin' to calm Loretta down and convince her to attend choir practice.

Claude dropped off for a nap after things quieted down. He awoke to a pain eating away at his hip. He adjusted his sitting position and got some relief. "Damn," he muttered upon seeing two old maid neighbors coming up the path toward the store. He couldn't stand them, especially the fat one. She talked so loud it hurt his ears.

The two walked single file up the path. Mousey, the short, prune-faced one sometimes disappeared behind the tall, buxom Mattie. Claude eased his head back and closed his eyes. With any luck, they would think he was asleep and walk right into the store and do their yakking with Loretta.

Mattie took the steps first, confirmed by the loud moaning of a loose board.

"Mr. Claude looks a bit white," Mattie said.

The women hovered inches above Claude's face. "Is he breathin'?" Mousey gasped. "I don't think so."

Mattie tugged his shirtsleeve. "Mr. Claude, talk to me. Are you okay?"

Afraid she might start hollerin' that he'd died, Claude raised his head and stared into beady eyes behind wire-rimmed glasses. "I'm fine. Now, go on inside. Loretta's dyin' to tell you about Ella's baby."

"Loretta can wait. I guess you've heard that the new teacher is Catholic. Us neighborhood Christians ain't wantin' a Catholic teachin' our precious children. We've gotta do somethin', so I'm gettin' a petition goin', and I'm here to get Loretta to help."

"The teacher won't last. Moonshiners will run him off," Claude said. "Now go talk to Loretta."

"Mentionin' lastin', you're old, Mr. Claude, and you ain't been baptized. Me, I'm ready to go. I got my casket picked out at the funeral home over in Eddyville. I go see it every Saturday when we go shoppin'. It's silver with real silk linin'. My dress is baby blue. I just love baby blue. You like baby blue, Mr. Claude?"

He had no idea what baby blue looked like and muttered, "I'm gonna be buried naked."

Both women giggled.

"Do we open you for viewin'?" Mattie asked.

Her question brought increased giggles from Mousey. Claude wished both women were wearing blue now instead of laughing and hollering in his ears. The longer Mattie talked, the louder she became. She leaned toward him and shouted, "Has Loretta seen Ella's new baby?"

"Not yet."

"Shame on her for not seein' her own sister's precious little baby. Wonder why Ella kept it a secret?"

"Ask Loretta. Fuss at her a bit for not seein' the baby before now," Claude said.

"I will, Mr. Claude, but don't forget you need to be baptized before winter. At your age, you could pass before spring weather."

His ears were hurting and the cabbage from dinner remained a problem, one he decided to share. He leaned to the side.

Both women stepped back. Mattie glanced at Mousey. She shook her head and pointed at Claude.

Mattie giggled. "Mr. Claude's got a problem, to say the least."

The old man bit his lip to keep from smiling. He leaned to the side again.

The women covered their noses and moved back. "My Lord, I'm goin' inside and get away from this," Mousey declared.

"I ain't finished talkin' about stoppin' that Catholic from comin' down here to teach our precious children," Mattie whined. "Am I the only one worried about a Catholic livin' here with us Christians? We've gotta get the petition signed and over to John Frank before the teacher arrives. Otherwise, we'll never get him out of here."

Mousey whispered, "Loretta won't help 'cause she's rentin' a room to him. Gettin' rid of him would be takin' money out of her pocket, and you know Loretta will squeeze the Indian head off a nickel."

Mattie rolled her eyes. "We all know Loretta has got to be the biggest frog on the lily pad. We'll start by braggin' about her bein' the only one with influence enough to get the petitions signed. Course we need to butter her up about being an aunt. Let me do the talkin'. I'm better at it."

Mattie jerked the screen door open and disappeared inside with Mousey on her heels. The old man smiled and leaned his ear toward the doorway. He counted. Loretta's outburst came on the count of three. Claude chuckled and treated himself to a peppermint from his bib pocket.

4

Faded blue pants hung loose around John Frank's long legs as Nick followed him into an inner office. The sheriff lowered his massive bulk into a chair behind a desk littered with papers. An eight-point deer head hung on the wall above his head. Nick couldn't imagine killing an animal, much less a person, which made all the guns in the rack beside the door more ominous.

The sheriff cupped his head in both hands and swung his feet up on the desk. A smile revealed uneven teeth beneath a drooping tobacco-stained mustache. "Just to tell you 'bout me, I head up the school board, been a two-term mayor of Eddyville, and my present job is sheriff of Lyon County." He smoothed his salt and pepper mustache with a thumb and forefinger. "You could say I've done pretty well for a country boy whose old man said I wouldn't amount to nothin'. You bein' from up North, I wanted you to know how folks live around here. I look out for my people, do what they want. They don't want coloreds livin' here so we don't have any, 'ceptin' Ducky and Mae, an old couple that live over by the mill where you're goin'. We have ways to encourage the young ones to leave and find work away from here." He paused. "Do I see disagreement in your eyes hearin' me say that?"

"I do disagree, sir. I believe in the rule of law which makes every man equal."

John Frank frowned. "I hope you ain't a troublemaker."

"I'm just a teacher, but I do have principles that I won't ignore."

John Frank tilted his head back and looked down his nose. "I respect a man who knows what he likes. I got nothin' against coloreds, but I can't say that about some of the people in my county. The way I see it, I'm helpin' keep the coloreds safe by movin' 'em away. There's people livin' here that would do harm to 'em in a cat's wink."

The man's reasoning was too ridiculous for words, but Nick held his disgust. His racial views would be better served over a period of time once he knew more about the people. He'd just listen and learn for now.

John Frank continued. "I'm gonna accept that you ain't here to make trouble. My advice is to teach the kids and stay out of people's business. The Feds may try to recruit you to rat out moonshiners. Not a good idea. People have been shot for less."

"As I said, I'm only here to teach."

"Then we'll get along fine."

The ferryboat whistle brought John Frank to his feet. "You've gotta go. The ferry's makin' its last trip for the day. Crossin' the river ain't safe after dark, especially after a rainstorm like we just had."

Nick left not knowing why the sheriff wanted the meeting. Nothing had been gained, other than for John Frank to feed his own ego and perhaps reveal his wacky racial views.

Fog hugged the far riverbank and darkness threatened when Nick emerged from the sheriff's office. In his haste to catch the ferry, his foot slipped off the narrow board and went ankle deep in the mud. He hobbled to firmer ground and kicked the mud from his shoe, but not before dampness crept in and wet his foot.

The barge rested upon the edge of the bank with the end gate dropped for loading. A tugboat bobbed up and down in the swirling current with its motor straining to hold the barge in place. A bearded captain stood behind the wheel and watched a deckhand prepare to cast off.

The old colored man sat atop the wagon with its wheels chained to the deck. Burlap bags covered the mules' heads, but they showed nervousness and shifted about in two to three inches of water that covered the deck. Nick took a deep breath and stepped on board.

His suitcase lay in the wagon bed behind the seat. He climbed up beside the colored man and introduced himself.

The old man spoke with downcast eyes. "I's Ducky. Dat be my boy, Eddie." He motioned toward the young colored man Nick had collided with at the station. Both nodded.

"Why are the mules blindfolded?" Nick asked.

"Old Nellie, she be high strung, and Jane be dumb enough to do what she do, so it best dey not see where dey be goin'." Ducky offered a warm smile followed by a chuckle.

The tugboat spewed oil fumes as it powered up and moved into stronger current. With each pitch of the barge the wagon rolled back and forth, straining against the chains. Queasiness rose in Nick's stomach after only a few minutes. The last thing he wanted was to upchuck. He hoped the beads of sweat that dotted his forehead weren't an indication that he was going to be sick.

A whining sound came from under the wagon seat. Nick leaned over to look and the black dog from the depot shot up and kissed him on the mouth. Nick patted the animal. "What's your dog's name?"

"Ducky don't have no dog."

"That's not your dog?"

"No, dat be yo' dog."

"But I don't have a dog," Nick replied.

"He think he be yo' dog. He done claimed you, Mr. Nick."

Nick patted the dog's head again. "What'll I do with him?"

"He'll keep critters away at da mill."

The animal tried to kiss Nick in the face again but settled down after a few pats on the head. Nick had heard that animals sense danger and the dog didn't seem frightened. He took that as a good sign as the boat powered up and moved further out into the current.

About midway across the river the boat suddenly lost power. The barge pitched and rolled as the current carried them downstream. Nick gripped the wagon seat and watched Ducky struggle to control the frightened mules. They jumped and thrashed about, even falling to their knees on the slippery deck.

A sudden swell lifted the barge and tossed Nick out onto the deck. He managed to catch his fall, but not before water saturated his pant legs and sent the book he carried into the river. Struggling to his feet, he latched onto the side of the wagon.

"Hold on tight," Ducky hollered. "It's gonna be okay."

Nick gazed up at Eddie. It didn't look okay judging by the young man's wide-eyed expression. And it wouldn't be okay with Nick until his feet were planted on solid ground.

The engine sputtered until it finally fired. Nick offered silent thanks and climbed back up onto the wagon. Ducky glanced at him. "Da Good Lord is watchin' over us."

Nick nodded, thinking that was exactly what his mother would have said.

Moving against the current at a turtle's pace, darkness was complete by the time the tug reached the dock.

"Welcome to 'tween the rivers, Mr. Nick," Ducky said as they stepped onto dry land.

Nick vowed to himself that he'd never cross the river again after dark or after a rainstorm.

Ducky removed the blindfolds from the mules and then lit a kerosene lantern that hung from the wagon's tailgate. They took to the winding road and were soon engulfed by fog, bringing with it loneliness and thoughts of home. Silence lingered except for the rattle of the harness and moans from the wagon when the wheels dropped into mud-filled ruts.

Half an hour into the trip, a gunshot shattered the silence and snuffed the lantern.

"Help us, Lord," Ducky whispered. "Eddie, get yo'self down in da wagon and don't you move, boy."

The dog growled and came out from under the seat.

"Hold the mutt or I'll shoot," a man ordered from somewhere in front of the mules.

Nick locked both arms around the dog's neck. He felt his own heart pounding. The voice sounded like that of the Vale character on the train.

A second man dropped the tailgate. Suitcase latches snapped in the darkness. "I've got it," the man said in a muffled voice. No one spoke until the sound of feet thrashing through the undergrowth faded.

"You okay?" Ducky asked.

"Yeah, who were they?" Nick climbed over the seat and felt around in the open suitcase. The man had taken something, but nothing was missing that he could detect by feeling around in the dark. Vale must have put something in the case while tinkering with it on the train. "Who were they?" Nick asked again.

"Some things best not talked about here 'tween the rivers," Ducky said.

"One of them sounded like the man on the train. Vale was his name."

"Ducky is gettin' old and can't hear good."

"Tell him," Eddie urged. "Loretta and Boyd own the mill where you're stayin'. Vale is her brother."

"Hush yo' mouth, boy. We got nothin' to say."

The Feds were looking for something in Vale's luggage at the station. He must have put whatever it was in the suitcase and retrieved it just now.

The wagon soon moved out of the fog onto the narrow ridge of hills that separated the Tennessee and the Cumberland. The stone and wooden gristmill soon came into view, half buried in the hillside. Moonlight painted the scene with the charm of a picture postcard. The sound of water trickling over rocks came from somewhere in the darkness beneath a large waterwheel that stood silent. A few feet up the hill lights flickered in the second floor window of a country store. This was what Nick had dreamed about seeing. For a moment he forgot about the troubled trip and was taken in by the night's stillness. He couldn't believe the sky held so many stars. He'd never in his life experienced such silence in the city.

Split logs embedded in the sloping grade next to the building formed steps to a small landing at the door to Nick's second floor living quarters. After saying good night to Ducky, Nick slipped out of his mucky shoes and socks to enter.

Dog circled and sniffed every corner of the two rooms. He finally focused on something of interest behind the potbellied stove and scratched to his delight. Nick spied a pan of water on the stove and washed the grime off his feet. Aided by an oil lamp he examined the contents of his suitcase. Nothing was missing, though his mother had added a Bible. Vale must have put something in the case on the train and removed it during the holdup. The man was obviously breaking the law and Nick wanted nothing to do with a smuggling operation.

A growl brought Nick back into the front room. The dog stared up at a stuffed animal head on the wall above a desk. Nick chuckled. "I hope your ability as a guard dog goes beyond a standoff with a stuffed moose. Bookshelves would be better."

Nick sank into an old rocker that answered to his weight. The room was a far cry from the one he claimed at home after his last brother moved out. A wave of loneliness returned. The dog placed its nose on Nick's knee as if he understood.

"Good boy." Nick patted the animal. "You are a boy, I hope." He bent to look. "Good. What am I going to call you?" He thought for a moment. "For now it'll be just Dog until we come up with a name that suits you."

A knock on the door brought another growl. Dog relaxed after reassurance from Nick that all was well. A tall man with a wide mouth, prominent cheeks, and piercing dark eyes stood in the doorway holding a covered tray in one hand and the other extended to shake. "I'm Boyd. Loretta sent you some grub, thinkin' you might be hungry after the trip."

Nick introduced himself, shook hands, and motioned Boyd inside. Aware of family connections, and due to Ducky's reaction after the robbery, Nick decided against mentioning the incident on the road.

"It's some fried ham and biscuits she cooked up." Boyd said. "You might as well know, Loretta don't cook much on Wednesday 'cause of choir practice. It's usually leftovers."

"Thanks. It's nice of you to bring food." Nick placed the tray on a shelf above the desk and didn't mention that he'd eaten at the boarding house. Dog reared up and sniffed.

"You need anythin'? Loretta said for me to ask."

"I could use more shelves for my books. They're being shipped. Maybe you could replace the moose with them?"

"No problem. Ducky will get on it first thing in the morning. Loretta said to tell you she'll ring the bell at mealtime. She's willin' to fix your meals so you can bring them here to eat, or you can eat at a table on the front porch in good weather. You'll see her daddy sittin' on this end of the porch from dawn to dusk. He's reached the senile stage and won't bother you."

Nick smiled. "We'll work things out."

"When you're of a need, the best place to take a bath is in the creek just below the water wheel. Nobody can see you from the road and no women go down that way."

Nick nodded. Bathing in a creek would be a new experience, but then his way of living changed the minute he arrived. His brothers had teased him about returning to the Dark Ages by warning him to be careful and not let his pecker get frostbitten squatting in the woods.

Boyd patted Dog who seemed to trust him enough to sniff his shoe. A good sign, Nick hoped.

"You have a good lookin' dog. Did you bring him with you on the train?" Boyd asked.

"No, he adopted me at the depot."

"I've got foxhounds." Boyd started to leave and turned back. "Loretta will show you the schoolhouse tomorrow. I'll leave so you can get some rest."

He extended his hand for another handshake and left, closing the door behind him. Nick stared after him for a moment. He liked the man. Boyd had looked him in the eye with a relaxed smile. His dark hair and tinted skin would suggest he was part Cherokee. Nick had read that the land between the rivers once belonged to them.

Dog reared up on the desk again and sniffed. He looked at Nick and whined.

"Okay, I'll divide it with you." A ham and biscuit disappeared in one bite. "You must be starved." Nick tossed another one and Dog caught it in midair. "There's one left and it should be mine, but you can have it. I've been more than fair to a dog without a name or a home."

Nick leaned his head back and closed his eyes. He never dreamed that people lived as he'd experienced today. The nagging thought of having made a mistake wouldn't go away. Where was the paradise Gramps talked about?

5

A door closing drew Claude's attention to the gristmill where a shirtless young man with a black dog emerged from the room above the mill.

"The new teacher," he muttered.

The man stood on the landing and gazed at the river for a moment before descending the steps. He followed the path toward the creek with a towel thrown over his shoulder.

"That's him," Loretta whispered from inside the screen door. She giggled. "He's short, but built well. He must believe in washin' by goin' to the creek like that." She came out and sat across from Claude with her gaze still on the teacher. "You feelin' okay this mornin', Poppa?"

"No, I'm dyin'."

"That's good, Poppa." She jerked around. "What did you say?"

"I didn't say nothin'."

She shook her head. "Poppa, stop bein' mean. You know I love you the most."

"Your ugly old mama said I was mean."

Loretta rose. "I ain't gonna stay and listen to you talkin' bad about Mama. I'll fix you and the teacher some breakfast. Then I've gotta wake my sweetie. Bless his heart, Boyd works so hard he's nearly dead on his feet some days. Don't know why Wednesdays take the most out of him."

She disappeared inside. Claude leaned back and closed his eyes. He didn't know how long he waited before The Bird glided in and perched on the edge of the porch. After catching the old man's eye it took flight and landed on top of Claude's head with a wing spread long enough to cover his eyes. Blackness surrounded him. He screamed for help, but heard no sound.

The elderly man was thrashing with both hands and babbling about a bird as Nick stepped upon the porch. He called to him and got no response. Nick gently shook his shoulder. The old fellow opened his eyes and looked around. He appeared confused as if in a strange place. "Who are you?"

"I'm Nick Kincaid."

The old gentleman pulled himself upright in the chair. Perspiration followed the age lines down his face. He still looked around as if lost.

"Are you okay?" Nick asked. "Can I get you anything?"

He pulled a dingy handkerchief from his bib pocket and mopped his neck and brow. "Was I dreamin' or was the damn thing really here?"

"I'm not sure."

"Oh, now I remember. It weren't a dream. The Bird was remindin' me of somethin' bad I did once. Did you see The Bird with its wings wrapped around me, chokin' off my air?"

What was the old man talking about? Not sure how to answer, Nick said, "No, sir, I guess I didn't see that."

He leaned back and looked up at Nick. "Now I remember who you are. You're the new teacher, ain't you?"

Nick nodded.

"Might as well not unpack. You ain't gonna be stayin'."

Nick chuckled. "Why do you think that?"

"'Cause you're a revenue man."

"No, I'm just a teacher."

"Did I tell you my name? It's Claude."

"Nice to meet you, Claude."

"The Bird said you're a decent boy in spite of bein' a revenue man and not stayin' long."

Nick laughed. "I'll like your bird if he says nice things about me, but assure him I'm not a revenue man." Claude reminded Nick of his own grandfather's mental decline. He felt pity for the old guy. Why shouldn't Claude talk to birds? "Is the bird your friend?"

"No. That Bird wants to kill me. And you're the first person who didn't think I was crazy for seein' it."

The jury was still out on the crazy part, but older people deserved a certain amount of tolerance. "Tell me more about the bird. When did you first see it?"

"Let me think of what age I was back then. Must of been goin' on nine when it first come to me. I ain't never told a soul before. Me and mama was workin' in the field when lightnin' hit. It took her down as quick as a snap. After we put her in the ground, I climbed a hill to the

47

big spring, stripped off naked, and sat in the water up to my chin. I was thinkin' about Mama and cryin' when The Bird come and sat on my shoulder. Its wings grew long enough to hug me. They felt like my mama's arms. I don't know why I'm tellin' you this. Do you think I'm crazy? Sometimes I wonder."

"It's fine that a bird visits you."

The old man's eyes brightened and that was reason enough to go along with the old fellow.

"I hope the people here don't run you off," Claude said.

"No sir, they won't. I don't run easily."

"Anybody for breakfast?" A woman with a narrow butt pushed the screen door open and backed out carrying a tray. With an ear-to-ear smile, she introduced herself as Loretta Birdsong and placed the tray on a table covered with a blue oilcloth that looked new. She would never be taken as Vale's sister. He would probably be considered handsome, and she was homely with a mouth too wide for her thin face.

"Bet you're starved with hardly no supper last night. I've got you some breakfast. Have a seat." Seeing that a large yellow cat occupied the chair, she quickly dumped the furry animal onto the floor and motioned for Nick to sit. As he dropped into the chair, she grabbed the table and said, "The mornin' sun is gonna blind you." Nick jumped up and watched her drag the table into the shade at the far end of the porch. He moved the chair over and thought about holding it with both hands before trying to sit, just in case she chose another location. "You can't see to eat with the sun in your eyes."

It felt odd with Claude about twenty feet away on one end of the porch and him on the other.

Loretta took the items from the tray and placed them in front of Nick. "I hope you like cathead biscuits and milk gravy with your ham and eggs."

Nick nodded. He'd never heard of cathead biscuits. He eyed the yellow cat that took a spot in the sun on the edge of the porch. No, no, there couldn't be a connection.

Compliments about the outlay of food brought another giggle from Loretta. With her eyes on Nick, she shouted, "Poppa, I'll fix your plate in a minute."

The outburst puzzled Nick. She'd shouted, yet the old man stared straight ahead as if he didn't hear.

"Poppa can't hardly hear nothin'."

Nick was even more puzzled. He'd spoken to the old man in a normal voice, yet Claude hadn't heard his daughter, even though she'd shouted.

Loretta exposed a flat, bony chest as she leaned forward and pointed. "The school house is over yonder on that hill next to the Methodist church." She hurried on. "We're good Methodists. Course that don't mean . . . Catholics are good too. What I'm tryin' to say—"

"Teacher, do you eat fish on Friday?" Claude shouted.

"Not always." The old man was alert now and he was shouting. What was his game?

Loretta turned toward Claude and shouted again, "Poppa that's not a proper question to ask a Catholic."

"Do you like catfish?" Claude shouted even louder.

Nick nodded. Which one was crazy, Claude or Loretta?

Loretta giggled. "Please overlook Poppa. His mind is leavin' him a little at a time."

Claude leaned forward and squinted. "Somebody is comin' and it's got to be Mattie, 'cause she still uses a buggy." He turned toward Nick. "Stay clear of them old maids. The fat one is a pain in the ass."

Nick blushed from ear to ear. Loretta covered her face. "Oh, Lord, Mr. Kincaid, I'm so embarrassed. Poppa, what am I goin' to do with you?"

The mare came at a fast trot and was reined to an abrupt halt. Both women climbed down and hurried toward the porch. The fat one led the way, gasping and dabbing perspiration with an oversize handkerchief. She shouted, "Loretta, we've got some news you don't want to hear, so I come right over." She came up the steps wiping her neck and cleavage. The tiny woman followed. Her small eyes darted around behind thick glasses like two black marbles in a bottle.

Loretta met the larger woman at the top of the steps. "Good Lord, Mattie, what is it? You'd think somebody died."

"Lord knows I hate to tell you this, you bein' the nervous, high-strung type."

Loretta's brow arched. "I'm not nervous or high-strung. Get on with it, who died?"

"It hurts me to say so, but your sister birthed a colored baby."

Loretta's face flushed and the veins in her temples shot to the surface. "A brazen lie!"

"It's the truth. I saw the hair, lips, and all. It's colored."

"Somebody's lyin' like a dog," she mumbled. Her lips quivered. "I need Boyd. Where's Boyd? Somebody get Boyd. He needs to look into this. I'm gonna have a stroke. My nerve powders, I need my nerve medicine." She staggered in the door and disappeared inside.

Nick could hardly believe what he'd just witnessed. He expected the two women to bring out a voodoo doll and start jabbing pins at any moment. They enjoyed their role as messengers.

"Tellin' her was the Christian thing to do," Mattie announced.

When no one agreed, she held up a handful of papers. "I guess it's too late to get Loretta to sign my petition. Whew, it's really hot today." She pulled the neck of her dress out and her hand disappeared down the front. She rolled her breasts from side to side and dabbed with the handkerchief as she crossed to Claude. "Mr. Claude, I want you to sign my petition."

"Let that man over at the table sign first." Claude pointed at Nick and smiled.

Nick's first impulse was to run.

Mattie came forward. "I should apologize for you hearin' what you just heard, but it was my Christian duty. After all, travelin' salesman have seen it all and done it all from tales I hear."

"I'm not, uh—"

"No reason you can't sign it. I'm Mattie Thornton, doin' God's work by gettin' a petition against the Pope to keep him from stealin' our little Christian children and turnin' 'em into Catholics."

She placed the petition in front of him.

Nick stared at the page, all blank except for "Help get rid of the Catholic teacher" printed across the top. Before he could respond, Mattie said, "I see Loretta is feedin' you. You must be a relative and not a salesman."

Claude boomed, "Meet the new teacher."

With an audible intake of air, Mattie grabbed her chest. "The Catholic?"

"He likes fish," Claude shouted.

Mattie threw her hands up and bellowed, "Help me, Jesus." With her feet planted apart and her chin thrust forward, she pointed at Nick. "Do you believe in Jesus?"

Nick stared open-mouthed. The woman was deranged. He turned to Claude who only smiled. "Catholics embrace Jesus," he said.

"Embrace? What does that mean?"

"Believe in him."

"Are you sure?"

"Yes, ma'am. I've been Catholic all my life. I'm sure."

Mattie squinted.

"It's true," Nick repeated.

She smiled. "Well, I didn't know that. That's a good thing."

"Did you know he likes fish?" Claude bellowed.

"You told me, Mr. Claude," she shouted. "So Catholics are like Christians?"

Nick nodded instead of explaining they were Christians. She extended her hand and gushed. "If I do say so myself, I'm the school's main supporter. You'll be seein' a good bit of me, 'cause you're gonna need my help. I wasn't blessed with kids because I wasn't blessed with a man, but I do more than my part to support the school."

"I appreciate that. The school needs community support." He hoped this woman didn't represent the mainstay of supporters.

Mattie giggled and asked, "If you're single, Mr. Kincaid, I know a girl that would be perfect for you."

Claude shouted. "He don't like girls."

Mattie's brow went up as she cut her eyes toward Nick. "Is that true?"

Nick froze for a moment. She could have an ugly sister at home, but saying he didn't like girls could be worse. "I *like* girls. What's wrong with you, Claude?"

"Maybe it's fish you don't like," Claude bellowed.

"I like both."

"Well then, I have the perfect girl for you."

"No, thanks, I'll find my own girl. I don't want to be matched up."

Mattie shrugged. "Just tryin' to be helpful. Come Mousey, we've got a lot of stops to make before night. I want the whole community to pray about Ella havin' a colored baby. They can't pray if they haven't heard."

Once Mattie's buggy was straight with the road, Claude turned to Nick. "That woman brings out the meanness in me."

Nick rose and crossed to Claude, thinking there was an abundance to bring out. The old man took pleasure in his daughter's pain, yet he seemed unaffected by having a biracial grandchild. Nick would have guessed Claude to be intolerant of coloreds. Two women inflicted pain on a neighbor and then called it a Christian act. Would he ever fit in with these people whose culture and views were so different? "The news about the baby upset your daughter, but it didn't seem to bother you."

"It ain't true. Ella would never lay with a colored. I'd hate to think about this community if one of our own had a black baby."

"But you said you knew about the child."

"Just havin' fun." Claude chuckled. "I also told Mattie you don't like girls."

Nick smiled. The old man was complex. He pretended to be deaf, enjoyed hurting his daughter, and seemed to be quite a prankster.

"That woman will tell everyone I don't like girls. Don't you know male teachers have trouble without any help?"

"Don't worry, I'm gonna talk to The Bird about gettin' you a special girl."

"I'm holding you to that, so your bird had better come through."

Claude laughed. "I was teasin' you about the fish and girls."

"What do I make of you? Your hearing is better than you pretend, but your daughter doesn't know. I've known you less than an hour and you've confused two ladies into thinking I don't like girls. I should push you off the porch and watch you roll down the hill."

Claude roared, "I was havin' fun, that's all."

"And you pretend not to hear. What's that about?"

Claude chuckled, "Let's keep that our secret. I like you, young fella, and I don't like many people."

6

Loretta took to her bed too upset to show Nick the schoolhouse after Mattie's visit. Nick decided to go alone, and Dog left the coolness under the porch to accompany him.

"Be careful," Claude called. "The sun's hot enough to fry an egg on a flat rock."

Nick gave a thumbs up. It was his first time to hear that expression, but a lot of firsts had occurred in the last twenty-four hours.

Perspiration saturated Nick's shirt before he reached the top of the first hill. He pulled his shirttail out and wiped his face and neck, convinced an egg would actually fry on a flat rock. In spite of the heat, excitement mounted as he neared the school. He envisioned a picturesque building in the woods, unlike the brick monstrosity he'd attended in Chicago with rooms stifling hot in the summer and drafty in winter.

A glimpse of the newly painted clapboard structure beneath a canopy of trees caused excitement to surge even more. It looked picture-book perfect until he reached the crest of the hill and saw the wooden cross over the door. Could the schoolhouse really be the unpainted, weather-beaten structure standing fifty feet beyond the church? "Signs don't lie," he muttered.

An old sow rooted for acorns under a nearby tree as Nick approached the school. She made threatening grunts and faced off with Dog while her brood scampered under the building.

It was difficult to wrap his mind around what his eyes were seeing. Hogs actually lived under the building. His brothers would never stop teasing him if they knew. No wonder John Frank had insisted a trip down for an interview was unnecessary. Nick considered himself an optimist, but his skepticism wouldn't support that claim at the moment.

He gave the schoolhouse door a shove and was met with a wave of heat that hit him in the face like opening a hot oven door. A fluttering noise sent him stumbling backward to dodge a large escaping bird.

His dad's stinging words came in a flash. "You're a fool for taking that job. People will screw you."

Nick took a tentative step inside and stood as his gaze moved around the room. A desk sat on an elevated platform with a small blackboard on the wall behind it. A length of stovepipe hanging through a hole in the ceiling suggested a stove stood in the corner behind a stack of benches and tables. An overturned bookcase lay face down with books scattered across the water-stained floor.

He moved further into the room until hearing a humming sound that came from the back corner. It sounded much like someone crooning to a baby. Pigs lived under the building. What kind of animal lived in it and made that sound? He picked up a broken chair leg and moved toward the noise. Cobwebs raked his face and heat from the tin roof thinned the oxygen and made breathing difficult.

Nick peeked around the stack of tables and thought for a brief second that he was hallucinating. A teenage girl sat cross-legged in front of a potbellied stove with her back toward Nick. Long blonde curls hung to her waist. She hummed and swayed back and forth while cuddling a doll against her shoulder.

Nick called to her, but she acted as if she didn't hear. He called twice more and then touched her shoulder. She jerked around. Soot covered her face and also the doll's. Fear sent her crawling into the corner behind the stove, clutching the doll against her breast.

"Don't be afraid. I won't hurt you. I'm the new school teacher."

Apparently she couldn't communicate. She was either deaf or retarded. He would accomplish nothing by frightened the girl and backed away to give her space. She jumped up with unexpected quickness and ran past him. He reached the doorway in time to see her disappear into the woods. What was she about?

All the unusual events since his arrival further questioned the soundness of his decision to come here. He dropped down on the schoolhouse steps. For an instant, he longed to be back in Chicago until he remembered that Kincaid would remind him forever about screwing up.

He wouldn't go back a loser. He'd make things work out by getting the community involved. If they wanted their children educated, the parents would help make it happen. "Dog, let's find a swimming hole and deal with this heat. It'll be my first time to swim in the raw. What about you?"

Dog ran ahead, occasionally sniffing at something beside the road. Nick picked up a rock and threw it into a patch of weeds a few feet in front of the animal. He ducked his tail and scampered back. Nick threw up his hands and laughed. "I've adopted a sissy dog. Kincaid would never approve of you."

7

The swim was the perfect way to deal with the heat, though Dog preferred to be an observer and only got his paws wet while getting a drink. Nick spent half an hour or more playing around in the cool water and felt much refreshed as he climbed up the embankment onto the road. He stopped and gazed at the distant hills. They were breathtaking with their many shades of green against a backdrop of clear blue sky.

The few people he'd met since arriving bordered on the bizarre, especially Claude who pretended deafness and seemed to wrestle with his own demons. All were fascinating characters. Perhaps each had a different story to tell. Jenny was the standout. He couldn't get her out of his head. He'd dreamed about her last night, a dream he welcomed, except next time he'd keep Liz out of it. She was the first girl he kissed and the only girl he'd ever slept with if he didn't count the dark-haired girl who worked at Rose's place. His brothers took him there to lose his virginity on his fifteenth birthday, and then burst into the room at an awkward moment. His only recourse to stop their pointing and laughing was to throw something. It turned out to be a lamp, an unfortunate choice since Rose booted them all out. But it provided his brothers the chance to tease him in an ongoing debate about his status as a virgin. They finally agreed that Nick was only half virgin since he never finished.

The sound of a car brought Nick back to the present. A Model-T topped the hill behind him. He moved to the edge of the road and kept walking. The car slowed as it pulled alongside.

"Hey, Teacher Man, you've been swimming? Your hair's wet."

Nick turned to see Jenny's dimpled smile, surrounded by dark tousled hair. Her complexion glowed in the afternoon sunlight with the softness of a rose-colored cloud at sunset.

"Yeah," he answered. "I'm glad to see you."

"You're glad to see me? Why?"

He felt his face grow hot.

She giggled. "You blush easily, don't you?"

He chuckled. "Guess so. I'd stop if I could." He blushed even more, causing her to laugh again. She had a flirtatious, teasing nature that he liked.

"I hear you have a room over at the mill."

"Yeah. How about you? Do you stay in Eddyville?"

"No, I live here between the rivers. As the locals would say, just two hills over. I board with two ladies." She smiled again. "Mattie gave you high marks after learning a Catholic offered no threat to the children."

Nick was surprised that she boarded with those two women but glad that she lived nearby. "I'm afraid Mattie was unhappy when she left."

"Just disappointed, since she was determined to match us up until Claude told her you don't like girls."

"What? No, no, no. The woman's confused. And Claude's senile. I like girls."

"Do you?"

"Yeah, I do, especially you." He smiled through a blush that burned his face.

She laughed and looked pleased. "Well then, how about a ride? I'll show you the most beautiful place between the two rivers."

He looked at Dog.

She pointed. "Him too. What's his name?"

"Just Dog."

She laughed. "Teacher Man, you may have a gift for teaching, but your skill for naming your pet is lacking." She laughed. "Get in."

The gears groaned as the car shot forward. The roar of the engine and the rustling air made shouting necessary for conversation as they continued past the gristmill up into the hills, turning toward the Cumberland side as they entered a narrow road where underbrush swept the sides of the car.

After going a short distance, they were forced to leave the car and follow a footpath through lush green foliage, where large boulders stood among the trees like posted sentries. Gushing water from a spring grew louder as they approached a large pool that created mini waterfalls as it overflowed down the hill.

Sun rays knifed through the trees and sent dancing lights across the forest floor. Nick thought of Claude. Could this be the spring where he'd grieved for his mother and first imagined that a bird gave him comfort?

Jenny stopped and pointed at the young girl that Nick had encountered at the schoolhouse. She sat with her feet in the water.

Seeing them, she scrambled up like a frightened deer and darted into a thicket near the pool.

Jenny ran after her, signing with her hands, but the girl never looked back.

"Who is she?" Nick asked as he approached. "I saw her at the schoolhouse a short time ago."

"Her name's Meglena Ireland. She knows these woods as well as any wild creature living here."

"I just saw her at the schoolhouse. How did she get here so fast?"

Jenny pointed. "Cut across that hill and you're at the school. Not far the way a crow flies."

"What's wrong with her?" Nick asked.

"She's deaf from a childhood disease. About a year ago the local doctor took her to Saint Louis to see a specialist. They could do nothing. She came back more disturbed than ever. Her speech is affected, and it makes communication difficult."

"That's sad," Nick said.

"I taught her what little I know about signing." She smiled. "My lesson came from a street corner beggar who gave me a card with all the signs on it. Poor girl, her father's an alcoholic and her grandmother's weird. Did I see something black on her face?"

"Yeah, soot. I found her in front of the schoolhouse stove smearing soot on her and the doll's face."

Jenny shook her head. "Meglena's a little lost bird that can't find its way back to the nest."

"Does she attend school?"

"Not anymore." Jenny grabbed his hand and pulled him toward the pool. "I don't want to feel sad today. Let's talk about happy things." Her hand felt soft like her smile. "What do you think of my special place?"

"It's poetry to the eye. I see why you like it. It's a perfect place to forget the world."

"That's why I come here."

The wind stirred the trees and sent a ray of sunlight dancing across her face. Their gazes met. She turned away and knelt beside the pool, letting water trickle through her fingers.

Nick sat on a rock beside her. "How did you find this place?"

"Claude told me about it. It's special to him."

"You know he sees a big silver bird."

"Yeah, he told me."

"Do you think that's strange?"

"Of course it's strange, but so are a lot of people." She laughed and flipped a handful of water toward him. The bulk of it hit him in the face. "Oh, I'm sorry," she squealed, overcome with laughter. "I didn't mean to get you wet."

Her apology sounded hollow against the mischievous sparkle in her eyes and her inability to stop laughing. He laughed along with her as droplets followed furrows down his face. She jumped up and sat beside him. Her leg pressed against his as her fingers brushed water from his chin. He felt his pulse quicken. "How did you end up down here?" he asked.

"I grew up in Cleveland. My mom and dad separated five years ago. I met a cheating dog just like my father and came here to get away. My aunt knew the Governor who gave me this job. I came here and loved the place and the people. What about you? What are you running from?"

"Maybe myself."

"What do you mean?"

"I had to get away too. I'm the youngest of three boys, the odd one according to my family. I didn't want to work with them at the meat plant. It's a dead-end existence. People with jobs like that often forget how to dream and end up just existing instead of living."

"Just existing?"

"If you don't dream about the kind of life you want, you'll duplicate that of your parents. The meat packing industry has defined three generations of existence for my family."

"What kind of life do you want?"

"Wow, what a question." He paused for a moment. "Love from someone special and respect from all my peers. I want to feel free, both in where I live and the right to express my ideas. I didn't want to be the guy who ground sausage for fifty years. That's why I went to school."

"Why a teacher?"

He cringed. "Do you think teaching should be just for women?"

"No, not at all."

"My father thought it queer that as a teenager I marched down the street with a group of women demanding equality in the work place."

Her mouth fell open. "You did that?" She smiled. "You're different."

"We're all different, yet alike. That's what makes people inter-esting."

"Why did you choose this place?"

"It must have been to meet you."

She smiled and glanced away.

"It was my grandfather. He worked the rivers in these parts as a young man. I always fantasized about a place like this when I was out of step with my family and the city closed in on me. I guess I'm looking to test myself and learn more about life. I'm the runt of the family. Does that tell you something?"

"What's wrong with being short? I'm short," Jenny said.

"It's okay for you. In getting a date, a short man is like an ugly girl at the dance, but you wouldn't know about that."

She faced him and smiled. "How sweet for you to say that and to be who you are."

"To be who I am?"

"I mean the march and all." She smiled. "To care. To be different."

He leaned forward until their lips touched. Then he kissed her, softly, lifting her to her feet and pressing his body against her. She pulled away.

"Why did you do that?" she asked.

The fire in her voice told him she was annoyed, but her kiss was real. "Involuntary, like my blush," he teased. "Couldn't help myself."

"We'd better go." She started walking away.

"Wait. I've wanted to kiss you ever since seeing you at the train station."

She turned and stared.

"I felt a connection."

"I bet you did. You're a man like all the others. I thought you were different."

"Different from what?" he demanded. She looked away. Silence settled in between them. He finally spoke. "You want to know what's different about me. I'm a short man who has to try harder to get a pretty girl to look his way. You looked and you kissed me back with the same feeling I felt. There's absolutely nothing wrong with that, and it's wrong for you to try to make me feel that it is."

"I'm sorry. I'm a flirt, a romantic, all the things I shouldn't be. It meant nothing. Just a kiss, okay?"

He followed her up the path in silence. He'd revealed some of his innermost feelings, something he seldom did. She'd teased and flirted like she wanted to be kissed. He never claimed to be the lady's man on the block, but Liz had never complained about his kisses. Was he such a bad kisser, along with being short?

8

Claude recognized the tapping sound of the truck before Loretta topped the hill. Boyd came out the door as she braked to a stop and climbed out. Seeing him brought a loud whimper as she rushed up the steps and threw herself into his arms. "Boyd, the disgrace is gonna kill me. I had to force my way past Ella to see that baby with my own eyes, and she still denied that the baby was colored with me lookin' at it."

Boyd folded his arms around her. "Hush, Loretta. Let it go. Hysterics won't change it."

She pulled away and turned to Claude. "Poppa, I hope you realize that Ella's disgraced the family. You should disown her like you've done Vale. I'm your only daughter now." She dabbed at her eyes and waited for a response.

"Your sister always wanted a baby."

An explosion of whining returned as she turned back to Boyd. "He can't hear shit." She shouted even louder, "Poppa, the baby's hair is nappy black."

Claude smiled and nodded. "Like Frank's, I guess."

She threw her hands in the air. "The old fool's gonna kill me yet." She buried her face in Boyd's chest and whined, "What am I gonna do?"

"Stop it. Listen to me. Frank ain't gonna let no man, black or white, lay with his wife and not shoot somebody."

"What are you gettin' at?"

"Ella's not the kind to cheat on Frank. Maybe some nigger forced hisself on her. Frank would stand by her if that happened, and he'd kill the son-of-a-bitch who done it."

"You're sayin' Ella couldn't help herself?"

"That's what I'm thinkin'."

"She'd be ashamed to tell me, her own sister." Her face brightened. "I can explain it that way at church and they'll understand."

"Don't know who could of done it. When did Eddie move away?"

"Why are you whisperin'?" Claude asked.

"It's nothin', Poppa," Loretta shouted. She lowered her voice. "Don't remember offhand when Eddie left. I could ask Mae. What are you gonna do now?"

"I'll talk to Frank on Monday if you'll watch the store."

The sound of a motor drew their attention to the road. Jenny's car came over the hill. She stopped and let Nick out before continuing on.

Boyd called to him. "I see you've found somebody to show you around."

Nick came up the steps. "I saw the big spring. I've never seen anything like it. It's magical."

Boyd chuckled. "Yeah, and with a pretty woman you can make your own magic."

Loretta punched Boyd on the arm. "Honey, you cut that out. Teasin' Mr. Kincaid like that. Mr. Kincaid, I'm sorry about not bein' able to take you to see the schoolhouse, but Mattie's gettin' the community together next Saturday to repair the buildin'. I can't help 'cause I'm still embarrassed out of my skin about my poor sister gettin' violated by some nigger. Course she couldn't help herself."

"I'm sorry, I didn't realize that was what happened."

Boyd spoke up. "The community is gonna repair the schoolhouse on Saturday. Then we're havin' a square dance and pie auction that night to raise money to pay for it. By the way, Ducky and Eddie is buildin' them bookshelves for you."

Claude spoke up. "What did you say about Eddie?"

Loretta leaned near his ear. "Boyd said Eddie's puttin' in bookshelves for Mr. Kincaid."

"Eddie's here?"

"Yes, Poppa. Remember, he was comin' for his mama's birthday."

"Tell Eddie to leave now!"

"Why do you want him to leave?" Loretta asked.

"People are talkin'. The Bird told me they're gonna be accusin' Eddie."

Loretta whispered to Nick. "That imaginary bird is gonna be the death of me."

9

On Saturday morning wagons and buggies filled the area next to the schoolhouse soon after the sun cleared the highest hill. Teams tethered under the trees shifted about, rattling harnesses and swishing at early morning flies as people clustered in groups and talked quietly.

Nick assumed their discussions were about him based upon occasional glances his way. They were polite, but remained standoffish. Boyd had advised Nick to work the crowd like a new preacher and engage each person, a strategy he soon questioned when conversation died as he approached. He was pleased when someone shouted, "Better get started if we're gonna get done today."

Someone else added, "Can't believe Mattie's not here to boss everybody around. She's never late."

"Count that as our blessing for the day," replied a thin-faced old fellow with an oversized mustache. His comment caused laughter to sift through the group.

The turnout pleased Nick, but their distrust was apparent by the way they shut down around him. He climbed up on the end of a wagon to confront their concerns. Nerves stirred his stomach as they gathered around.

"I thank you for coming. It shows an interest in your children's education, one I share. I shook your hand as a stranger this morning, but I want to live in your community as a friend. I'm only here to teach your children. I'm not with the government. I'm not a revenue man. If I've ever been within a mile of one, I didn't know it. I don't care if you raise corn, make whiskey, or fish for a living. I'm here to teach your children. Prohibition is foolish, as is any other law that tries to dictate morality."

Their expressions remained unchanged until he realized they might not know the meaning of morality and added, "The government has no business telling you how to live your life." He paused and surveyed the group, noting there were several approving nods. "Any questions?"

After a long pause a man shouted, "Let's get to fixin' the school-house."

The group dispersed with shouts of agreement. Perhaps it was a first step toward gaining their trust.

Women disappeared inside carrying brooms, mops, and buckets. Men swarmed the building, and soon the sound of hammers echoed through the hills. For nearly an hour Nick watched men whispering. Sometimes two and, at other times, three men huddled in conversation until Nick came near. He wondered if his little talk did any good, and then an old man hollered, "Mr. Teacher, we need to learn you how to talk Southern." Nick turned to search out the speaker and saw an old man with a toothless smile wave his pipe.

A man on a ladder hollered down, "Yeah. You ain't ever gonna find a woman to court with that Yankee talk."

"And her daddy gonna shoot yo' behind off, talkin' like you do," a voice on the roof added.

The first laughter came. Nick knew his few words had earned him a chance to prove himself. Now time was on his side. "Youse guys ain't up to snuff without my Yankee charm," he shouted.

"Youse got us there," a man mimicked, causing more laughter.

"Hey, I see Mattie's horse and buggy comin'," someone shouted from the rooftop.

A moan ran through the group.

Mattie's buggy arrived in a cloud of dust. She left Mousey the chore of tying up the horse. Wearing striped overalls filled to capacity, she limped toward them with the aid of a hickory stick. "Didn't aim to be late, but my old red cow got loose and I've been chasin' her. Twisted my hip." She turned to a large red-faced man. "Her calf is due soon. When she comes in heat again, I'll let you service her. You've got the best bull around."

The man blushed redder. She hobbled away ignoring the ripples of laughter among the men. Like a cat stalking its prey, she circled the schoolhouse and used the hickory walking stick to point out defects that needed repairing.

By mid-morning Mattie's sharp-tongued criticism caused Nick to fear an open rebellion by the men. He understood why Mattie was never blessed with a man. He had to take action and motioned for her to follow him a short distance away from the group. He spoke in a whisper. "Repairs on the outside are going well, thanks to you. But there's a tremendous amount of cleaning to be done inside. Is there someone other than you capable of taking charge and making sure the job is done correctly?"

Mattie's brow went up. "By golly, you're right. I'd better check it out. Nadine Jackson is in there bossin' everybody around and she don't know her butt from a hole in the ground when it comes to dealin' with people." She turned back toward the men. "Y'all keep doin' what you're doin'. I'm gonna do some checkin' inside."

Once she disappeared inside the door a man hollered, "How did you manage that?"

"Just used some of my Yankee charm," Nick teased. The men laughed.

Repairs on the school were completed in time for Nick to stop by the creek for a swim before dressing for the evening festivities. He was pleased with the repairs, especially the plans to return the following Saturday and paint the schoolhouse. The community wanted the children to have an education. Good news for Nick and a major step forward to assure success.

He'd never heard of a pie supper and learned from Loretta that the man who bids highest on a girl's pie gets a piece of pie and maybe a kiss if he's lucky. Remembering his experience at the spring, he didn't expect a kiss, but he was determined to get some answers from Jenny. Damn it, he saw himself as a good kisser.

The heat of the day failed to surrender to the August night, and the breeze that stirred could have come from an oven. Moths fluttered around the lanterns that hung in the trees next to the church. Pie boxes covered in bows and colored tissue paper filled a long table at the end of a half circle of benches taken from the church. Mattie herded couples over to meet Nick, even though he'd met most everyone that morning.

"Mr. Kincaid is a good Catholic who believes in Jesus," Mattie kept repeating. Nick finally whispered to her that it wasn't necessary to mention his religious affiliation and that he would depend upon her to respond to any concerns members of the community might have about him being Catholic.

"I'll take care of it," she whispered back like a conspirator.

Claude arrived in the back of Boyd's truck, sitting in his chair like a king on a throne. Nick helped Boyd lift Claude and the chair to the ground.

"If I had a lick of sense, I'd be in my rocker over there on the porch instead of here," Claude gasped. He mopped sweat from his brow with a shirtsleeve. Loretta questioned his manners for not using a handkerchief and drew a glare from him that needed no enforcement with words.

"I'll get you some lemonade, Poppa," Loretta said. She turned back to Nick and lowered her voice. "In spite of Ella havin' that baby, I'm gonna hold my head up and try to pretend it ain't happened, 'cause it weren't her fault some nigger forced hisself on her."

Nick wondered when the rape theory had been confirmed. No coloreds except Ducky and Mae lived between the rivers. Ducky's age eliminated him. Who could have raped her?

Nick's thoughts were interrupted when Boyd pulled a handkerchief from his pocket and mopped his face. "I have to agree with the old man. It's hot as hell with these trees around. No air gettin' through."

An angry outburst from the shadows near the church silenced everyone as all eyes looked in that direction. Vale had shouted something about protecting women from niggers.

"Sounds like them boys hidin' in the dark is puttin' somethin' extra in their lemonade," Boyd said.

Nick smiled. He'd seen a Mason jar being passed around earlier.

"Hell no, I ain't had too much to drink," came another outburst from Vale. "People are sayin' my sister laid with a nigger. Wouldn't that piss you off?"

"Damn it, shut your mouth," another hissed.

"Vale's drunk," Boyd said.

Claude's lips trembled.

"You all right, Claude?" Nick asked.

"No, I ain't. The Bird come to me this morning." He paused, looking thoughtful. "Maybe it was last night. I told Ducky he should send Eddie away, but I fear he ain't believin' me."

Nick didn't know how to respond and looked at Boyd who shrugged. Nick couldn't tell the old man there was no bird. He whispered to Boyd. "Eddie lives in Chicago, right?"

"He lived here when Ella got knocked up. That's got some of the boys all stirred up."

Jenny arrived wearing a light green dress that turned heads. She looked beautiful. Nick took notice of the green and yellow pie box she placed on the table. He planned to buy her pie, even if it took every penny he had. She'd have to talk to him, then. He couldn't get past her reaction to their kiss at the spring. Why would she think he wasn't good at kissing? What happened between them was more than just a kiss and she needed to admit it.

Mattie hobbled to the edge of the light and hollered toward the men in the shadows. "Come and gather around if you ain't drinkin'. If you are, take your butts home, 'cause we don't want you here." She pointed. "Men on that side and ladies over here. Us women did the bakin' so you men have gotta do the buyin'."

Vale called out, "Hey, Little Partner, you gonna sit with the women? You've been hangin' with the ladies all night."

Nick's anger surged and his hands automatically balled into fists. He stared in the direction of Vale's voice. Mothers had converged around him all evening with questions about school and their children. He'd had no opportunity to join the cluster of men.

"Pay no attention," Boyd urged. "His tongue gets loose when he drinks, but all in all, Vale's a decent guy."

Nick nodded, though he questioned Boyd's assessment of Vale. His head told him to stay calm. Getting into a fight wouldn't be a good example for a new teacher.

Vale shouted, "Bein' a teacher qualifies you to sit with the women."

The crowd fell silent. No one had ever challenged him like that without Nick taking him on. Anger moved him a few steps toward Vale when someone grabbed his arm and turned him around. "Don't do this, Teacher Man."

He tried to pull away. "Please, Nick, don't do this," Jenny begged. Her eyes pleaded. Silence lengthened. "Please," she repeated. "Let it go."

He finally nodded and Jenny led him away.

Vale laughed. "Okay, Little Partner, you stay with the women folk where it's safe."

Loretta rushed over to Boyd and whispered, "Get that fool brother of mine away from here. I have to put up with the stares and whispers about Ella. Now my brother's drunk as a skunk."

"You're bein' the bigger man," Boyd said to Nick. "Everyone knows that."

"Everyone except Vale," Nick answered.

Jenny smiled and pointed toward the table. "You want to know which pie is mine?"

"I've already made it a point to know."

Her smile suggested she was pleased, which was more puzzling. Did she want to eat pie with him or was it just her way to keep him out of a fight?

When Jenny's pie went up for auction, Nick made the first bid. Before the auctioneer could continue, Mattie interrupted. "That pie is sold to Mr. Kincaid. Come sit over here next to Jenny." Mattie applauded and others joined her. "Don't they make a perfect couple?"

A man yelled, "Guess that Yankee charm works after all." Nick blushed through more laughter and hand clapping.

Once the bidding ended, Nick and Jenny sat on the schoolhouse steps and enjoyed the cinnamon custard pie by lantern light. They chatted as if the incident at the spring never happened. Whatever bothered her there seemed to have passed. But Nick still needed an explanation. He pushed the last bite of his second piece of pie into his mouth. "And you can also bake a great pie."

"What do you mean, also?"

"You're also beautiful."

She looked away.

He lowered his voice. "About the kiss at the spring, we need to talk."

"Let's not get into that."

"Something wonderful happened between us and you cut it off. Why?"

She brushed pie crumbs from her lap. Nick waited. "I was afraid of where the kiss might go."

"Where did you want it to go?" he asked.

"You know how men are."

"I only know about myself. I thought you liked the kiss as much as I did."

"Look, Nick, you know."

"No, I don't know," he whispered. "I need you to tell me."

"Can't you just leave it alone?"

"No. I really need to know."

She faced him. "I was hurt once and I won't be again."

The edge in her voice didn't go unnoticed. "Being hurt is bad, but when you like a person, you have to put your heart on the line. I knew you were special the first time I saw you. Then you smiled. I knew I was going to do everything I could to get you to feel the way I feel." He chuckled. "If you can't tell in this light, you should know I'm red as a beet right now, saying things I never thought I could say."

She flashed a quick smile.

"Nobody has a patent on not being hurt. I don't know what some guy did to you. But I'm not him. If you let him go and give me a chance, you'll see how great it can be."

"It's all too soon."

"No, it's not. I have this feeling about you."

He reached for her and she pushed his hand aside.

"No," she whispered and rose. "It was just a silly kiss. Thanks for buying my pie."

He watched her walk away. She was far from over the hurt left by the other guy. But her kiss was real and she had shared pie with him. It was a start.

10

The sawmill boiler belched a cloud of white smoke as Boyd braked the truck and rolled to a stop beside an open shed. Jed Morris stood in the office doorway. He leaned out and sent a tobacco chew flying off to the side. "What brings you over my way?" he called as Boyd approached.

"Need to speak to Frank," Boyd answered.

Jed raked graying curls away from his face and motioned Boyd inside. Brown tobacco juice stained his salt and pepper beard.

Boyd took a chair pushed tight into the corner as Jed squeezed in behind a desk with its top buried beneath stacks of papers and ledgers. He reached underneath and came up with a jug. "Want a shot? It's the sweetest batch I've tasted in a long time."

Boyd waved aside the offer. Jed turned up the jug. Droplets spilled from the side of his mouth, sprinkling his shirt. He smacked his lips. "Bet I know why you want to speak to Frank. It's about that nigger baby, ain't it?"

"Could be."

"Rumors are flyin'. Frank and Artie had a fist fight this mornin'. That's why I've got Frank workin' down there by himself. Keepin' distance between 'em. Course Artie was just tryin' to help."

"What happened?"

"Everybody's heard the rumor 'bout the colored baby. Artie asked Frank if it was true and that's when it started."

"If some colored had his way with Ella, it was damn shore against her will," Boyd said.

"Goes without sayin' if Frank is standin' by his wife like he seems to be. We've got to do somethin'. The boys are willin' if you know what I mean." Jed said.

"We need to get all the boys together for a chat one of these days. Nobody knows who could have violated Ella. Ain't no coloreds been around in years, 'cept Ducky and he's too old. Besides, he wouldn't do somethin' like that."

"What about his boy, Eddie?"

"He lives up in Chicago."

"Yeah, but where was he nine months ago when somebody did it to Frank's wife? I been talkin' around and some of the boys said he was livin' here 'bout that time."

"I don't want to think it was Eddie."

"There ain't another nigger in these parts that's young enough to get a hard on 'cept that boy."

"Ella must of told Frank something," Boyd said. "I'm hopin' he'll tell me what happened. Eddie split some wood for Frank several months ago before movin' to Chicago. The timin' is right, but I just can't bring myself to think Eddie would do somethin' like that. He's visitin' back here now. Been tryin' to decide if I should mention it to him."

82

"If you do, he'll lie and take off."

"I suppose so."

"You never know what them people will do. They're high sexed, like animals. I'd never allow one around my women folk. John Frank's done a damn good job keepin' things peaceful here 'tween the rivers. He told me to ask around and see if I could find out what nigger did that to poor Ella. I had to tell him Ducky's boy was the only nigger who could of done it."

Boyd stood. "We don't want to get rumors started about the boy until we know. I'll talk with Frank. Maybe me bein' family will make a difference, and he'll tell me what he knows."

"If you find out anythin', just give me the word." He pointed at a rope hanging on a nail by the door. "I got a few boys who will make damn shore that no nigger ever touches another white woman again."

"I'll try to talk to Frank," Boyd said.

"I was gonna ask him myself until he punched the daylights out of Artie."

Jed followed Boyd outside and wished him luck.

The smell of freshly cut wood scented the air as Boyd walked down toward the river. On both sides of the road stacks of raw lumber waited to be loaded onto a boat. Frank glanced up with his lip swollen to one side and then looked down.

"What brings you here?" he asked, keeping his eyes on a tally sheet as he counted and recorded the boards in the stack.

"You all right, Frank?" Boyd asked.

"Why wouldn't I be?"

Boyd took the last cigarette from a pack and pecked it against the back of his hand. Talking to Frank was like talking to the camel

83

whose picture he crumpled into a wad and tossed onto the ground. Cupping his hands around a match, Boyd pulled fire into the cigarette and slowly exhaled. "Since we're family and all, we need to stick together, support each other, you know. I was wonderin' if you needed to talk to somebody."

"Nope. Don't have nothin' to talk about."

Boyd took a long drag. "Ella and the baby doin' well?"

"Yep."

"There's a rumor."

Frank jerked his head around. His face twisted into deep furrows and anger flashed in his eyes. "Ella never laid with no nigger, you understand."

"Course not, Frank. I come as family, hopin' I might be of help. There comes a time when everybody needs family behind them."

"Me and Ella make it just fine by ourselves. We don't need nobody."

"A lot of people say the baby . . ." Boyd's words trailed off when Frank took a step toward him. Boyd held Frank's gaze for a moment, then Frank resumed counting.

"Guess I'd better be gettin' back home." Boyd snuffed out the cigarette with the toe of his shoe and walked away.

The screen door banged shut.

Ella called from the other room. "That you, Frank? I'm puttin' the baby down for a nap."

Without answering, Frank hung his cap on a nail beside the door and smoothed his hair down with both hands. He unbuckled his overalls and let them fall to the floor, then sat at the kitchen table.

"Your supper's ready. I'll be there and dish it up in a minute," Ella called.

"Take your time." He touched his tender upper lip. Artie had given him a solid punch in the mouth. For good reason, now that he'd had time to think about it.

Ella came into the room. "Frank, honey, I've asked you a hundred times to leave your overalls on the chair out on the back porch. You know that's where I wash 'em. They're always covered in sawdust and I don't know what. We've got a baby now." She picked them up and tossed them out the door. "You're sittin' there with your head down. Somethin' wrong or you just tired?"

"Nothin' wrong."

"You didn't bring no sunshine home with you, did you?" She removed covers from pots on the stove and filled his plate. "You're havin' a vegetable supper. You want some sliced tomatoes?"

"No."

Frank looked up as she set the plate in front of him.

"What happened to your lip?"

"It ain't nothin'."

"What do you mean it ain't nothin'? It's all swoll up." She leaned to touch his lip.

He turned away and averted her hand.

"What's goin' on Frank? You been in a fight?"

"I said it ain't nothin'."

"I can see it's somethin'. Why don't you want to tell me?"

"Just a little scrap with Artie."

"Artie's your best friend since you both was kids. What happened?"

"Just drop it," he shouted.

85

His outburst brought tears to Ella's eyes. He felt guilty. He'd never hollered at her before, not even the time she'd left the gate open and goats destroyed the garden.

"It's about the baby, ain't it?" she asked.

Frank scooped a spoon of fried corn and started it to his mouth. He suddenly pitched the spoon onto his plate, then rose and headed toward the door. "I ain't hungry."

Ella followed him out. He dropped down on the edge of the porch. She sat beside him and burrowed her face against his neck and shoulder until he slipped his arm around her. A dove cooed in the distance.

"The Bible talks about lovin' all children. A baby don't know black from white or green from yellow. I love the child. Why can't everybody love a baby?"

Tears painted wet lines down her cheeks. Frank spoke softly. "You know that baby girl is colored by all accounts."

"She's a baby first. I know she's a little bit colored, but what's first is what's important."

"People are talkin'. Some think you laid with a colored."

"I would never lay with a colored or anybody else. I love you, Frank." A soft sob erupted. "What are we gonna do?"

"I don't know," he mumbled, hugging her close.

11

The steady drone from the engine grew louder as the ferryboat neared the dock across from Fanny Hartman's boarding house. Her cooking was so good on the day Nick arrived it was a treat to have lunch there again. He pushed his empty plate aside and gazed out the window at a scene far different from the hustle and bustle of Chicago. He loved the slow pace that his new life offered.

Laughter came from below the ferry landing where two boys took turns swinging on a rope and dropping into the water. Up near the depot Eddie loaded boxes onto the wagon while the mules occasionally shook their heads to ward off nits and flies that braved the noonday sun.

The swinging doors to the kitchen popped open as Fanny charged into the room with a bowl of blackberry pudding in one hand and a pitcher of iced tea in the other. She glided around the cluster of small tables, each covered with a starched white tablecloth. She moved with the ease of a dancer in spite of her advancing age.

Nick and a portly man wearing a dark blue suit were the only people remaining in the dining room following the noon meal.

Butter dripped from the man's chin as he rotated an ear of boiled corn while his large teeth scraped kernels from the cob.

Fanny paused to refill the man's iced tea glass as she floated by on her way to Nick's table.

"You're gonna try some of my blackberry puddin', ain't ya?"

Nick nodded, though he was stuffed.

"Blackberry season is near over. Probably the last blackberry puddin' I'll be makin' this year." She whispered, "I added a little sweet cream to your puddin'. Hope you like it."

Nick nodded and smiled.

She leaned forward and looked out the window. Her soft cottony hair framed a wide face that held twinkling blue eyes. "Is that Eddie I see over at the depot?"

"Yeah, Boyd needed supplies picked up and Eddie came in Ducky's place. He wanted to buy his mother a birthday gift. I hitched a ride with him to pick up books for school."

"You tell Eddie to come to the back door so I can fix him a plate."

Nick frowned, ready to express his views against racial prejudice, but before he had time to open his mouth, she added, "I fed him here in the dining room once and Ducky threatened to beat the boy."

"Why do you call him boy? I'll be twenty-three my next birthday and he's a couple of months older. I don't consider myself a boy."

"Well, I never thought about why. In these parts, everybody always refers to a young colored man as boy. He's really a man, a bright one too."

"Yes, he is. I learned that by discussing literature with him on the way over. He's well read."

"He got to hangin' around Vale too much 'fore he moved to Chicago. My mother's older sister, who's gone to glory, used to teach at Woodson too." She leaned forward and lowered her voice. "Guess there's no need to keep it a secret anymore. After school in the evenings, she taught Eddie from the same books she used every day at school. He was a bright child accordin' to Aunt Laura. Course we never talked about it before."

"Not many coloreds living around here now, are there?"

"No. I'm sorry to say a lot of people twist the Good Book's meanin' when it comes to treatin' coloreds right. Most moved out over the last twenty years. Course, John Frank encouraged the young ones to leave."

"Why?"

"When he took office, goin' on sixteen years ago, most coloreds had left. Some bad stuff was happenin' to the young ones. John Frank says he don't have anythin' against coloreds. I'm not supposed to tell this, but when he got elected as sheriff his plan was to leave the older coloreds alone and move the young ones out. Even give 'em money to live when they left. Nobody knows this, but he worked with a colored group in Chicago that got jobs for 'em. He figured that was the way to keep peace and give coloreds a chance for a better life."

Nick wasn't surprised to hear that John Frank helped them get jobs. He still had the sheriff pegged as a self-serving man and figured he did it for his own self-interest. "Was Eddie forced to move away?"

Fanny paused and twisted her lip. "Don't think so. He was the only young one left 'tween the rivers and never caused no trouble. There's nothin' for coloreds to do around here. Not much for whites 'cept the whiskey business and the government wants to close that down." She glanced at the man in the corner and lowered her voice to a whisper. "Rumor has it that Cleve Underwood over there is a government man tryin' to stop whiskey makin'."

"A revenue man?"

She nodded. "Course he says he's a salesman, and thank God for 'em. Salesmen passin' through keep me in business." She glanced at the near empty bowl of pudding. "You want more?"

"No, I'm fine. It's really good."

She smiled. "I better check on the kitchen. I sometimes forget I have bread bakin'." She hurried away.

The sheriff was a racist regardless of the twist he put on things. Nick couldn't accept that the man actually believed he was offering a service by sending young coloreds from their homes. Nick knew he'd speak out on the matter at the right time. Perhaps over time he could change such thinking.

The scraping sound of chair legs scooting across the wooden floor drew Nick's attention to the man across the room. He rose from the table and came forward. "Couldn't help from overhearing you mention books. Are you the new teacher?"

"Yes. Nick Kincaid's the name."

"Cleve Underwood."

"Glad to meet you." Nick flashed back to John Frank's advice about not making friends with revenue men.

"I hear you're from Chicago," Cleve said.

Nick nodded. "You don't sound like a local yourself."

"Cleveland is my home. My company assigned me here and I travel this end of the state showing my samples and taking orders, dry goods, mostly." Cleve chuckled. "I could tell by your voice that you weren't from here." He extended his hand to shake.

John Frank eased through the doorway and stood watching. Cleve cleared his throat. "I'll see you around, Kincaid. Nice to meet you."

Cleve put his hat on and acknowledged John Frank with a slight nod.

John Frank returned the acknowledgement and watched Cleve go. He spoke while staring after the man. "I see you made a new friend." He crossed and dropped down into a chair opposite Nick.

"We just met. I wouldn't describe him as a friend."

John Frank grunted. "What did you two talk about?"

Without looking up, Nick ran his spoon around the bowl and came up with the last bite of pudding. He hoped John Frank had a sense of humor. "We both agreed that this county has a sorry ass sheriff."

A scowl spread across John Frank's face. It gradually melted into a smile and then he roared with laughter. "You little son-of-a-bitch, nobody in this county has the balls to tease me like that unless they know me well. You're all right, son."

Apparently Nick's teasing had gained favor. The sheriff smoothed his mustache into place with his thumb and forefinger, a gesture he continued to repeat. "Cleve would like to see my ass in a federal prison for not stoppin' people from makin' whiskey. That will never happen. Do I turn my back while people make it? Yeah. I don't enforce the law because my people have to eat. Times can be hard livin' here. A man plants bottomland each spring, hopin' for a good crop. The river floods and washes it away. Come winter, he's huntin' for possums to feed his family."

The sheriff's interest in the welfare of the people was sort of weird. He could take teasing. Maybe Nick's assessment of him was wrong. Perhaps there was a heart beneath his inflated ego. "You really care about your people?" Nick asked.

John Frank frowned. "Shore I do. Why would you think otherwise?"

Nick shrugged and then added, "I have an issue with your attitude toward coloreds."

John Frank glanced around and lowered his voice. "I ain't got nothin' against colored folks. Like I told you before, I get 'em out of here to keep down trouble."

"You don't protect them. You allow them to be run out."

"I'm protectin' 'em by sendin' 'em away. You think about that. You and me ain't gonna agree about this today and if you repeat this talk, I'll call you a liar and everybody will believe me."

Nick pushed the bowl away and tossed his napkin onto the table. The good sheriff had a warped sense of justice, but Nick felt he had no choice but to retain a working relationship.

"Now, if you're finished," John Frank said, "walk up to the office with me and I'll give you them new books for school."

When they left the boarding house, Jenny stood in front of the general store talking to Vale and another large, tall bearded stranger. Someone Nick had never met. Nick loved the way Jenny tilted her head and smiled while talking, but he didn't like her talking to Vale. She saw Nick and hurried into the store as if trying to avoid him, which only added to his frustration. He couldn't make her like him, but the urge to go into the store and finish the pie supper conversation was under consideration when he heard Vale with slurred speech say, "Partner, I'm speakin' to you. "

"I'm sorry, I didn't hear you." Nick said. "What did you ask me?"

"Is what they're sayin' about my sister true?"

"I wouldn't know. You should talk to your sister about that and not me."

"I make a habit of stompin' every nigger lover's ass. Should you be on my list?"

Nick stiffened for a fight and John Frank stepped between them. "Vale, the teacher made his point, and a good one I might say. So let it go."

"Sheriff, I just want to know which son-of-a bitchin' nigger did Ella, 'cause he's a dead man." Vale pointed toward the depot. "Brady says the only nigger young enough would be that boy loadin' the wagon."

"Wild speculation don't help nobody," John Frank snapped. "You've got a gut full of whiskey. Go sleep it off." He lowered his voice. "You'd better hear me. You start somethin' and I'll lock yo' ass up." He turned to Nick. "Now, let's get them books."

John Frank's office was up a side street directly in line with the depot. Getting the books took only a few minutes. Nick came out the door with a box of books under each arm and saw Jenny waiting across the street. She met him midway.

"We need to talk." She was careful not to meet his gaze.

"You've been on my mind. What's on yours?"

"I've thought about what you said. Maybe I'm scared of liking you too much."

He smiled. "I could never like you too much."

"I don't know you."

"I don't know you either, but I want to."

"You've probably had a lot of girlfriends."

"Just one. She was nothing like you." His comment brought a quick smile.

"Can we start by being friends?" she asked.

"I assumed we were already."

Her face relaxed and then she gasped and pointed toward the depot. "What are they doing to Eddie? Oh, my God, stop them. I'll get John Frank."

The man with Vale had Eddie pushed against the side of the wagon with his arm pressed against Eddie's throat. Vale was screaming in Eddie's ear.

Nick dropped the books and ran. "Let him go," he shouted.

Vale staggered forward to meet Nick. "Stay out of this." He drew back his fist to meet Nick's charge, but Nick gave a quick left jab that caught Vale in the mouth and took him down. Brady let Eddie go and faced Nick whose blow struck the side of the big man's face. He staggered, but regained his footing.

"You son-of-a-bitch," Brady roared. A lightning punch connected with Nick's jaw. He went down hard with his face rooted in the dirt. He rose to his knees just as Vale's boot caught him in the ribs and sent him sprawling. Nick gasped for air as pain shot through his side. Nick heard a thud and saw Brady crumple to the ground beside him. Eddie stood on the wagon above him and waved a two-by-four wagon standard. Nick scrambled to his feet as Vale advanced with an open blade. He grabbed Vale's wrist and both went down, sending the weapon flying. Nick rolled on top of Vale and shot two hard punches into his face. Nick felt someone grab him by the leg and drag him away.

"Break it up, boys," John Frank shouted. He positioned himself between Nick and Vale.

Jenny dropped to her knees beside Nick. "Are you okay?" she asked. Her hand trembled as she dabbed a cut above his eye with a handkerchief.

"I'm fine." He struggled to his feet, though the pain in his side felt like a rib had been torn out. When he felt dizzy for a moment, Jenny grabbed him around the waist.

"Are you sure you're okay?" she asked.

"Yeah." She dabbed blood from his swelling lip. "I'll get beat up again if you continue to hold me like this."

Blood dripped from Vale's nose and dotted his shirt. His steely eyes gazed at Nick. "I ain't through with you, Partner."

A moan came from Brady. He rolled over and sat up.

Eddie stood holding the wagon standard. John Frank looked up at him. "The teacher dropped two boxes of books in the street up there. Get 'em. I want you and the teacher on the ferry in five minutes. We're gonna put a river between this fight before somebody gets hurt."

12

A moth fluttered through the open door and circled the oil lamp in the center of the kitchen table. Mae smacked at it with a dishtowel, only to see it escape into the shadows. Cupping her hand to catch crumbs, she wiped the faded red oilcloth that draped the table.

Thoughts of her son warmed her heart. Eddie had bought her a birthday present in Eddyville. He didn't fool her one bit by pretending to pick up supplies for Mr. Boyd. The only good thing about being a year older was Eddie's visit. Now that he was here, she hated the thought of him returning to Chicago. He needed to find him a good woman to care for him and not go messing around with them honky-tonk women in the city. She'd seen pictures of them in the paper.

Men's voices floated up the hill from the gristmill through the open door. She paused and listened. Ducky and Eddie were talking loud like they were arguing about Mr. Nick's fight with Vale. She'd applied a poultice to the teacher's head to stop the swelling. He must be a good man, standing up and fighting for her boy. She would send some peach cobbler down to Mr. Nick after supper to show her thanks.

Mae reached her long slender arm into the oven and removed a pan of cornbread and dumped the hot steaming pone onto a plate just as Ducky and Eddie came in the door. They sat at the kitchen table without saying a word.

"Is the teacher doin' well?" Mae asked.

"Gonna be fine," Ducky snapped.

Mae cut her eyes toward her husband. He sounded like his dark mood might be after him again.

She studied the two men a moment before turning away to fill bowls from pots on the stove. Ducky seemed troubled and Eddie was too quiet. Something wasn't right. She set plates in front of them. "Ducky, what's goin' on? You two is actin' like somethin' be bad wrong." She looked at Eddie who glanced at his dad and then looked away.

"Eddie's leavin' tonight," Ducky declared.

"No, I'm not," Eddie shot back.

Mae bristled. "Ducky, why you want my boy to leave?"

"He hit Big Brady on da head with a wagon standard. I fear dey be after him."

Mae gasped. "I knows da teacher got in dat fight, but you too?"

"Don't worry. I'll leave tomorrow after we celebrate your birthday," Eddie said.

Mae sank onto a chair by the table and twisted the bottom of her apron into a wad. "Eddie, maybe you should go in the mornin'. The sheriff might lock you up or worse for hittin' a white man."

"No. The sheriff saw the fight. He won't do nothin' to me."

"There be Mr. Claude's vision of a hangin' to think on," Ducky barked. He turned to Mae with eyes like dancing balls. "The boy's gettin' uppity livin' in the big city."

"No, I'm not. I'm grown up and I'm no coward."

Duck jumped to his feet. "You think I be a coward?" He drew back his hand.

Mae screamed, "Don't you hit him."

Ducky froze. Deep furrows raced across his brow as he glared at his wife.

"I never in my life called yo' hand about nothin'," Mae said. "But I is now. I gives you a son to love and not beat. Black folks don't need to beat der own. Been too much beatin' in da past."

Ducky dropped into his chair with eyes downcast.

Mae had embarrassed her husband. She went against the Good Book. She'd have to do some praying and ask her husband to forgive her.

Ducky's hand trembled as he took a fork and started eating. Eddie looked from his mother to his father. He touched his dad's arm. "You've made me the man I am. I remember that you carried me on your back through the woods in the dark so Miss Laura could teach me to read. I can still see you sittin' on her back porch noddin' off while waitin' for me. I learned to read. It opened my eyes to possibilities. I'm gonna live in the white folks' world and have a good life."

Ducky rose and hurried out the door. Eddie started to follow.

"Wait," Mae called. She motioned to a chair beside her. "Come, sit. Yo' daddy needs to be alone. He'll carry dem words to his grave, but he won't let you see him feelin'. He closes down fast as a door drops on a rabbit trap where feelin's is involved."

"I know."

"Yo' daddy's feelin's come out for what he do for you. A man has to feel proud and powerful inside 'fore he be soft and kind on da outside. Yo' daddy's a kind man."

"He's always been afraid to stand up."

Mae sat up straight with her chin thrust out. "Maybe he be wiser than you, boy. We be from a tribe of tall Africans. Your granddaddy was brought over from a place called Goree. The story goes that he spent forty days and forty nights on a ship shackled in irons."

"Mama, I've heard the story before."

"But you ain't feelin' it. When your daddy was still under foot, too little to even work in the field, his daddy was took in the night and dragged away tied behind a horse."

"I know about that, Mama. Nothin's gonna happen to me before I leave. Daddy is afraid because of what Mr. Claude said. The old man is losin' his mind, sayin' he talks to a bird."

"Watch out, now. Old folks sometimes have da gift."

Eddie chuckled. "Not the kind of gift I have." He pulled a red and yellow silk scarf from inside his shirt. "Happy birthday."

A breeze from the door moved the scarf about. The silk threads in it glimmered in the lamplight.

Mae took it and bathed her hands in its softness. She pressed it against her cheeks. "You outdid yo'self, boy. It's the prettiest thing I ever seed. I needs to save it to put around my neck to be buried."

"No, it's for you to wear now. I'm savin' my money so I can move you up to Chicago. Then I'll buy you all the pretty scarves you want."

"The Lord did bless me by sendin' you." She spread her arms and wrapped the scarf around him as he hugged her.

Mae stiffened when she saw Ducky watching from the doorway. Eddie turned and faced his dad, who stared at the floor as he spoke. "Boy, you knows how dem loose planks jumps around on dat old Donaldson bridge every time a wagon rolls cross it?"

"Yes, sir."

"Dem boards always seems to be loose ever since you was little. Dat old mule Jane don't minds 'em, but Old Nellie acts skittish when she crosses. Maybe I be like dat old mule. I feels like I been walkin' on loose boards all my life."

Eddie rose.

Ducky threw up his hand. "I never be a feared for me. It be for you and Mae. So I acts like a cowed dog whenever I needs to. I forgot you already be a man choosin' yo' own path."

The knock aroused Nick from a light sleep. A pain above his right eye reminded him of Mae's poultice tied tightly against his brow.

"I'll be right there," he called after a second knock came. Nick grabbed a lamp from the desk and cracked the door. Claude leaned on a cane, gasping for air, his face pale in the moonlight. "You've got to help Eddie." He faltered. Nick grabbed his arm and led him inside. The old man dropped into the rocker. "You've gotta talk to Eddie. Nobody listens to me." He looked up at Nick. "The Bird come to see me again. All its feathers was plucked except the long silver ones on its wings. It sat on my shoulder and pecked at my ear until it bled. He leaned his head to the side. "See."

Nick held the lamp near and saw that dried blood covered the top rim of Claude's ear. The old man had probably scratched it.

101

"People comin' to the store is makin' talk against Eddie." His voice trembled. "Some say he was with Ella, but I don't believe it. You gotta make Eddie leave."

"He is leaving. Ducky is using Boyd's boat to row Eddie across the river in the morning."

Claude slumped in the rocker with a loud sigh. The faint sound of Loretta calling caused the old man to frown. "Tell that woman you ain't seen me."

Nick peeked out the window and saw a lantern moving down the hill. A second call sounded much closer. Dog barked and scampered to the door.

"Even your dog thinks Loretta is a varmint that needs to be chased away."

Loretta called, "Mr. Kincaid, is Poppa up there?"

Nick turned and whispered to Claude. "You might pretend to be deaf, but I can hear. I have to answer her."

"Tell her to go away. That skinny-assed woman is a pain."

Nick opened the door and motioned to Loretta. She hurried up the steps and shot in the door.

"Poppa, have you lost your mind wanderin' off in the dark? What's wrong with you?"

Claude sat stone-faced and stared straight ahead.

"He ain't hearin' me." She shouted, "Poppa, I've come to take you back to the house." She removed a handkerchief from an apron pocket and wiped her face. "Poor, Poppa. His mind's slippin' away more each day. Livin' in his own world, you might say." She took Claude's hand. "Come, Poppa, let's get you back up the hill."

Nick watched them go. He couldn't help but like the old man.

13

A pain in his hip brought Claude out of bed well before dawn. He sucked on a peppermint and watched the glow in the eastern sky become more intense. His mind soon drifted back to when he stood by his father's bed and watched the dying man wrestle with death. His father opened his eyes and looked up at Claude.

"You get nothin'. Yo' brother, Daniel, gets all my leavin's. I done made it legal."

Daniel smiled at Claude from across the bed. Though anger twisted Claude's gut, he pressed his lips tight against the news. He'd followed a plow and team across the rocky hillside since turning seven just like his brother. He had scars on his back from his daddy's whip and his sweat had dropped into every open furrow. The old son-of-a-bitch would deny him now.

The old man turned to Daniel and struggled to speak. "My daddy . . . stole gold pieces from the Union army. It's hid . . . in a tree scarred from . . . a lightning strike. The one that stands up on—"

His words faded, as did his breath. He lay still. Horror flashed across Daniel's face. He grabbed the dead man by the shoulders and shook him. "Where, Poppa? Which tree?" he screamed.

Claude walked outside and left his brother pleading for his father to speak. Excitement welled in Claude's chest and left him breathless. "Buzzard Hill," he muttered.

He knew the tree. Lightning peeled a gash from top to bottom during a thunderstorm. Leaves grew on half of the tree and the other half remained a skeleton of dead branches.

Daniel came out the door with his good fortune mirrored in his face. "The farm belongs to me now. You can stay and work for your board if you want." He started toward the stables and called back over his shoulder. "I'm goin' to see Mr. Garner about building a box for the old man. You go up the hill and start diggin' a hole next to Mama."

Claude didn't answer. He waited until his brother rode out on the bay mare. Once Daniel turned the bend in the road, Claude jumped to his feet and raced up the hill faster than he'd ever run. If the old man had told Daniel where to find the gold, Claude intended to get there first.

Stumbling and falling, he pressed on through briers and under-brush, snagging his pants and shirt. Blood oozed from scratches on his arms and face. He reached the spring, gasping for air. He cupped his hands and scooped a handful of water. Sucking his palms dry, he then splashed his face and continued the climb.

The tree stood alone in an open space. Claw-shaped roots pierced the rocky hillside, thirsty for the taste of moisture deep beneath. Large boughs spread like an open umbrella, some drooping within a few feet of the ground.

Drenched with sweat from the climb, Claude circled the tree and searched for a knothole. No holes, nothing. He again scanned the tree, moving around it slowly. Again, nothing. Could this be Poppa's deathbed joke?

He straddled a drooping bough and scooted along until reaching the tree's trunk. A handful of straw stuck out from a limb that grew some twenty feet up, most likely a bird's nest. He pulled himself from limb to limb and found three eggs in the nest. "You old son-of-a-bitch," he screamed. In a fit of anger, he jerked the nest from its perch and hurled it away in disgust, watching it tumble from branch to branch and break into pieces as it sifted down.

Claude wiped away sweat and tears with his shirttail. He blinked several times before the knothole came into full focus. It was real. The nest had covered a cavity in the tree. Rough bark scraped his arm as he reached inside. His fingers touched something. He forced his arm further in and scraped it even more until he was able to grasp something. Could it be? His hands shook as he withdrew the dried leather pouch. He forced it open and screamed, "I had the last laugh, Poppa. I found the gold."

A board on the porch squeaked and Claude jerked awake. Loretta stared down at him. "Here's your breakfast."

She placed the tray across his chair. "Just biscuits, molasses, and bacon this mornin'. No eggs. A varmint got in the hen house or else the hens are takin' a vacation." She giggled as she sat across from him. "Was you dreamin' just now? 'Cause you was talkin' up a storm."

Claude felt the hair rise on his neck. Had he said something about the gold? "Guess I might of been snorin' and you thought I was talkin'."

"No. You was talkin' about Uncle Daniel as clear as daylight."

The old man tried to appear calm, but his heart pounded. He took a long sip of coffee. Fearing the answer, he asked, "What did I say?"

"Somethin' about a tree and a pouch."

He stopped his hand from trembling by sopping a biscuit in molasses. "Can't figure what you're talkin' about."

"You know Uncle Daniel walked the hills forty years lookin' for the gold. I thought it might be about that."

"Daniel was crazy."

"Some folks didn't think so."

"Some folks didn't know Daniel like I did."

"A tale is still goin' around about the Union Army losin' some gold."

"That's just a tale." Claude laughed. "My crazy brother was a damn fool."

Loretta rubbed her lips together and stared for a moment. "Poppa, if you knowed about the gold, you'd tell me, wouldn't you?"

"Loretta, how come you ask that? After all, you're my oldest daughter and the one that loves me best."

She smiled, as if pleased with his response, but Claude doubted that she fully accepted his answer.

The sound of a horse and buggy drew all eyes toward the road. Loretta twisted her lips and rolled her eyes. "Here comes the biggest mouth 'tween the rivers. I'm the best Christian in the whole community, but I'd like to slap her in the mouth for spreadin' that stuff about Ella."

Mattie climbed out of the buggy and Loretta hollered, "Come on up. We got hot coffee."

Mattie labored up the steps. "Maybe a sip of coffee with an extra spoon of sugar might perk me up. I'm movin' slow this mornin'."

"Got some hot inside. Be right back." Loretta disappeared.

Mattie leaned close to Claude's ear and shouted, "How you feelin', Mr. Claude?"

"I died this mornin'."

"Mr. Claude, you're always tryin' to pull my leg."

Loretta returned and handed Mattie the mug.

"I come over to hear the latest about Ella," Mattie said. "Has she confessed to givin' herself to some colored?"

Loretta drew herself up like a snake ready to strike. "My sister didn't give nothin' to nobody. If it happened, and I'm not sayin' it did, some colored forced hisself on her."

Mattie tilted her head and gave a woeful sigh. "Loretta, sweetheart, I've seen the baby. It's colored. You gotta accept facts."

"It's not colored until I say it's colored."

Mattie shrugged and started to respond until the sound of a motor drew her attention. Jenny came up the hill and drove past the store without looking in their direction.

Loretta stretched her neck. "Where is she goin'? Just drove right by without wavin'. She's stoppin' at the mill? She don't have nothin' to grind, does she?"

Mattie giggled. "It's the new teacher. Jenny worried a good bit about Vale beatin' him up. I think she likes him more than she's willin' to say. Bet she's here to check on him."

"She wouldn't be goin' to see him alone in his room. Oh, my Lord, she's goin' up the stairs."

Mattie hurried to look. She giggled again. "He's standin' in the doorway and ain't wearin' no shirt."

"That girl's gonna ruin herself." Loretta rushed over to Claude. "Poppa, come and do somethin'."

Claude heard, but he pretended to be asleep.

She turned back to Mattie. "Poppa's asleep or just deaf as a dead man. What's happenin' now?"

"She's goin' inside."

"She'll ruin her reputation," Loretta whispered. "We best keep this between ourselves."

A waste of words, Claude thought. Women can't keep nothin' to themselves.

"Just a little bump on the head. I'm fine," Nick said. He opened the door wider and motioned. Jenny stepped inside. Their gaze connected until he remembered that he wore no shirt. He grabbed one from the back of a chair and hurriedly fumbled into it.

"Vale did that to you?" She pulled his shirttail aside and lightly touched his black and blue ribs. Her hand felt cool and soft. "Should you see a doctor?"

"It's just bruised." He felt the heat from a blush and began to match buttons to buttonholes while staring at her. His pulse quickened at the thought of taking her in his arms.

"Wait, you've missed a buttonhole." She pushed his hands aside and lined up the openings. The tips of her fingers brushed against his chest. He smelled the light scent of lilac, a reminder of their first kiss at the spring. Her closeness sent his arteries pumping even more. He reached for her and she abruptly turned and moved away.

"We didn't finish talking the other day before the fight with Vale," Jenny said.

"No, we didn't."

Their eyes met again. She quickly moved to the window and pushed the curtain aside. "I had a boyfriend before. I thought I loved him."

"I don't care about your previous boyfriends."

"We were together, you know?"

"Do you still love him?"

"No," she blurted.

"Then we don't have a problem."

She faced him. "It was about trust."

"There is nothing wrong to expect trust and for it to be earned."

"My mother trusted my father. He left her for another woman after nearly twenty years."

Nick remained silent for a moment. "Was he a good father?"

"He left my mother."

"He wasn't her father."

The response startled Jenny. She rubbed her hands together and turned back to the window. "He hurt her."

"And you were hurt by what happened between them."

She nodded. "Dad loved baseball. When I was a kid, he put me on his shoulders and walked three blocks to the stadium every Saturday during the season. It's one of my earliest memories. We had a hot dog at the game and ice cream on the way home." She was silent for a moment and then continued. "I usually had mustard or ice cream on my dress. My mother fussed. My father would say, 'Dorothy, Jenny had fun she'll remember the rest of her life."

"And you have remembered it."

She turned toward Nick and leaned against the windowsill. "When I think back, my mother worried over unimportant things, still does. My dad didn't worry about anything."

"Maybe he told no one about his worries."

After a pause she nodded. "Maybe so. My mother had nothing good to say about him afterwards."

"My grandmother once said to forgive someone is the same as forgiving yourself, and you don't even have to tell them."

Jenny wrinkled her nose. "I don't know what that means."

"I'm not sure either, but it must be profound since Granny said it."

Jenny smiled. "Nick, you're honest and you make sense. That's one of the reasons I like you."

"That's encouraging. But I wish you trusted me."

"I don't know you."

"There are things we know and some we take on trust. I know we'd be good together. I see it in your eyes. If you've really looked at me, you've seen it in mine." He reached and took her hand. She didn't resist. He pulled her to him. He touched her lips ever so lightly with his, one, two, three times. Then their lips met as he pulled her into his arms.

"No, Nick, no. Let me go." She pulled away.

He threw his arms up and shouted, "Damn, Jenny, what are you trying to do to me?" He jerked the door open and shot out onto the landing.

She followed him to the doorway. "I'm sorry, Nick."

He leaned against the railing, frustrated. He took a few moments before facing her. "Maybe I was wrong about us. You'd rather remain bitter toward your father who loved you. Probably still does. As for the guy you thought you loved, maybe he was a creep. I don't know. But for whatever reason, you keep hanging on to him or at least the feelings you had."

"That's not fair."

"What's not fair is for you to give me hope and then take it away. Don't pretend there can be something with me unless you're willing to take a chance. You've got to decide." He turned away and glanced toward the store in time to see Loretta's and Mattie's heads disappear behind the corner of the building. He heard Jenny's footsteps descend the stairs until the crunch of gravel reached his ears. Without looking her way, he went inside, slammed the door, and dropped into the rocker. Dog came over and licked his hand. He leaned back and closed his eyes. "Damn," he muttered, "I didn't want her to leave."

He heard the door open and looked up. Jenny stepped inside. He rose.

"I'm afraid," Jenny said. "The way I feel scares me." She paused as if expecting him to speak. When he didn't, she continued. "We just met. Things were moving so fast."

"I'm sorry. I should have been more understanding. I'm glad you came back." His impulse was to smother her in his arms. Whatever happened now was up to her.

"I came back to be with you."

He opened his arms. She moved into them and he felt the warmth of her body against his. He kicked the door closed and their lips met.

14

A boat moved slowly up the Cumberland as Nick watched from his doorway. He understood his grandfather's never-ending infatuation with the beauty of Kentucky. The quiet sound of bubbling brooks and the splendor of rolling hills elevated his spirit, yet hidden among its beauty were elements of bigotry that seemed foreign to such a place.

The sound of a screeching bird drew his attention toward the hill behind the store. The blue jay had a nest near the path that led up to the cabin. She'd sounded an alarm as Mae passed by carrying a basket of laundry stacked up to her chin. Her long legs searched for firm footing with each step, yet she moved with such dignity in spite of the cumbersome basket and the difficult climb.

Nick checked his watch. Jenny should be arriving soon. He walked up to the store and found Claude asleep. The old man jerked awake as Nick stepped upon the porch. "Didn't mean to wake you."

Claude raked back his ruffled hair. He looked pale and hollow eyed. "Must of dropped off. Didn't sleep much last night."

"Are you feeling all right?"

"Aches and pains. Some days I feel like I'm fixin' to die."

Loretta came out the door carrying a straw basket. "Here's your picnic lunch, Mr. Kincaid. It's so cute for you to surprise Jenny with a picnic." She set the basket on the table and eyed her father. "Poppa's been actin' real strange all day, have you noticed?"

Claude always acted strange, but aware he heard her every word, Nick chose not to answer.

"Don't know what's comin' down," Loretta said. "Mae's been out back cryin'. She ain't done a spoonful of work since Eddie left. Then Poppa just about destroyed his room."

Nick wanted to ask what had happened and offered a questioning frown. Loretta cut her eyes over toward Claude and lowered her voice. "Last night we heard this thrashin' around downstairs. Boyd jumped out of bed and went runnin', thinkin' maybe somebody had broke in the store. Poppa had took a hoe and was beatin' the place up. It was pitch black. His room was a mess with flour and sugar spread everywhere. Even beat my mama's picture off the wall."

Nick whispered. "Did he say why?"

"I'm plum ashamed to tell you why. He thought he was chasin' that bird he says he talks to."

"That Bird tried to kill me," Claude shouted.

The outburst startled Loretta. Claude didn't look her way. It was as if he was talking to himself.

"I thought for a minute he heard me talkin' about the bird. He's gettin' sicker in the head all the time."

"My head's fine, Loretta."

She gasped and looked from Claude to Nick. "Lord help, Poppa did hear me. It's a miracle." She knelt before him. "Poppa, I've been prayin' for a miracle. You can hear."

The old man leaned forward. "Talk up, Loretta, you know I can't hear."

She jumped to her feet. "Poppa, you must of heard. Mr. Kincaid, didn't you hear Poppa hear? I mean, Poppa, you heard me."

The old man continued to stare straight ahead. Loretta looked confused. "I guess he didn't hear." She sighed. "I've got to finish supper. You have fun on your picnic."

She went inside and Nick turned to Claude. "Shame on you for teasing her like that."

He ignored Nick and asked, "Did I tell you The Bird come last night? Woke me up. It landed on my pillow, naked except for the wing feathers. The son-of-a-bitchin' bird lowered its head and spit on me." He pulled the top of his shirt open. "See where the spatter hit? Burned like fire."

Red splotches and blisters covered his chest.

"It raised its wings like this," he said, raising his hands above his head. "Then it started growin' until it was bigger than me. Had blood red eyes. I rolled out of bed and tried to run, but it wrapped its wings around me, squeezin' my air off. I couldn't breathe. I grabbed a hoe leanin' in the corner and beat it off until Boyd and Loretta got there. Them two said they didn't see a thing and The Bird had nearly killed me. Do you think Boyd and Loretta wants The Bird to kill me?"

"I'm sure they don't." It was sad to see the old man's reality slipping away. Nick was glad that further discussion about the bird was spared by the sound of Jenny's car. Claude shaded his eyes. "Who is that comin' up the hill?"

"It's Jenny," Nick said. He grabbed the basket and headed down the steps.

Claude called out, "You have fun, boy, while you're young."

15

Water bubbled over rocks in a nearby brook as Nick and Jenny snuggled on a blanket with her head nestled on his shoulder. She opened her eyes and smiled. An afternoon breeze moved a wisp of her hair against his face. He blew it aside. She laughed and touched his chin. "You've got a dimple."

He chuckled. "It's not a dimple. All the men in my family have a cleft chin. You're the one with dimples. You show them every time you smile."

She giggled.

"And when you laugh."

She sat up. "What time is it?"

"About an hour of light left, I'd think."

She jumped to her feet. "We've got to go." She grabbed the corner of the blanket and pulled. He rolled onto the grass and sat up. She dropped to her knees and gave him a quick kiss. "Come on, I want to show you the sunset from the top of Buzzard Hill."

The sun hung low and the wind stirred the treetops as they drove along the spine of the ridge between the two rivers. The sound of a boat horn drifted up from somewhere beyond the hills on the Tennessee side.

The evening sky glowed orange as they spread the blanket on a wide flat rock that faced toward the Tennessee River. Jenny settled into his arms and out of the quietness came a twittering that grew in volume until it reached a deafening pitch. A flock of black birds, numbering in the thousands, passed overhead and descended beneath the hill.

"Where did they come from?" Nick asked as he rose.

"They come through every year going south."

"My God, I can't believe the number." Nick pulled Jenny to her feet. They watched the flock descend into a large tree that stood alone in a clearing on the next hill. The tree turned black, pulsating like a breathing thing as birds fluttered to balance on spindly branches too fragile to hold their weight.

"I have never seen this many before," Jenny muttered. "It's unbelievable."

"Let's take a close-up look."

Nick took her hand and the two soon found the descent difficult. Not only was the hill steep, but vegetation growing out of the rocky hillside made it nearly impossible to navigate their way around and under thick underbrush. The climb up the hill was more demanding. They often lost their footing, and at one point crawled underneath a thicket of prickly bushes for a few dozen yards.

The tree stood alone in a clearing a few hundred feet from the tree line. When they stepped out into the clearing, the tornado of birds shot straight up in the air. Half of the tree was green and the other half had dead branches that looked like bones plucked clean and dried by the sun.

Jenny pointed to an object that hung from a dead limb. "What's that?"

"Not sure," Nick answered. "Stay here and I'll check." He was looking directly into the sun and couldn't be sure, but the hanging object was shaped like a man. An eerie feeling crept up his back.

"Look above you," Jenny cried.

Buzzards circled. The stench grew stronger as he circled the tree and put the sun behind him. "Mother of Jesus," he gasped. Feet hung from beneath a gray wool blanket that draped the body like a poncho. Nick's stomach churned with nausea.

"What is it?" Jenny called.

Nick didn't answer. Eddie's shoe lay on the ground beneath the body. He'd worn it during their ride to the mill on the day of their arrival. He'd propped his foot on the wagon sideboard and Nick remembered the silver colored shoestrings.

Jenny called again. "What is it?

"Stay there," he shouted. "I'm coming back."

Her eyes searched his as he approached. "It's Eddie," he whispered.

She gasped and buried her face in his chest. He held her close. Neither spoke. His head filled with questions. Vale had threatened to do this. An impulse to leave and take Jenny came first, and then rational thinking took over. Someone had to pay. Eddie deserved justice.

16

Mae's screams carried down the hill to where Nick and Claude sat on the porch as still as wax figures. Dog rose up and snapped at a large bug that buzzed a lantern hanging by the door. Nick rose and crossed to the end of the porch. "Who did this, Claude?" Nick asked, barely audible.

The old man cleared his throat. "We best not talk about it."

"Why not talk about it? The community should demand that John Frank prosecute those responsible."

Claude didn't respond.

Nick rose and circled the porch. He'd read about lynchings. An average of two a week occurred throughout the country the year before. Why hadn't such knowledge tugged at his very soul before? Was it because the victims had no faces and the hangings were happening somewhere else, to someone else? Eddie's hopes and dreams must have been much like Nick's own.

Nick looked up at the stars and whispered a prayer, one he'd learned as a little boy.

Claude broke the silence. "I told Ducky what the Bird said. Why didn't he listen to me?"

Nick wanted to scream at the crazy old man, to tell him that hate killed Eddie and not an imaginary bird.

The light from a lantern moved down the hill from the cabin. "Someone's going down toward the stables," Nick said.

"That'd be Ducky goin' to bring his boy home, I 'spect."

"But Loretta said she'd ring the dinner bell and get neighbors here to help as soon as Boyd gets back with John Frank."

"Ducky ain't waitin' for no white man's help," Claude said.

The lantern disappeared inside the barn.

"Ducky doesn't know where to find the tree," Nick said.

"Everybody knows about that big tree that lightnin' hit."

"He can't get the body down alone. It's hanging too high."

"He's gonna try."

"He needs help." Nick jumped off the porch and raced across the yard. The moonlight allowed him to avoid stepping in the flowerbed by the garden and to duck under the clothesline.

Ducky had the collar around Old Nellie's neck when Nick opened the door and stepped inside the barn. The old man's dark eyes were filled with rage as he turned and faced Nick.

"You don't have to do this," Nick said. "Boyd's gone to get help."

"No white man's hands is touchin' my boy ever again."

"I'm sorry, Ducky."

"How you be sorry? Has yo' son been hung up like a hog at killin' time?" The old man turned away and harnessed the mules in silence. Nick watched, unsure of his role. Ducky's wet cheeks glistened in the lantern light. His hands trembled with each rattle of the chain as Ducky fastened each buckle.

Once the mules were hitched, the old man climbed onto the wagon seat without a word and tapped the lines. He left Nick standing by the door.

Nick hesitated a moment and then raced after the wagon. He grabbed the end gate and lunged headfirst, sprawling flat in the wagon bed. He climbed across the seat and sat beside Ducky who looked straight ahead and never acknowledged his presence.

Anguish etched deep furrows in Ducky's face. He held the reins steady and the mules moved at their own pace. Neither spoke as the team strained against their harness and moved up the steep hills. Shadows and rocks took on ominous shapes. Nick thought of comforting words, but he knew Ducky would reject them all. Grief had captured the man.

"You knows who do this?" Ducky blurted.

The suddenness of the question startled Nick. "No, but I'll not stop until I find out."

Ducky smirked.

Silence returned for the remainder of the ride.

The tweet of birds was heard while Nick and Ducky were some distance away. They'd returned to the tree.

Ducky ignored the deafening twitter and pulled the wagon under the tree. The old man started praying for the names of the killers. He rocked back and forth with both fists balled above his head. Nick finally placed a hand on Ducky's shoulder. He ended by beggin' the Lord to show him their faces.

Ducky backed the wagon under the body and climbed over the seat. Nick held the lantern high. The old man stared for a moment and then wrapped his arms around his son's body and pressed his face against the blanket. The birds fell silent. Sickness stirred in Nick's stomach and he pressed his jaw tight to keep nausea at bay.

After what seemed to take forever, Ducky fumbled in his pocket and came out with a knife. He tried to support his son's body with one arm and cut the rope with the other. Seeing Ducky's lack of progress, Nick scrambled over the wagon seat and reached to help.

"Don't touch him," Ducky snarled.

Nick drew back.

The old man strained under the weight as he struggled to cut the rope. "Help me, Lord, help me," he moaned. His body trembled from the effort.

Nick jumped up on the wagon seat with the lantern in one hand and attacked the rope with his own knife. It was dull. He used a sawing motion until the last fiber snapped and the body dropped, taking the old man to his knees in the wagon bed. Ducky cradled his son and cried softly.

Nick moved down onto the wagon seat and tapped the reins. The mules moved forward.

17

Boyd's wagon carried Eddie's body up the hill to the gravesite behind the cabin. On a steep incline Ducky tapped Old Nellie with the reins and the mules lunged forward. The pine box started sliding and would have pushed Claude off the tailgate had Nick not rammed his shoulder against the box until Boyd rushed forward and the two pushed it back onto the wagon.

The mourners continued the climb in silence, except for the rattle from the shifting harness. Loretta carried a basket of zinnias cut from the bed beside the garden. John Frank lagged a few steps behind, breathing hard from the climb.

A rickety cane-bottomed chair was placed beside the open grave for Mae. Ducky stood behind her, his face cast in grief. Mae sobbed quietly into a handkerchief as Boyd read a few words from the Bible. After Nick and John Frank lowered the pine box into the ground, Ducky stepped forward with a shovel. He scooped it full and held it over the open grave, slowly tilting it to allow the gravel and dirt to pepper down onto the pine box. Mae cried out with such force that her wails must have been heard a mile away. Loretta dabbed the corner of her eyes with a lace-trimmed handkerchief, while trying to comfort Mae with pats on her arm. Jenny clung to Nick's arm with her head pressed against his shoulder. Her warmth against him reaffirmed life and how precious it was.

Ducky dropped each shovel of dirt into the grave and often paused to wipe his eyes. Circles appeared under his arms and across his back. Nick offered to help, but Ducky wanted no help as he performed this final act of love toward his son.

Claude sat on the wagon's tailgate and watched. A sudden puff of wind tugged at his sparse hair. He pointed and called out, "Look yonder." A black cloud of birds moved toward them and without a sound settled into the trees at the edge of the clearing.

The sun was dropping fast and dark shadows took shape beneath the trees by the time Ducky finished filling the grave. He drove the crude cross into the ground, and then fell to his knees. Filling both hands with dirt, he raised his arms slowly and spread his fingers. The dirt showered down on his head as he called out, "Lord, show me the men who kilt my son," he begged. "And I'll send them to hell where the devil waits."

After Loretta scattered flowers over the grave, Ducky requested that he and Mae be left alone with their boy. Nick glanced back and saw them kneeling beside the grave, clinging to each other.

No one came. Where were the neighbors? The Woodson community should have been there demanding justice.

Nick faced John Frank the moment the group stepped inside the store. "Sheriff, who killed him? You've got to know."

The room fell silent with all eyes on John Frank. "Not sure yet, but I'm workin' on it," he answered and moved past Nick.

"What the hell does that mean?" Nick demanded in a loud voice.

The sheriff turned back with a frown. "An investigation takes time. I can't go accusin' innocent people."

"Come on, Sheriff, you're savvy to everything in the county. I think you know or at least have an idea who did it."

John Frank nodded. "Yep, I reckon I do. But I can't go too fast or my people will vote me out of office."

Nick threw up his hands. "This is not about votes. It's about doing your job . . . upholding the law. You know damn well there are racists in this community who want you to do nothing. But the law expects you to arrest the guilty party and see that they're tried for murder. "

John Frank's eyes narrowed and his face reddened. "You watch it, boy. I know my people and I'll do it at my own pace."

Jenny reached for Nick's hand. "It's time for us to go."

He pulled away. "Sheriff, you don't intend to do a damn thing, do you?"

Boyd stepped in front of Nick. "Jenny's right, Nick, you need to go. We're all tired. Maybe we should deal with this at another time."

Nick's gaze moved around the room and returned to rest on Boyd. "You're a leader in the community. Will you demand justice?"

Boyd stared into Nick's eyes and said nothing.

"Answer me, Boyd." Nick looked around the room. "Is there no justice for coloreds between the rivers?"

Jenny tugged on Nick's arm and whispered, "Stop it, Nick. Come on, let's go. We're all too tired to think."

"Maybe some supper would help everybody," Loretta added. "I'll fix you some, Mr. Kincaid."

"I'm not hungry," Nick snapped.

John Frank stepped forward. "Let me give you some advice, boy. I brought yo' ass here and I can send it away. Don't want to. People like yo' teachin', and I want to keep you. You do yo' job and I'll do mine, my way. You ain't learned our ways yet. Best to keep quiet."

Nick bit his lip and looked away. He'd said enough. Maybe too much in the heat of the moment, but he wasn't willing to let things go indefinitely.

A moment of silence followed. John Frank checked his watch. "Guess I best get back across the river before Burt shuts down the ferry for the night. You'll be hearin' from me." He gave a little nod.

Cold air rushed in as he opened the door. Loretta shivered. "Boyd, we'll need some firewood brought in for a fire in the mornin'."

"It's gonna frost tonight," Claude added.

"Poppa, we might as well move you inside until spring. The birds won't be singing no more this year. They'll be goin' south for the winter."

Nick took Jenny's arm and led her out the door without a word. The faces of his students, all smiling and innocent, filled his head. Where were their parents today?

He walked her to the car in silence and opened the door for her to climb in. "No one in the room, not even Boyd, gives a damn about justice for Eddie."

Jenny faced him. "It's not that simple, Nick."

"The hell it's not. Boyd didn't speak up. He didn't say a damn word. And you were silent . . . couldn't wait to shut me up and drag me out of there."

"Nick, that's not fair. I want justice, but there are people who will hurt you. You can't let your anger make you say inflammatory things. Give John Frank time."

"I can't believe you. I'd almost think you're on their side."

"And I think you want a fight. Well, it's not going to be with me. I'm not staying here to listen to you spout off and act like an immature hothead." She climbed into the car. "Get some rest and calm down."

"Go on and pretend it didn't happen," he shouted.

She ignored his outburst and drove away.

18

Frost was still visible in shaded areas when Nick went up to the store for breakfast the next morning. The front porch was stripped bare of furniture and a few sticks of firewood lay where Claude's chair had been. It now sat in the back corner of the store next to the large pot-bellied stove.

A faded patchwork quilt draped Claude's shoulders. His squinted eyes relaxed as Nick approached and a smile spread across his face. "I was wonderin' if you'd ever wake up."

"Slept in," Nick muttered. He took a tin cup from a shelf above the table and poured coffee from the pot brewing on the stove.

Claude yawned. "I didn't sleep much last night, myself. Waited for The Bird, but it never come."

Nick didn't want to hear about the bird. He wanted to know who killed Eddie. "Claude, it took more than one man to hang Eddie's body in that tree. Do you think an organized group was involved?"

Claude looked thoughtful for a moment. "I can't say for sure. Could of been two or three men that got together outside any group."

The front door opened and a short, dumpy woman slipped inside. She looked around like a timid child in a strange place. Ends of fuzzy brown hair stuck out from under a white scarf tied under her chin. Chubby hands clutched a blue wool sweater together at the neck. She hesitated until seeing Claude peeking at her from behind the stove

The woman called softly, "Poppa, it's me."

"Ella, honey, I couldn't see who you was 'cause of the glare from the window."

Ella knelt beside Claude. "Poppa, did I 'cause that colored boy to get hung?"

"Folks think the colored baby belonged to him."

She slipped her scarf off and fluffed a wad of unruly hair off her face. "I caused somethin' bad and I didn't mean to cause somethin' bad. I just wanted the baby to love. Frank told everybody I had her, when I didn't."

Nick felt sick to his stomach. A little white lie with good intentions caused the death of an innocent man.

Ella wiped her eyes with her coat sleeve. "What can I do, Poppa?"

"Nothin' can be done now, honey."

Nick spoke up. "Yes, it can. Get the community to speak with one voice and demand justice. The law would have to move against the guilty. We can't excuse murder and still call ourselves Christians. Some people here in Woodson know who lynched him."

"You best be careful about namin' names," Claude cautioned. "Some wouldn't hesitate to shoot you in the back."

"I'm so sorry," Ella cried. "I wanted to tell the sheriff the truth before now, but Frank wouldn't let me."

Loretta hollered from the top of the stairs. "I hear talkin', who's down there?"

"It's me," Ella said.

Loretta clomped down the stairs with an angry outburst, "You've disgraced the whole family. Our mama is up in heaven cryin' her eyes out about you havin' that baby!"

"I didn't have no baby," Ella said.

Loretta's jaw went slack. "What?"

"Somebody put the baby in my woodbin. I got Frank to tell everybody I had the baby when I didn't."

Loretta clapped her hands. "Praise be Jesus, we have nothin' to be ashamed about. You would of saved me a lot of shame and grief if you'd told the truth before. Course we need to come up with somethin' to explain you takin' in a colored baby."

"I caused that colored boy to be killed.'

"Well, yes, you did cause it, but the best part is that it never happened. I mean you bein' with a colored. We can put the whole thing behind us. Let the law deal with who done it. I'm so happy." She laughed and reached to hug her sister.

Ella pulled away. "Loretta, don't you understand? I caused Eddie to be killed."

"That's unfortunate of course, but just be happy you didn't disgrace us all. We can figure our way out of you takin' that baby." Loretta looked around. All eyes were on her. "What is everybody starin' at me for? What did I say? Did I say somethin' wrong, Mr. Kincaid?"

"Why would you think that, Loretta? You're just being your sweet self, no doubt proving that you are a narcissistic bigot of the highest calling." Nick turned and headed toward the door. He heard

Loretta giggle and say, "I don't know what that means, but it was a compliment, I'm sure, 'cause he likes my cookin'."

19

Childish laughter filled the schoolyard while Nick watched the children engaged in various games during the afternoon break. Thoughts about the lynching had flashed in his head a thousand times since learning that Ella wasn't the birth mother. The day had passed without one comment or question from the children about the killing. The community's code of silence apparently included the children.

A puff of smoke caught Nick's eye as it floated from behind the boy's outhouse. Jimmy Lawrence and Colby Wallace were the prime suspects. This would be their second offense.

Nick tapped the bell beside the door and all playground activities ceased. Students formed a single line and entered the building. The two smokers' identities were confirmed when they came from behind the outhouse, fanning smoke. Nick stopped them at the door. "How were the smokes, gentlemen?" Both boys looked as guilty as charged. "You'll learn your punishment tomorrow."

When all students were seated, Nick's gaze moved around the room until there was complete silence. He pointed to a little bright-eyed girl with braids. "Helen, before recess you had a question. You may ask it now."

"I told mama you said a man invented a rocket that could leave the earth and go into space. Mama said if it did that, it would go up to heaven."

Nick smiled. "Not that far, Helen. A physicist, Robert Goddard, invented a type of liquid fuel and believes in time rockets will be used for high altitude flight. It's the groundwork for a whole new field of study. Who knows, maybe one of you might become a physicist and work on such a project."

"Do you think the nigger that got hung went to heaven?"

All eyes turned toward the little first grader. Not even the squeak of a chair was heard. The boy leaned his head on the table and covered his eyes. Either the attention embarrassed him or perhaps he remembered that Eddie's death was a forbidden subject. The other students remained deathly quiet.

"Yes, I'm sure he did," Nick said.

"My daddy said niggers don't go to heaven," another little boy behind him stated.

Nick took a moment to arrange his thoughts, knowing the boy would never believe his father could be wrong. "Jim, people have different ideas about heaven. When you're grown up, you'll form your own opinion. It might be different from others, even your family. First of all, the young man lynched was a Negro, not a nigger. I would hope you say Negro from now on. His name was Eddie. He was a smart young man. I attended his funeral and saw his mama and daddy cry just like your parents would if it were you."

"Why would you go to his funeral?" Stan Green, an older boy, asked.

Stan was one of the brightest students in the class. He'd sounded angry when he questioned. "Eddie was about my age, a man just like me except for his skin color. The person who murdered him should be in jail. Someone broke the law. If that person had killed a member of your family, you would expect the law to act. It should act the same for Eddie. Under the law there should be no difference between Eddie and your father. Do you remember us talking about all men being created equal and that we are governed by the rule of law?"

An older boy spoke up. "That don't mean nig . . . Negroes."

"The word should be *doesn't* mean, not don't mean. Yes, it includes Negroes."

"The Good Book says it don't," another boy added even louder.

"The Bible doesn't say that," Nick answered.

"There were slaves in the Bible and we turned 'em loose," another boy added.

A choir of voices agreed.

"Hold it," Nick said. "Unfortunately, there have always been slaves somewhere in the world, black, white, red, yellow. We live by the rule of law. Life, liberty, and the pursuit of happiness is one of the most famous phrases in the Declaration of Independence. Those three aspects are listed among the 'inalienable rights' of man. That means all men have the same right under the law."

Stan rose and tucked his books under his arm and headed toward the door.

"Stan, where are you going?" Nick called.

He turned back. "My daddy told me to leave school for good if you started holdin' up for that nigger."

"Wait, Stan. Think about all we talked about, the scholarship, college?"

"School is not for me." He turned and hurried out the door. Other students followed, all older except for a little girl who was yanked from her chair by an older brother. A total of six left.

Nick felt heartsick for a moment. He wished he'd said nothing, until remembering what Father O'Riley had said when Nick was a youngster. "Kincaid, your scores are good, among the top in the class, but you have no voice. The real measurement of a man is not about height or size. A little dog will face off with another dog ten times its size. It's about having the courage and character to applaud what's right and challenge what's wrong. You sat there and never questioned. Bring your voice with you to my class. Debate is healthy in a republic such as ours. It will serve you well to remember that the rest of your life. It's good to question."

Nick realized that all the students were focused on him, waiting for him to speak, to have a voice. He glanced at the vacated seats, knowing he'd done the right thing, and also knowing a difficult time lay ahead before change would come to the people living in Woodson Chapel.

20

A few nights of an early October frost had brushed the green hills with shades of red, yellow, and orange as Nick climbed up on the wagon seat and tapped the reins. He was on his way to get an update on the sheriff's progress. Waiting for John Frank to act had exhausted Nick's patience. The sheriff hadn't shown himself since the day of the funeral, nearly three weeks before. Nick was determined to prod the lawman into moving the investigation forward. Ducky and Mae were walking shadows and their sadness renewed Nick's commitment to fight for justice each time he saw them.

The drive into Eddyville proved uneventful. Aware of Jane and Nellie's temperament, Nick never relaxed until he reached the ferry and saw spirals of smoke floating over rooftops that dotted the hillside above the town's main street. He decided against taking the wagon and team across the ferry and tethered them to a tree.

While waiting for the ferry, a wagon and team arrived driven by an elderly man with white scruffy hair. He climbed down from the wagon and glanced at Nick without speaking.

"Good morning," Nick called.

The man nodded and continued to place blindfolds on the mules for the crossing. He finished and turned to Nick, "Ain't you new around here?"

"Been here a few months."

"What's your business, if it's any of mine?"

"I teach at Woodson."

The man's hard-faced expression softened into a smile. He stepped forward and extended his hand. "I'm Jed Harris. My grandkids go to your school and like your teachin'."

"I'm glad to hear that."

"The girl is learnin' to read real good." Jed laughed. "I had you pegged as a government man 'fore you got here. Hope you ain't one."

Nick smiled. "No, just a teacher."

"I own a sawmill a few miles upriver. Didn't mean to be unfriendly, but I don't want the government in my business or my neighbors. At first I thought you might be one of 'em."

"No, not me. Boyd's brother-in-law, Frank, works for you, doesn't he?"

"Shore does." He turned his head and sent tobacco juice flying into the river and then wiped his mouth on his shirtsleeve. "Frank's wife's done a hell of a bad thing by layin' with a nigger. That's against what the Good Book teaches." A smile crept though his tobacco stained beard. "The matter has been fixed, thanks to the Lord above."

"What do you mean?"

Jed chuckled. "I mean there's one colored boy that won't be pokin' his pleasure in no white woman again."

Anger boiled up and reddened Nick's face. His impulse was to punch the old bastard, but a bloody nose was not the solution for ignorance. He kept his voice level. "Eddie didn't sleep with Frank's wife."

"Then how come the baby's black?"

"Ella didn't give birth. She found it left in her woodbin."

Jed's brows arched. "Woodbin?" He spit his chew into the river. "Any woman would claim that who'd spread her legs for a young black buck."

The hate behind the words stunned Nick. "You probably know who lynched the young man."

Jed's eyes narrowed. "Mr. Teacher, you don't understand our ways here 'tween the rivers. You ought not to say somethin' like that." A surly smile crept across his face. "It could be dangerous."

Nick ignored the veiled threat. "The law says someone must pay for killing an innocent man."

Jed scoffed, "No colored boy is that innocent. The baby damn shore had a nigger daddy from what I hear."

"The killer is going to prison," Nick declared. "I won't stop until that happens."

The old man's face turned red. "Somebody needs to talk some sense into you 'fore you get shot." He climbed onto his wagon and stared straight ahead. Nick didn't care that he'd made the old bastard angry. He made a point not to acknowledge the man's presence during the crossing.

The town looked deserted except for a lone wagon and team tied in front of the general store. The odor from smoldering coals came through the blacksmith shop's open doors as Nick passed on his way to see John Frank. He found the sheriff's office locked and went down to Fanny's boarding house to inquire about John Frank.

The door triggered a bell as Nick stepped into the deserted dining room. Fanny soon popped through the kitchen's swinging doors. Flour covered her hands and a smudge dusted her cheek. She used her forearm to rake white hair away from her face.

"Mr. Kincaid, it's good to see you. Take a seat and I'll bring coffee."

She disappeared into the kitchen and soon returned with clean hands and a mug of coffee. "Can I fix you some breakfast?"

"No, thanks, I've eaten. I'm looking for John Frank."

"You ain't heard? Somebody shot him last night."

"Shot him?" Stunned by the news, it took a moment before Nick found his voice. "Will he be okay?" If someone shot the sheriff to slow down the investigation, Nick's life was in more danger than he'd realized.

"Yeah. Thank God it didn't kill him. He'll be laid up for a couple of weeks."

"How did it happen?"

"Ambushed. He was in his boat fishin' and somebody shot him right here." She pointed to her shoulder. "The bullet caused a flesh wound, they said. Thank God whoever did it was a bad shot."

"Why would someone shoot him?"

She lowered her voice. "It could be from an old grudge, but he thinks it's from askin' too many questions about the lynchin'." She slipped into the chair across from Nick and leaned across the table. "I ain't told nobody this, 'cause I ain't sure. But I believe Eddie was here in Eddyville to catch the train the mornin' he disappeared."

"Why do you think so?"

"My upstairs bedroom window faces the street. I heard a car and peeked out. It looked like Vale's, but the fog was openin' and closin' so I couldn't see real good. Then I saw a man with a suitcase comin' up the riverbank toward the depot. Couldn't swear that it was Eddie, but I thought it was him at the time. I still do."

This was the first indication that Eddie made it to Eddyville. Ducky had walked with him to Boyd's fishing boat before daylight that morning. The boat disappeared and no one knew if he'd made it across the river. "If it was Eddie that means he was either killed here and hung to look like a lynching or actually lynched across the river."

"Like I said, I can't swear it was him, but a little bit later, I was tackin' the dinner menu up outside the front door when I heard voices and scufflin' up near the depot. That was before the six o'clock train. I thought to myself, who is fightin' this early in the mornin'? Fog had pushed back in and I couldn't see nothin' and didn't recognize the voices. A little later the sun burned through and I noticed a suitcase on the depot platform with a belt holdin' it closed. It set there until up in the mornin'.'."

Nick felt a chill crawl across his back. Whoever killed Eddie probably did so in Eddyville.

"Someone wanted to stop the investigation by shooting the sheriff. Did John Frank know which side of the river the shot came from?"

"He said this side because of the position of the boat."

Nick had expected a different answer. He was told the Nightriders were never active anywhere except between the rivers. Vale lived in Eddyville. He'd killed a man before and swore he'd kill the man who slept with his sister.

"Would the ticket agent know if Eddie purchased a ticket or even arrived at the depot to catch the train that morning?"

"I don't know, but I'm not sure you should talk to Henry. Just 'tween you and me, that whole Walker family don't like coloreds, or people who do. Maybe you should leave it alone."

Nick's gaze caught hers until she looked away. "Do you know something I should be concerned about?"

Fanny didn't answer.

"Do you know something that I should know for my own safety?"

She leaned closer and whispered. "I've heard table talk about you. Some people don't think you're who you say you are." She puckered her brow. "I trust I ain't talkin' to a government man."

"No, you're not."

"Some say you're pushin' too hard for an arrest. That's somethin' a government man might do. Be careful who you talk to and what you say."

Footsteps on the stairs drew their attention. Fanny rose as Cleve appeared. He took each step by holding onto the railing and rotating his large bulk from side to side. He smiled and called out as he approached. "I've committed a salesman sin by sleeping late." He chuckled and pointed to a chair. "May I join you, Mr. Kincaid?" Nick nodded.

"You want the usual. One boiled egg with biscuits and sausage gravy." Fanny giggled and turned to Nick. "Mr. Underwood has the same breakfast every mornin'."

"I do indeed, Fanny. I'm a creature of habit."

She hurried toward the kitchen. Cleve turned his gaze toward Nick. His clear blue eyes stared with such intensity that Nick glanced away. "Do you think rumors are dangerous, Mr. Kincaid?"

"They can be," Nick answered. The question struck Nick as an odd way to open a conversation. But then Cleve was mysterious.

"The whole tragedy over at Woodson was fueled by a rumor, a little white lie. Do you believe it's ever okay to lie?" Cleve asked.

"I suppose most people filter their comments to spare the feelings of others. I'd never tell a lady she had an ugly baby if that's what you mean."

"Wise as well as considerate, sir. I've heard that you've been extremely vocal about demanding justice for the young Negro man that was murdered."

"We do live by rule of law in this country."

He tilted his head and looked over his glasses. "That we do, my friend. There's a rumor going that you think members in your community have an obligation to turn in the person who murdered the young man if they know his identity."

Nick took a moment. Where was Cleve going with such questions? "Yes, I should think a law abiding citizen would turn in someone for breaking the law for such things as murder."

"How about making whisky? Are people to pick and choose which law they want to follow?"

Nick sat back in his chair and folded his arms. Was this an attempt to recruit him to work for the Feds? "A pure constitutionalist would say there is no difference," he answered.

Cleve smiled. "Just something to think on." He pulled himself up with some effort. "I usually step out for a breath of air while Fanny prepares my breakfast." He pursed his lips and looked thoughtful.

"Woodson is a place where people protect whiskey making. They've been known to protect murderers. Perhaps you should talk less about the lynching." He tipped his hat. "Good day, Mr. Kincaid."

Nick watched him go. Had he been interviewed to help the Feds, or warned, maybe even threatened?

Fanny returned, wiping her hands on her apron. "I've got his egg boilin'. What's he havin' to say?"

"I'm not sure myself." Nick rose. "But the train out there will leave soon, and I'm going to Paducah to talk to John Frank."

Fanny hollered after him. "You watch yourself."

Henry Walker pushed the ticket across the counter toward Nick, tilted his head, and looked down his nose. Freckles dotted his baldness and a thin band of shabby red hair shaded his ears. "Ain't you that new teacher over at Woodson Chapel?"

Nick nodded. He felt uneasy about identifying himself after what Fanny said about Henry.

The man shot Nick a yellow-toothed grin. "Goin' to Paducah, huh?"

Nick nodded again.

"If you're lookin' for excitement, you can go over to colored town and get yo'self pleasured for nearly nothin'. Ask somebody for directions. Everybody knows where to go."

"Thanks, but I don't think so."

He whispered. "Guess you heard about the nigger bein' hung." His thin-lipped smile was frozen in place.

Was Henry trying to tell him something by mentioning the lynching?

146

"We're all big hunters around here. I hope you remember it's huntin' season, so be careful in the woods. We wouldn't want an accident to happen to somebody like it did to that nigger boy." Henry's voice matched the coldness in his eyes.

"That was no accident, but you know that and more, I imagine." He turned away and headed toward the train.

A whirlwind of thoughts filled Nick's head during the short train ride into Paducah. He'd never been a crusader for coloreds, had never known that many. This was his first time to witness such an injustice. The sheriff being shot and then the not-so-subtle warnings from Henry concerned Nick, but the values taught to him about right and wrong by his parents challenged him. To walk away was unthinkable.

Nick paused in the doorway of John Frank's hospital room. The sheriff lay on his back with his mouth open and eyes closed. Anna Louise nodded in a chair by the window. She opened her eyes and looked around. Her lipstick had worn off except for a thin red line around the outer edges of her mouth. She rose and extended her hand. "Mr. Kincaid, it's nice to see you."

"How is he?" Nick asked.

"Just a flesh wound. He's gonna be fine," she whispered. "Some blood loss, that's why he's pale. Just needs rest accordin' to the doctor."

John Frank shifted his shoulder and grimaced. He blinked several times and opened his eyes. "Oh, it's you, Kincaid. I thought I heard talkin'."

"Sorry about what happened. Do you know who might have shot you?"

"A dozen or so who don't want me lookin' into that boy's killin', I would guess. The word is, you've been shootin' yo' mouth off about justice at school and everywhere else. Are you tryin' to get shot? Stop it and let me do my job."

Anna Louise spoke up. "Mr. Kincaid, I don't want John Frank upset talkin' about that unfortunate happenin'."

John Frank cut his eyes toward her and snapped, "Anna Louise, go get yo'self some coffee."

"But John Frank, I think you should rest."

"Go!"

She grabbed her purse from the table and disappeared out the door. He took a deep breath. "Damn women. They try to boss you at the blink of an eye. If you're wantin' me to tell you who murdered Eddie, I don't know. If you're wantin' to find out who I suspect, I've narrowed it down to about twenty-five men and I ain't ready to name none of 'em."

"Then you've been working on the case."

John Frank frowned. "You asshole, do you still think I don't want to solve the case?"

"No, I didn't mean that."

"The hell you didn't. I showed patience when you was gettin' on my ass about solvin' the case the day of the funeral. You're still doin' it and I'm about to get pissed."

"I want the killers punished."

"I want it too, for me. Look, Kincaid. You and I want this case solved for different reasons. I'm not crazy about niggers myself, but it's in my best interest to solve this hangin'. Somebody went over the line by killin' that boy. I'll own up to coverin' my hide. I have to keep people in line without rilin' up anybody. Otherwise, my ass could be mud in the next election."

"You're savvy to everything that happens in this county. I'm disappointed you haven't narrowed the suspects down to two or three by now. You must be close to knowing the killer or killers."

"Hear me, Kincaid. The case is active . . . I'm workin' on it." He grimaced and grabbed his shoulder. "Damn the pain! Look, I don't feel worth a shit and I ain't gonna fight with you. Hear me, ease off! I'm still at twenty-five suspects. And here is why. Years ago, slaves livin' between the rivers worked the iron foundry over at Birmin'ham crossin'. After they got freed, a group of white men banded together and was stronger than the law for years. They caused most coloreds livin' between the rivers to move to cities like Chicago."

"Were they the KKK?"

"Maybe an offshoot. The Nightriders have always been active in a loose-netted way. Ain't been no coloreds around to be a problem, but they still dole out punishment to a man who won't work and take care of his family or one who beats his wife. Helps me keep order without affectin' votes."

"Why does it have to be all about votes with you?" Nick couldn't keep the disgust from his voice.

John Frank shrugged. "It's our system and it works."

"That's crap," Nick muttered.

"Damn it to hell, somebody is gonna kill yo' ass if you don't back off. I've got dozens of suspects just because they don't like niggers. Tell me which one I'm supposed to arrest. Then there's Vale. He vowed to avenge his sister and he still tops my list."

"Why? Ella didn't give birth to that baby."

"Who knew that when the lynchin' took place? Did you?"

Nick shook his head. The answer to that would eliminate Vale or make him a prime suspect.

"Listen, boy, I know what I'm doin'. The killer could be anybody, even Boyd."

"Boyd? What are you trying to sell me? I can't believe that."

"Why not? He used to lead the group. May still do so."

Nick's mouth felt dry. "Are you serious?"

A nod. "Damn right, I am."

Nick trusted Boyd and had voiced his suspicions and theories about the murder to him. It might explain Henry recognizing Nick. Someone had been talking, but to think it had been Boyd was a punch in the belly.

"This is just between us," John Frank said. "It's most likely one or two from that group. Maybe members of the community know, maybe they don't. Either way, nobody is gonna talk, not even people who don't belong to the group. People between the rivers have a code of silence that everybody follows because they want to, or because they're afraid not to. Havin' said that, just don't forget that Vale is highly respected by the group and had more reason than most to kill the boy, 'cause his sister was involved. That don't mean he did it. It just means he might have a reason."

"How can I help?"

"Keep yo' ears open and yo' mouth shut." He paused, allowing his dark-eyed stare to punctuate the statement.

Nick left the hospital disturbed by what he'd heard. He lived in a community supported by an underlying secret society to judge and punish outside the law. Not unlike the Chicago mob who made their own rules and punished accordingly. The two were worlds apart, yet similar in that both had no respect for the rule of law.

The train back to Eddyville departed a half hour late and with it came a surprise. Vale sat on the front seat and smiled when Nick boarded. "Hey there, Partner, I'm just gettin' back from Chicago, yo' hometown. What brings you to Paducah?"

"Personal business," he answered and continued through to the next coach. Vale followed and sat across the aisle.

"Maybe we should talk about that fight we had," Vale said.

"An apology should go to Mae and Ducky. It was their son you were beating up and someone murdered later."

Vale leaned forward. "I've never apologized to a man in my life. I was drunk when we fought. I'm now on record that I had nothin' to do with Eddie's killin'. You'd better damn sure keep that in mind when you're runnin' yo' mouth."

"But you know who did."

Vale settled back in his seat and sighed. "No, I don't. Look, Partner, you'd better believe that. I'm tryin' to make things right with you. Loretta and Boyd say you're all right. Talk is goin' 'round that there might be a bullet waitin' for both you and John Frank."

"Someone shot and wounded him yesterday," Nick said.

"Well, I'll be damned. Don't surprise me. You'd better take what I'm sayin' serious. You're talkin' too much, so be careful and watch yo' back. That girlfriend of yours come beggin' me to put out the word and save yo' ass, so I've been doin' that."

"Jenny asked you to protect me?"

Vale nodded.

"I can take care of myself. Keep your fucking advice to yourself."

Vale rose. "Look at yo' face red as a beet. You're pissed at me 'cause that girl is crazy about you. She wants you alive, you sucker."

He left Nick simmering and moved to the front of the coach. Jenny knew he detested the man. It was like cutting his balls off by going to Vale. He could damn well take care of himself.

21

Nick entered the store and was met with a wailing sound much like that of a distressed animal. It came from Claude slumped in his chair behind the stove, draped in a blanket.

Nick hurried forward. "Mr. Claude, what's wrong?"

The old man rose and spread his arms like a bird. The blanket fell to the floor and left him naked.

"What's going on?" Nick asked again. The old man mumbled something and stared into space. Nick grabbed the blanket and spread it back around Claude's shoulders. "Talk to me, what's the matter?"

With an unexpected move, Claude wrapped his arms around the hot stovepipe. Pain twisted his face and odor from the scorching horsehair blanket filled the room.

For a second Nick's brain didn't connect with what he was seeing. "What the hell?" He grabbed the old fellow and pulled him off the stove.

Groaning, Claude staggered backward and fell into his chair.

"Holy Jesus," Nick shouted. "What have you done to yourself?"

Loretta called from upstairs. "What's going on down there?"

"Claude's burned himself. Come quick."

The old man lay back in the chair with his arms spread and palms turned outward. Parched skin with red splotches started at his wrist and moved upward.

"Why did you do that?" Nick kept asking without getting an answer. The image of the old man anchored to the hot stove was surreal. He covered Claude's nakedness with the blanket as Loretta came hurrying down the stairs.

"Poppa, I've told you a hundred times to be careful around the stove." She hovered while examining the redness that continued to grow. Tears pooled in Claude's eyes. "I'm on fire," he whined.

"Boyd's bringing some lard," Loretta said. "It'll help stop the burning."

Claude looked at his arms and then up at Loretta. "What happened to me?" His voice wavered and his gaze darted around the room as if he didn't recognize his surroundings.

"You fell against the stove," Loretta said. "I've warned you to be careful."

Nick whispered, "He didn't fall. He hugged the stovepipe."

Loretta gasped. "What?"

Nick nodded.

Boyd came down the steps two at a time, carrying a bucket of lard. Loretta grabbed a handful and gently rubbed it on Claude's arms and chest.

"How did it happen?" Boyd asked.

Loretta rolled her eyes. "Poppa hugged the hot stovepipe."

Boyd gave Nick a questioning look.

Nick nodded. "Just grabbed it and held on until I pulled him away."

Loretta leaned down in Claude's face and shouted, "Poppa, why did you burn yourself?"

"The Bird led me to the devil's furnace."

Loretta turned back. "He's sayin' that bird caused it."

Claude shouted, "The Bird told me who killed Eddie!"

Boyd pushed past Loretta and faced the old man. "Don't you be callin' out any names and accusin' people." He glanced at Nick. "Likely as not, he'd name you or me as the killer considerin' his mental state."

Nick felt goose bumps on his neck. Boyd had stopped the old man from talking. Nick looked Boyd in the eyes. "Does Claude know who did it?"

Nick expected a facial expression, something to change, but Boyd only chuckled. "Claude knows nothin'. The poor man's mind is goin'."

Claude began to cry. "I need to talk to Ella before the bird kills me."

"Poppa, I can give Ella a message," Loretta said.

Claude frowned and stared up at her, but said nothing.

"What did you want to tell her?" Loretta asked. Claude didn't answer. Frustration puckered her brow for a moment, but she recovered quickly and smiled. "Poppa, you just relax. I'm goin' to fix you a special breakfast. We can talk about your message for Ella while you eat. You know Boyd killed a hog yesterday. I'll fix you some fresh sausage, along with eggs, sweet hoecakes, and butter-milk biscuits." She gave the old man a quick pat on the shoulder and hurried up the stairs.

Boyd moved over beside Nick and leaned against the counter. He took the top from a rock candy jar and tilted it toward Nick. He declined. "How did you make it with Jane and Old Nellie goin' into Eddyville yesterday?" Boyd asked.

"Everything went well," Nick said. "I didn't take them across the ferry."

"Is John Frank goin' to be all right?"

Nick looked at Boyd. It was odd that the news about John Frank had reached Boyd so soon unless someone had made a special trip to tell him. "How did you hear about John Frank?"

"I don't remember who told me now."

Nick waited. If Boyd had made a slip it never showed in his expression. He looked thoughtful for a moment. "It must of been somebody comin' by the store yesterday or last night. Not important." The silence that followed was broken by dogs barking somewhere out back of the store. "What's important is me feedin' my foxhounds right now." He looked at Claude and then pointed at his own head and made a circular motion as he walked away.

In the future, Nick would remember to slide the desk in front of his door before going to sleep.

Nick pulled the coat collar snug around his neck and watched the last child disappear down the path behind the church. His thoughts returned to Boyd who had stopped Claude from naming men who might be involved in the lynching. He was also evasive about how he knew the sheriff had been shot. Even more disturbing was the threatening note tacked to the schoolhouse door when Nick arrived that morning. It demanded that he leave Woodson or die. The many suggestions that he watch his back had seemed less daunting until now, but the note had frightened him enough to briefly consider going home.

He listened for Jenny's car. They had planned to meet immediately after school and it was unusual for her to be late.

Nick went back inside to wait. He studied the note again. It was written on brown butcher paper, the same kind Boyd used at the store. He also printed just like in the note. The door shot open suddenly and startled him.

"Hey, Teacher Man." She smiled and moved into his arms. She must have sensed his lack of enthusiasm and pulled back. "You're not still angry with me are you?"

He handed her the note. "Read this."

"Oh, my Lord," she muttered. "What are you going to do?"

"What can I do? Threats are coming from all directions. First, it was Jed Harris, then Henry Walker, and even Cleve Underwood got into the act. I'm not sure it was a threat from him. More like a warning, I'd say. Even John Frank warned me to be extra careful. This all happened in one day. With the sheriff shot and me living at the mill . . . even some of Boyd's actions worry me. The sheriff told me he used to head up the local Nightriders. I don't know whom to trust."

She threw her arms around his neck and held on for a moment. "You've got to think about your safety."

He gently removed her arms. "It's not just about me. Two weeks ago I started with twenty-seven students. Now I'm down to seventeen. It's sad that parents have involved their children. A little girl that left before you arrived cried and turned in her books. She said her daddy won't let her come back to school."

"You can't be concerned about the children now. You've got to leave. It's that simple."

"It's not that simple," he snapped.

"It should be," she said forcefully. "You've been too verbal about justice for Eddie. Now you have no choice but to leave."

"Wanting justice is being too verbal? I can ignore the threats."

"Don't be stupid. You've got to go."

"Stupid, huh? Oh, that's right, Vale will protect me."

Jenny stepped back. "What are you talking about?"

"You asked him to watch my back."

She smiled. "Nick, that didn't mean anything."

"It did to me. You don't think I can take care of myself."

She rolled her eyes. "Look where you're taking this conversation. Good people live here, but there are some that will hurt you. I don't want you to go, but you've got to."

"No, I don't have to. I'm capable of making my own decision."

"Damn, Nick." She turned away for a moment. When she turned back, tears welled in her eyes. "Nick, we're talking about your life." Her voice crumbled. "You dumb bunny, I don't want you hurt." She turned and ran for the door.

He watched her go. What had he just done? He had no right to throw insults as he'd done. She was on his side.

22

A horse neighing and the clamor of hooves awoke Nick. He quickly rolled out of bed and peeked out the window. Men on horseback dressed in white were clustered in front of the gristmill. If they were there for him his only escape would be to drop from the bedroom window and grab onto the waterwheel as he fell.

The riders talked in muffled tones as their horses shifted about. Seconds passed, but it seemed forever before the group moved up the hill toward the store and stopped. Nick pushed the desk away from the door and slipped outside.

A snow cloud floated past the moon and its shadow covered Nick crouched on the landing. Boyd soon appeared on the store's porch holding a lantern. "How did it go?" Nick heard him ask.

John Frank was right; Boyd was still connected to the Group. Nick strained to hear but understood little of their short conversation, not enough to conclude what it was about.

A movement under the tree near the store caught Nick's eye. He dropped flat on the landing. Frost covered boards burned his belly like fire. A man eased out of the shadows with a long barreled rifle and came toward the gristmill steps. Nick's mind clicked with options. Should he crawl inside and go out the back window or remain still and attack the man on the stairs? He chose the latter.

Nick lay with his hands spread, ready to spring up, grab the gun, and go down the steps on top of the bastard.

Ducky called in a loud whisper, "Mr. Nick, you be up der?"

Nick came up off the landing, wilted with relief. "Yeah, Ducky, I'm here."

The old man climbed the steps. "I could hear dem talkin' to Mr. Boyd from where I's hid. They ain't after you. Mr. Boyd, he say to spread the word that Vale say to leave the school teacher alone."

It didn't explain the note tacked to the schoolhouse door, but a decision to leave Woodson Chapel didn't have to be made for fear of Boyd. If he controlled the Nightriders, what Nick had learned tonight offered a certain amount of protection. It also confirmed that Jenny's request to Vale had been honored, something that he'd take up with her later. "Who were they?" Nick asked.

"Too dark to see. Dey faces was covered. I's been keepin' an eye out for you, Mr. Nick. This ain't nothin' I ain't seed before. You can get some rest now. Dem men won't be back tonight."

Nick jerked awake with every squeak and moan made by the old mill. Getting back into a sound sleep proved impossible. At first light he went up to the store to confront Boyd about the nightriders. He sat by the stove and sipped coffee while waiting for Boyd to come down. His willingness to talk would determine if he could be trusted.

The door opened and Mattie entered wearing a heavy black coat that reached to the floor. Her pumpkin face nested in a long red wool scarf that circled her neck. She raised fog-covered glasses and smiled.

"Mr. Kincaid, I was hopin' to see you." She giggled. "And how are you and Jenny doin'?"

"Fine," he answered, puzzled why she'd asked the question.

In the midst of wiping her glasses, she stopped and tilted her head. "A little love spat between you and Jenny, I'm guessin'."

"Did Jenny say so?"

"Not to me. She's real private and wouldn't say anythin' to anybody. I'm not one to be nosey, but I felt there was a little problem, bein' your matchmaker. Jenny acted nervous and all put out about somethin' when she got home yesterday. It come to me it was because of you."

Her lack of nosiness could be questioned, but Jenny would never confide in Mattie, certainly not about their love life or the disagreement yesterday.

"Now that winter is comin' on, you two don't have a proper place to court. Come and use my front room if you want. I told Jenny she could."

"Thanks for the offer," Nick said, though he'd never take her up on it. He could imagine Mattie on her knees peeking through the keyhole and reporting what she saw to the whole community.

"Did you hear about a member in our community gettin' his comeuppance last night?"

"What do you mean?" Nick asked.

"Old man Benchwald got a good lashin'. This was the second time he got caught beatin' on his wife. He was warned once but he got drunk and did it again."

161

"You mean they whipped him instead of turning him over to John Frank?"

"They shore did. Besides, he's as mean as a snake and not even a Christian."

Nick smiled at her inference, though he understood what she meant. He wanted her to leave before Boyd came down. There could be no discussion with Mattie present.

She lowered her voice. "Let's just say our neighborhood men put family first, but I ain't namin' no names." She spied Claude behind the stove and shouted, "Mr. Claude, I didn't see you over there quiet as a mouse. Loretta was tellin' us at choir practice about you slippin' and fallin' against the stove. You've gotta watch your step, Mr. Claude. You're gettin' old."

Claude turned his gaze toward Nick. "I'm already old. I told you that woman was crazy."

Mattie giggled. "I meant you get feebler with age. Accidents happen."

"Weren't no accident. The Bird made me bear hug the stove."

She turned to Nick. Confusion rumpled her face. "Did he say hugged?"

Nick nodded.

She whispered, "Why would he want to hug the hot stove?"

Nick shrugged.

A smile spread across Mattie's face. "I just caught Loretta in a little fib. She said accident. Bless her heart. No wonder she's a wreck with a brother like Vale, a sister that claims a colored baby, and now a daddy that's crazy as a June bug. I must remember to discuss her condition with my prayer group so we all can pray for her."

The sound of footsteps on the stairs cut the conversation short. Loretta appeared, followed by Boyd. She saw Mattie and gushed, "Mattie, I didn't know you was down here."

"I was askin' Mr. Claude how his burned arms was doin'," Mattie said.

With a nervous giggle Loretta glanced at Nick and answered, "He's doin' fine. You stirrin' so early this mornin'. What can I get for you?"

"I noticed a board bucked up there by the stove. Did Mr. Claude hang a foot on that and fall?" Mattie asked.

Loretta grabbed Mattie's arm and pulled her toward the front of the store. "Come, I've got to show you a new bolt of material we just got. I was savin' it for myself, but I feel like the color would look good on you."

Nick smiled at the charade until noticing Boyd's stare. He lowered his voice. "Who were your midnight visitors?"

Boyd cleared his throat. "You saw them, did you?"

"Yeah, I thought they might be coming after me."

"You have nothin' to worry about from those men."

"Does that mean I have reason to worry about other men?"

Boyd avoided his eyes. "Maybe not. I'm tryin' to do what I can."

"What does that mean?"

"It means you run your mouth about Eddie and people are stirred up."

"What people? Do you know them?"

"I don't know who killed Eddie if that's what you're askin'."

Silence settled in except for jabbering at the front of the store.

"Can I trust you, Boyd?" Nick asked.

Boyd's dark eyes narrowed. He paused as if preparing a response. "That's a fair question. Every friend or enemy I have here 'tween the rivers will tell you that my word is my bond. You can trust me. I can't be totally sure some idiot won't try to get at you."

"You mean just because I want a killer brought to justice?"

"Are you forgettin' the boy was colored and some thought he slept with Ella?" Boyd looked him in the eyes until Nick stuck the note up in his face.

"Read this and tell me I have nothing to worry about."

He took the note and read. "Do you know how to shoot a gun?"

"No. I grew up in the city, remember?"

"You could always leave and go back there."

He leaned toward Boyd and whispered, "There's no way I'll be run off."

Boyd smiled. "That's the answer I expected. I'm gonna teach you to shoot. What are you doin' after school?"

"Nothing planned."

"Good. We'll do some shootin' up on the hill until a handgun feels like it's attached to your ass. See you later."

Nick turned his cup up for a sip and watched Boyd disappear up the stairs. The coffee was cold. He'd just agreed to learn to shoot. He'd never been big on guns or hunting for sport. A shiver ran up his back at the thought of being hunted.

23

"Damn it, Jenny, stop the car. Please, let's talk," Nick said as Jenny gripped the wheel with both hands and stared straight ahead.

She braked the car to an abrupt stop. "What's to talk about? You've decided to stay here and give some extremist a chance to shoot you in the back. I simply wanted you to leave until things die down."

"I thought about going home, I really did. I want you to understand, I can't be a quitter. A man's got to feel he measures up."

"Bull crap. The need to measure up is not exclusive to men. Women want that also. It's dumb to expose yourself to danger. It's not a measurement of your manhood."

"It feels right to stay. If I were asked to fight for my country, I'd be afraid, but I'd go. I'm scared to stay here, but it's the thing I've got to do."

She folded her arms and rolled her eyes.

"Jenny, I've got to be true to myself. Shakespeare said, 'This above all: to thine own self be true.' That's what I'm doing."

"No one is threatening to shoot Shakespeare," she snapped.

"That's real cute."

"Nick, damn it, I'm not a nag. I'm afraid for you."

"I can take care of myself. Apparently you don't think so by asking Vale to watch my back."

"Not that again. Don't you understand? I'm in love with you."

The word caught him by surprise. His mind raced. They'd never talked about love. The gears groaned and the car lunged forward. He'd hesitated a moment too long before responding.

"Wait, wait, we're not finished talking."

"We're finished."

"Please, stop the car."

"No! I just made a fool of myself again."

"Stop the damn car, please!"

Jenny stopped the car. Nick raked a mop of hair back. "I wasn't ready for that."

"I got that."

The hurt in her voice deepened the frustration he felt. He sighed. "Maybe I can explain it this way. I do care for you."

"Care for me? I care about Mattie's puppy, but I'm not in love with it. There's a difference, Nick. Just so we understand each other, I can take care of myself. I don't have to have a man."

"Wait, wait. I'm sorry." He cleared his throat. "The truth is, I was . . . maybe even a little jealous of Vale."

"What does that have to do with me being in love with you? For your information, I went to him because I didn't want you shot in the back. I want you to leave now for the same reason. If that challenges your manhood, you've got a problem I can't solve."

"It's not about my manhood."

"Sure it is. You think Vale's competition. Get this, Nick. Neither one of you own me. I chose you."

She was right. He'd always thought of his mother belonging to his dad. He swallowed. "That's true, I don't own you. And I do see Vale as a threat. I've disliked him from day one. That probably won't change. I don't want the way we feel to change either." He gently touched her cheek and wiped away a tear. "I'm glad you chose me. I just need a little time, please. I don't want to lose you."

She hesitated. "We'd better go or we'll be late." She looked at him with a tender kind of sadness in her eyes that made his heart skip. He reached to kiss her and she pulled away.

"Not now, please."

Beside the narrow lane that led down to the Ireland house, a pen of goats had scraped clean all the winter green from the hillside and stripped the bark from the tree trunks. An old bony red cow stood in the fence corner. The gray weather-bleached farmhouse looked as unloved as the old cow. Smoke drifted lazily from the chimney of the boxy two-story structure.

A yellow spotted hound rose up from the porch and barked. Alfia Ireland emerged and quieted the dog with a threatening kick. She wore a black dress, her shoulders draped with a dingy white wool shawl. A large wooden crucifix dangled on a chain around her neck. She stood motionless and watched Nick and Jenny approach the porch.

"Miss Ireland, remember me?" Jenny said.

"I know who you be."

"This is Nick Kincaid. He teaches over at Woodson."

Alfia's dark eyes shifted toward him. She nodded. "What can I do fer ye?"

"Is Meglena all right? She hasn't been coming to school," Nick said.

"Meglena ain't been herself."

"What's wrong with her?" Jenny asked.

"That's private."

"We just wanted to see if we could help her," Jenny added.

The old woman's gaze shifted to Nick and then back to Jenny. "God is the only help for my granddaughter. She ain't right in the head."

"What do you mean?" Jenny asked.

The old lady crossed herself and kissed the crucifix. "Meglena has to be watched until the spell is broke."

"What kind of spell?" Jenny asked.

Alfia shifted as if she would leave.

"Please, we just want to help."

"Your prayers can help."

"May we see her, talk with her?" Nick asked.

"Best you don't."

"Miss Ireland, she's been smearing soot over her face," Nick said.

"I know," Alfia snapped.

Nick and Jenny waited. The old lady's mouth twitched and she caressed the crucifix with both hands. "A demon is wantin' her for sure. Last week she stripped herself naked, covered her body with soot, and said she wanted to be colored."

"Why do you think she would do that?" Nick asked.

Alfia's face tightened into a deep frown. "Don't know. Meglena babbled about that nigger boy gettin' hung for layin' with that white woman. Her daddy caught her and that same nigger boy swimmin' together last summer."

Nick could hardly contain his surprise. It connected Eddie to Meglena, but she seemed like a child, much too young to give birth.

The old lady looked as if she had revealed more than she intended. Anger spread across her face. "That was awhile ago," she barked. "She ain't bright enough to know not to swim with a nigger. Her daddy lashed her good and she ain't done it since."

"May we see her?" Nick asked again.

"We take care of our own."

"Just to talk—"

"We be decent people. Meglena won't be comin' back to school this year. Maybe next. The Lord keep you safe." Alfia turned and disappeared inside.

They left the Ireland farm with more unanswered questions than answers gotten. The old woman had connected Meglena and Eddie. Before the car cleared the yard Jenny said, "The baby could belong to Meglena and Eddie?"

"It's possible, but she seems too young to have a baby."

"Oh, it's possible," Jenny said, "but I can't see her grandmother not knowing. And if she knew, she'd kick the girl out. No one is a bigger racist than that old woman."

Speculation about Meglena and Eddie dominated their conversation until Jenny suddenly turned off the main road.

"Do you know what you just did?" Nick asked.

"What?"

"You turned onto the road to the cabin."

169

"So I did." She smiled.

Nick had found the deserted cabin weeks before. He and Jenny had been meeting there after the weather became too cold for picnic outings. He soon had a crackling fire going in the large stone fireplace that kept the chill at bay in spite of the drafty cabin.

After Nick and Jenny made love, they cuddled under a blanket, bathing in their closeness.

"Hey, that tickles," he said as she walked her fingers across his naked chest.

She giggled and cradled her head against his shoulder. He closed his eyes and relished the quietness of the moment. Maybe he was in love. He was happiest when Jenny was near. He wished he knew what being in love felt like.

He turned and faced her. "Why don't you go to Chicago with me for Christmas?"

She rose up on an elbow. "Why?"

"To spend the holidays."

"I'm going to my home for Christmas."

"When did you decide that?"

"Been thinking about it for a while. I might talk to Dad. What you said about letting him know how I feel makes sense."

"I'm glad. It may turn out well for both of you."

"Time will tell."

"Couldn't you still swing by Chicago either going or coming?"

She frowned.

"What's wrong?" he asked.

"Nothing."

"Something's wrong, I can tell." He waited.

"Do you want me to go to Chicago for your family's approval before you know how you feel about me?" Before he could respond she added, "I'm sorry. I don't know why I said that."

"My family would love you."

"I'm getting mixed signals. You can't tell me you love me, but you want me to meet your family."

"I need time. Can't you accept where we are with each other for a while? Don't try to analyze everything."

She fell back and looked up at the ceiling. "Once, when I was five or six, I climbed a tree in the backyard. I was swinging from a limb. I couldn't pull myself up. It was too high from the ground to let go. That's how I feel now."

"What did you do?"

"I screamed for my mother."

Abrupt pounding on the door brought both of them up to a sitting position.

"Anybody in there?" a voice called from outside.

"Oh, my God, that's Vale," Jenny whispered. She clutched the blanket under her chin as Nick grabbed his pants. He shuffled into them on the way to the door and opened it just enough to slip outside. Vale stood grinning. Nick knew he'd seen Jenny's car parked down the hill.

"I'm out doin' a little rabbit huntin'. I didn't know you was a hunter. You findin' what you was huntin'?"

Nick felt the redness creep across his face. "What do you want, Vale?"

"Here 'tween the rivers a good neighbor would invite a huntin' buddy in out of the cold."

"We can't be hunting buddies when we've never hunted together."

"Whose car is that parked apiece down the hill?"

"I don't know what you're talking about."

Vale laughed. "I saw the car, Little Partner, or else I'm hallucinatin'."

"I know all about hallucinating. A couple of weeks ago, I took a shortcut through the woods and smelled sour mash. I followed the scent to a cave and saw mules tied up outside with kegs strapped against their sides. It was one hell of a hallucination."

Vale's eyes squinted. "You told anybody?"

"How could I tell anyone about something that exists only in my head?"

Vale stared. Nick held his breath, wishing he hadn't mentioned the still. He might have given Vale a reason to leave him here with a hole in his head. He checked Vale's pockets for a bulge from a weapon. It was there. Seconds passed.

"Can we trust each other?" Vale asked.

"I'd be embarrassed for anyone to know about your hallucination, and it would cost you if certain people knew about mine. I suggest no one ever knows about either one."

Vale shifted. "Just to make sure we're clear, Little Partner, you're sayin' you're willin' to live by the code we follow here 'tween the rivers by keepin' quiet about another person's business?"

"That's what I'm saying. Your code, plus my own."

"Yo' own? What's yo' code?"

"I wrote a letter to be opened if something happens to me."

"What do you mean?"

"I'm not saying you, but some folks are bothered by me pushing for justice for Eddie. And of course there's the map to the still that I copied from my hallucination."

Anger flickered in Vale's eyes. "You're lyin' through yo' teeth."

"Maybe, but you can't be sure."

Vale's face relaxed. "You slick little bastard, I gotta admire the way you think. You're smart enough to be my partner."

"I'm smart enough not to be."

Vale took a moment and then extended his hand. "Shake on it."

Nick pumped his hand hard. If Vale could be trusted, Jenny's reputation would be protected, though he saw no softness in the man's eyes. He'd still have to watch his back.

24

Nick filled the stove with green logs and closed the damper to preserve embers for a quick fire in the morning. He always tried to have the schoolhouse warm before the children arrived. Dog jumped up from the corner behind the stove ready to go the minute Nick reached for his coat. He seemed to know what was happening around him even when asleep. Nick gave him a pat on the head at the door. "You're my best buddy."

The wind came in strong surges, a good reason for Nick to give the schoolhouse door an extra push to secure the latch. He scanned the woods in case someone with a gun waited behind a tree, though he doubted anyone would be after him in such weather.

Trees swayed in the blustery wind and leaves spiraled past his head as if each one had its own flight plan. Frigid air nipped at his face. He buttoned the top button on his coat and turned the collar up, glad that the wind would be behind him for the walk back to the mill.

Nick's mood matched the dark clouds that huddled to the north. Jenny's insecurity about their relationship remained at the forefront of his thoughts. He'd also been plagued by yesterday's visit with Alfia Ireland, especially hearing about Eddie and Meglena swimming together last spring. He would talk with Ducky and Mae today. Perhaps they didn't know about the incident.

Nick stopped and stared at a wind-blown figure standing in the road some distance away. It brought to mind a picture of biblical Moses. Claude stood naked except for a blanket around his shoulders that billowed in the wind, threatening to lift him off his feet had he not supported himself with a cane. His shaggy hair stood on end as if each strand would be plucked from his scalp.

Nick hurried forward and broke into a run. "Claude, what are you doing out in this weather?"

Claude ignored Nick and continued to look up at the trees. His cheeks were red, and his whole body shivered with each gust of wind. Nick slipped out of his coat and draped it around the old fellow.

"What are you doing out here?" Nick asked.

"I'm lookin' for birds."

"There are no birds here. Let's get you back to the house." Nick reached for Claude's arm but he pulled away.

The old man's eyes continued to search the trees. "I don't see no birds, but I heard 'em singin'."

"The birds have gone for the winter."

A frown deepened the wrinkles across Claude's forehead. "Mama always said it was time to die when the birds stopped singin'. Is it my time?"

"No, Claude, the birds will be back in the spring."

"How did you know about the spring?" He whispered, "Don't tell Loretta that's where I hid it."

"I won't tell her. Let's go back inside."

176

The old man turned his face into the wind and his eyes teared. "It's four stone up from the bottom of the spring and three to the left. I want Ella to have it all."

"What are you talking about?"

"What?"

"I've got to get you inside right now. You'll be sick."

Claude shook his head and braced his legs. "No, I'm goin' swimmin' at the spring."

"It's December. You'll have to wait until warm weather. The birds will be back then."

"Will the birds sing again?" Claude asked.

Nick nodded. "Birds always sing again for someone somewhere."

With Nick's help the old man started back up the hill. Nick heard a keening in the wind. There was no mistaking Loretta's shrill, whiney voice.

Nick shouted, "Your dad's here. He's okay."

Loretta came weaving forward, breathless by the time she reached them. "Poppa, you 'bout scared me into a heart attack. Where was you goin'?"

The wind swayed Loretta and Nick took her arm to steady her.

"Whew. I am a bit wobbly." She faced Claude. "Where in the devil was you goin'?"

"To find the birds."

"Me catchin' pneumonia and you're lookin' for birds when there ain't none this time of year."

"We need to get him inside," Nick said.

A strong puff of wind lifted the blanket.

"Oh, Poppa, you ain't got no drawers on. Cover yourself, for heaven's sake."

Once inside, Nick guided Claude into his corner rocker. His mental lapses were coming more often. Loretta brought more quilts and then gave him a hot toddy. He drifted off before Nick left to go up the hill to see Ducky and Mae.

Deep shadows hugged the log cabin walls when Nick entered. Mae sat in the glow of an oil lamp with supper dishes still on the table. She began to clear them away. "Mr. Kincaid, I'm glad you come. Can I get you coffee?"

He declined. Ducky motioned him into a chair across the table. Mae wiped her hands on her apron and sat beside her husband, her face filled with anticipation. "I'm hopin' you come with news about who kilt my boy."

"I'm sorry. I don't have any news."

Ducky growled, "Woman, stop hopin'. I tells you a hundred times, we ain't ever gonna know."

"Hush yo' mouth sayin' such. I've prayed and justice will come in its own good time."

"I want justice too," Nick said. "I need to ask you some questions and you've got to be honest." Nick glanced from one to the other.

Ducky's eyes narrowed as he leaned into the light. "We always be honest. But nothin' will bring our boy back."

"I didn't mean that you weren't honest," Nick said. "We can't change what happened, but knowing the truth might give you some peace."

"There'll be no peace till my boy's killer be six feet under," Ducky said. "I pray to the Good Lord every day to have my gun aimed at the men who did it."

"Hush talkin' like that," Mae said. She turned to Nick. "You ask yo' questions. We'll answer." Mae cut her eyes toward Ducky. "We both will answer."

Nick cleared his throat. "When did Eddie go to live in Chicago?"

"Last fall," Mae said.

"I'm told that Eddie knew the Ireland girl."

"No, it's a lie," Ducky said. "He never knowed her."

Mae looked at Ducky and their gaze held for a moment. "Eddie knowed the girl. Ducky, tell him about that day."

"Woman, leave sleepin' dogs be."

"This not be about dogs, it be about my boy." Her voice was even and determined when she added, "Tell him, old man."

Seconds passed.

"I won't tell anyone unless it will bring Eddie's killers to justice," Nick said. "Please trust me." He waited.

"That boy never touched no white girl. I taught him to stay with his own kind," Ducky said.

"Did Eddie and the Ireland girl swim together?" Nick asked.

"No, never," Ducky barked.

"Tell him the truth," Mae pleaded.

Ducky rose and hurried out the door without a word. Mae shook her head.

"I'm sorry. I didn't mean to upset him," Nick said.

"Ducky, he have trouble gettin' past stuff. Been hard for him to trust all his life. He's gone to my boy's grave now. Needs to talk to him. I'll tell you what my boy told me."

Nick nodded.

"Last spring Eddie was fishin'. It was a hot day. Not knowin' somebody was around, he stripped down and jumped in the river. He looked up and that crazy girl was standin' on the bank without a stitch on. Eddie told her to go away, said it several times. She just stood, starin', like she didn't hear. She wouldn't leave. He covered his private parts with his hands and crawled out of the river. Her daddy come up as Eddie was grabbin' his clothes to leave. Da man throwed his fishin' pole at my boy and started cursin' and threatenin'. Eddie run."

"Are you certain it happened that way?" Nick asked. "I have to be sure."

Mae raised her head and straightened her back. "My boy knowed not to lie to his mama."

"Alfia Ireland said they were caught swimming together."

Mae spit air. "A lie. The girl's daddy come to us, threatenin' our boy. Ducky give him five gallons of molasses and two sides of bacon. Da man told us that was what would keep him satisfied. We still feared for Eddie. That's when we sent our boy away."

25

Winter settled over Woodson Chapel with a light dusting of snow a few days before Christmas. The glum and starkness of the day mirrored Jenny's feeling. She sat in the car snuggled under a heavy blanket with a clear view of the schoolhouse door. A north wind stirred the trees and leaves took flight across the school yard, some rising several feet into the air before disappearing among the naked trees.

Jenny waited to be sure the last child had left before entering the building. She slipped inside the door without a sound and watched Nick erase the blackboard. He turned back and grinned upon seeing her. "Are you okay? Mattie said you went into Eddyville to see the doctor."

"It's the time of year for colds and sniffles," she said.

He pulled her toward him and started to kiss her until she broke away. "I don't want you to catch what I've got."

He reached for her again. "I'll take my chances."

"No, please," she said, moving further away.

"What's wrong?"

"Nothing."

"Something?"

"It's just a gloomy day. You're leaving. I'm leaving."

"It's just for a couple of weeks. I'll miss you. Since you leave tomorrow, let's go up to the cabin for the evening."

"No. I've got to pack."

"But I had something planned."

"Sure you did."

"What does that mean?"

"Nothing." She forced a smile. "I just came to say goodbye." Tears flowed onto her cheeks.

"Jenny, what the hell is wrong?"

"They're going to kill you, Nick."

"No, no, they won't. I'm careful." He pulled her into his arms. "Don't you understand? When I see the hurt in the face of that old colored couple, I can't stop trying to get justice for Eddie."

She pulled away. "What about us?"

"What about us? I don't understand. Things are fine with us."

She paused briefly. "Yeah, yeah, everything's fine with us." She forced a smile, again. "I just wanted to tell you bye and to wish you a good trip home."

He pulled her to him again and she returned his kiss in full measure. He exhaled. "Wow. Come on, let's go up to the cabin. It's stocked with blankets, candles, and plenty of firewood. Loretta's preparing a special basket supper for us. I meant for it to be a surprise."

"No, I can't." She gave him a hug and quick kiss. "Please be careful. I love you." She hesitated a moment. He said nothing and she hurried out the door.

Nick shouted, "Have a good Christmas. See you in two weeks."

Jenny never answered. Why couldn't he have said I love you too? Tears blinded her as she climbed into the car. She was still having bouts of crying spells when she reached home.

Mattie emerged from the hen house with a basket of eggs and came forward. "You've been crying. I'm afraid to ask what the doctor told you."

"He just confirmed that I'm a fool."

"Oh, no."

"Yeah, I'm pregnant."

"What did Nick say?"

"He just wanted to take me to the cabin and sleep with me."

"I'm about to shoot me a school teacher for taking advantage of your innocence."

"Please, Mattie. I'm not that innocent. I'm just in love with the nicest guy in the world who is not in love with me."

"Baby, here 'tween the rivers, we have ways of dealin' with the likes of that teacher. Give the word and he'll be waitin' at the court-house ready to say 'I do' by noon tomorrow."

"No, Mattie. He'd do the honorable thing if I told him, but I don't want to marry the guy if he's not in love with me."

"You ain't even told him. Girl, he needs to pay for what he's done to you. "

"For what I allowed him to do. No, I can take care of myself. I'm not some delicate little flower. I'll have the baby and he's never to know."

26

Nick's old bedroom remained the same, except for the frilly curtains his mother had added. He'd returned from an afternoon with his brothers and found his mother had gone to the market. It seemed a perfect time to catch a quick nap.

Ten days of activities with family and friends had been enjoyable, but now he was anxious to get back to Jenny. She wasn't her usual warm and bubbly self when they were last together. No doubt she was bothered by something, perhaps anticipating the loneliness he now felt from them being apart. He wished he'd asked her to marry him that day before she left, but he'd wanted to surprise her and had hung a sign over the fireplace that said *Nick wants to marry Jenny. He's in love with her.*

It was good to put Eddie's death aside for short periods of time, mostly because of family distractions and John Frank's assurance that the killer would be arrested soon now that the Feds were assisting with the case. Nick had promised Mae that he would get Eddie's personal items while in Chicago, and with only one day left, that meant a trip across town tomorrow.

Nick hadn't told his parents about Jenny. He wasn't sure why he'd waited unless it was to postpone Kincaid's negative reaction. He'd shared the news with his brothers earlier, and just as he expected, they teased him about being a half virgin and suggested the three celebrate the news by getting drunk and maybe even by getting laid, a suggestion that he declined.

Nick rose up in bed and listened. His mother had returned. He had to tell his parents about plans to marry Jenny. His mother would be pleased for him, but there was no way to predict Kincaid's response.

Nick descended the stairs and found his mother putting groceries in the pantry. She turned and glanced at the wall clock. "Kincaid will be home soon." She motioned for Nick to sit. "Did you have a good time with your brothers?"

"Yeah, they beat me at pool, as usual, if that indicates a good time."

Kathleen laughed. "They give you a hard time, but that's because they love you. Kincaid figured you three would go out this evening, so I didn't plan much for dinner."

"I need to talk to you and Kincaid about something before I leave."

"You sound serious, like something's wrong."

"No. It's actually an announcement that may surprise you." He paused. "Mom, I'm going to ask this girl to marry me. Her name's Jenny. I'm crazy about her, but I'm a little scared."

"Oh, Nick, you've found someone?"

"Yeah. I think about her all the time."

"I'm so happy for you, but why are you scared?"

"I sometimes fly off the handle and say hurtful things. Then I feel guilty."

"You can't always be perfect or expect it from her."

"Kincaid gives everyone hell, including his sons. But I've never heard him say one hurtful word to you or you to him."

"Why would we want to hurt each other? You always find what you look for in a person. There's so much good about the big bear I married. I have little reason to give much attention to the negative."

"How can you say that? You're at his beck and call."

"I love doing things for him. Look what he does for me. We're partners."

"But Jenny and I sometimes argue. We don't always agree."

"I should hope not." She laughed. "You're different people. Love demands respect and sometimes compromise. I'm happy for you, Nick. You'll make a wonderful husband. Are you sure this girl is really in love with you?"

"Yeah, she knew before I did."

Kathleen rose and pulled a cigar box from the top of the cabinet. After digging around she held up a ring. "Gramps gave this ring to your grandmother when he returned from Kentucky. She wanted you to have it when you found the right girl."

"It's beautiful. Wow!" Nick shook his head as he stared at it. "Just think, Gramps gave her this ring years ago when he was just about my age."

"I hope you and Jenny will be as happy as they were."

"I'm sure Jenny will love it."

The kitchen door opened and Kincaid stepped inside and stopped. "I figured you and your brothers would be partying tonight since you're leaving and it's the weekend."

"I turned down their offer. I needed to talk to you."

Kathleen motioned to Kincaid. "Sit here. Nick, talk to your father about your plans. I've got to turn down the beds anyway. We'll eat when I finish." She disappeared up the stairs as Kincaid slipped into the chair across from Nick. "Are you in some kind of trouble?"

Nick smiled. "Some men would think so."

"What is it? You might as well spit it out. What kind of trouble did you get yourself in down there?"

"I'm getting married."

Kincaid's eyes widened slightly. "You don't need my permission."

"I'm not asking your permission, but I need some advice."

"What did you do, knock up some bimbo and now she wants you to marry her?"

Nick came to his feet. "Damn it, she's not a bimbo. She's a nice girl."

"Okay, okay. Sit down and tell me about her. What does her old man do?"

"I don't know. I don't care. I'm not marrying him." Nick rolled his eyes. "Just forget it." He headed toward the stairs.

"Where in the hell are you going? If you want to talk, talk, damn it."

Nick turned back. "I've never been able to talk to you. I've wanted to. I'm a grown man now and we still can't have a civil conversation. I just wanted a little advice."

"You've never in your fucking life wanted my advice. If you've got a question, go ask your mother like you've always done."

"I already know what she thinks. She thinks you're the most wonderful man on the planet. I want Jenny to feel the same toward me and thought you might give me some tips on being the kind of husband you've been." Nick turned and left, but not before seeing Kincaid drop his head and cup his face with both hands.

Nick flung himself spread-eagle across the bed and expelled a rush of air. He wanted to be back at Woodson Chapel. He wanted to see Jenny.

27

Jenny lay across the bed and stared at the ceiling of her old room. Her eyes were red from crying. No way would she give up her child, regardless of her mother's rants about the shame of being an unwed mother. It hurt to know that she was more concerned about what her friends would think than the feelings of her daughter.

Jenny ran a hand across her stomach and once again tears filled her eyes. She would never say bad things about Nick to their child or allow anyone else too. He'd marry her if he knew about the baby, but she wouldn't place all the blame on him. It was as much her fault as his.

She could find a job and work until the baby arrived, but to afford her own apartment, plus child care, posed an impossible problem in the future. Dorothy had made it clear that Jenny either put the baby up for adoption or find her own place to live. With such an ultimatum, Jenny had no choice but to turn to her father for help. She'd had little contact with him after the divorce, and it wasn't because he didn't make an effort to have a relationship. She'd accepted her mother's side of the story, but now maturity and time gave her a different perspective.

Jenny borrowed her mother's heavy black coat from the front closet and faced the blustery wind on the walk to the corner bus stop. Her head was wrapped in a gray wool scarf and even with the thick coat she felt the chill of a typical Cleveland January.

It took less than half an hour to reach the Police Department where her father worked as a dispatcher. Unsure of his reaction after years of being apart, she waited near the employee entrance for the three o'clock shift change. She couldn't let herself think about the possibility that he'd want nothing to do with her.

Her thoughts had drifted back to Nick and their time together when she heard someone call her name, a voice that she recognized all too well. Her old boyfriend, Dave, of nearly five years ago stood smiling.

"Jenny, I didn't know you were back. How are you?"

She forced a smile. "Fine," she said, feeling the awkward discomfort of seeing him again. He was still handsome, tall with muscular shoulders, looking much like the high school quarterback of her past, except now he wore a police uniform. He cleared his throat and looked down.

"Jenny, I understand if you don't want anything to do with me. I'm sorry for what happened. I acted like a real low life. We had something good and I threw it away."

She didn't respond but took pleasure in hearing that he felt a certain amount of regret.

"Did you marry the girl?" she asked.

"No, but I do take care of my kid. She'll be five soon. I see her most every week. I'm still single. Guess I never got over you." His gaze caught hers.

Jenny looked away.

"I'm not the same guy I was back then. Do you think we could . . . I mean, maybe be friends?"

"I don't see why not." She flashed another quick smile. What else could she say? To refuse would mean she still felt some kind of emotional ties.

He smiled. "Good. I went to the Academy and became a policeman, as you can see by the uniform."

"You always wanted that. Congratulations."

"I always wanted you and screwed up in the worst way. Remember how we talked about a little house and kids?"

Jenny glanced away, again. She wished he would leave before she started crying. It wasn't a house and kids with him, but one with Nick that flashed in her head.

"I have so many regrets, but I don't have a right to expect your forgiveness. Thanks for still being my friend. There's your old man on the way out the door. To this day he refuses to speak to me. I'll see you around . . . *real soon.*"

She nodded. Maybe he had changed. She watched him walk away and then turned as her father drew near. Pete Waclaw looked the same, perhaps more bald. Even in the winter, he refused to wear a cap. He was still physically fit, probably due to his workout routine. While growing up, Jenny couldn't remember a time when he didn't go through his daily workout. She stepped forward.

He was nearly upon her when he stopped and stared. A frown wrinkled his brow. "Jenny, is that you?"

She nodded.

"Are you okay?"

She nodded again. Tears rolled onto her cheeks.

He spread his arms. "Baby Girl, what's wrong?"

Hearing him call her Baby Girl brought more tears. She reached to hug him. He'd always called her Baby Girl and it felt especially nice to hear today.

His strong arms pulled her close. They'd made her feel safe when she was little. Why had she forgotten?

"You're crying. Is something wrong?"

"No, it's just that I'm glad to see you. And I'm sorry it's been such a long time."

"But you're here now. I've missed you," he whispered. "You're cold. I can feel you shaking. Let's get you to where it's warm. Do you still drink hot chocolate with two marshmallows?"

She nodded, touched that he'd remembered.

Pete slipped his arm around Jenny's shoulders as they walked the block and a half to a diner where off-duty policemen hung out. Talk was sparse, mostly about when she arrived in Cleveland and life in Kentucky.

Four or five officers in uniform, along with about the same number of civilians, were there when they entered the small place. Pete guided Jenny to a booth in the corner somewhat removed from the chatter and laughter that filled the small room.

"I can't tell you how good it is to see you," Pete said. "Having you here makes for a perfect Christmas."

They slipped into the booth and faced each other.

"Your mother can't have you all the time while you're here," he said, flashing a smile. "We've got to spend some time together. How long are you here?"

Jenny removed her scarf and averted her eyes as she spoke, "I'm staying. I've decided to move back home."

"Oh, I'm surprised. You seemed so excited about living in Kentucky as we talked on the way over here. Is Dorothy telling you she's on her deathbed to get you back?"

"No, no, it was my decision. But what about you? What's happened in your life?"

"Not much. I've got enough time behind me to retire, but I don't plan to. Still love my sports. I follow hockey in the winter, baseball spring and summer, and football in the fall."

Jenny flashed to her mother's constant complaints about his interest in sports during her childhood. She suddenly realized just how much her mother tried to control everything around her, even her father's taste in sports. There had been words, if not a fight, before and after most games. "What about your personal life? Do you have a girlfriend now?"

"No, Baby Girl. In spite of what Dorothy may have told you, I'm the faithful type. I've never been a cheater."

"Then you're no longer with Cathy?"

Pete frowned. "Of course I'm with her. We've been married for nearly five years. Didn't Dorothy tell you?"

Jenny's heart dropped. She and the baby sharing a place with him went out the window now that he was married. "No, she never told me, but I'm glad for you if you're happy."

"I'm very happy. The only thing that's been missing is you. Now you're here. I want you to meet Cathy. You'll like her."

"I don't know about that. She might not like me."

"Of course she will. You're having dinner with us tomorrow night. I'll pick you up at five, okay?"

"Well, I'm not sure."

"Not sure of what? You don't have to get anyone's permission anymore. Not mine, not your mother's."

That was true. Her mom would have a fit, but this time she'd do it anyway. Jenny nodded. "Okay."

Jenny arrived back at her mother's place and was met with a reminder not to bring mud into the house, though she'd already slipped out of her shoes from habit. Her mother appeared and with a quick glance checked her shoes.

"Where have you been? I called the house and got no answer."

"I was out," Jenny said. She moved past her mother toward the stairs.

Dorothy followed. "Where have you been?"

Jenny faced her. "I went to see Dad."

Her mother paled at first, then turned red. "Why?" she demanded. "You have no business with him. I hope you didn't tell him you got yourself knocked up."

"No, I got cold feet and couldn't tell him. What reason did you have for not telling me he was married?"

"That slut! I don't think they're really married."

"He said they were and I believe him. I'm having dinner with them tomorrow night."

"No you're not! If you do, find yourself another place to live."

Jenny was stunned for a moment until anger kicked in. "Are you throwing me out? Do I need to pack my things now?"

Jenny waited.

Dorothy grabbed her head. "You've got my pressure up." She rubbed her temples. "This could bring on a stroke. You know my mother died from one. My head's splitting open. I can't believe you'd ever put Pete before me. He never cared about you, never acted like you existed."

"As I remember, he came to the door a number of times and you told him I didn't want to see him. I'm sorry that I allowed you to keep me from him. There's no reason I can't have a relationship with both parents."

Her mother dropped into a chair and began crying. Jenny had seen her act this way before and realized she was only playing the victim to get her way.

"Can't you see what you've done to me?" she whined. "I can't show my face once people know you're pregnant. You're my baby. I'd give my life for you. Don't my feelings count?"

Jenny cupped her stomach. "That's the way I feel about my baby, too. I'd give my life for it, so why would I want to give it up to strangers?" She turned and continued up the stairs. Her mother's crying grew louder.

Pete and Cathy's modest house was decorated for the Christmas season. A tree filled with colorful balls and bows stood in the corner. A poinsettia sat on the coffee table between two large candles and soft Christmas music came from the radio in the corner. Even Cathy's apron was covered with symbols of Christmas. She welcomed Jenny with a hug as Pete watched, looking pleased.

"I finally get to meet you," Cathy said with the warmth and ease of an old friend. "Please come in. Pete's told me so much about you, I feel like I know you."

Cathy was a tall, slim woman that moved with such grace and projected genuine warmth with her twinkling blue eyes set in an oval face. "I hope you're hungry." She pointed toward a chair, one of four that surrounded a small table draped in a Christmas red tablecloth. "Pete's always starved when he gets home from work, so I try to have dinner ready. Besides, the kitchen table is a perfect place to relax and enjoy friends and family, along with the food."

A large platter with a roast, surrounded by a medley of garden vegetables, sat in the middle of the table with a basket of homemade rolls beside it.

As Pete and Jenny took their seats, Cathy held up a bottle of wine. "I've been saving this for a special occasion and nothing could be more special than tonight." She poured the wine and turned to Pete. "Honey, you make the toast."

"Welcome home, Baby Girl," Pete said as glasses touched.

It was the happiest Jenny had felt since being home. The dinner conversation centered on Kentucky. Topics ranged from whiskey making to the absurdity of prohibition and to the difference between urban life and country living. The wine, the dinner, and being away from her mother had allowed Jenny to completely relax until Pete said teasingly, "Baby Girl, you've grown into a beautiful woman. I'm surprised some nice Kentucky guy hasn't chased you down."

Emotion grabbed her and a flood of tears rolled onto her cheeks. She stood. "Excuse me. I need to use the restroom."

Cathy rose looking concerned. "It's down the hall, honey. Are you okay?"

Jenny nodded and hurried away, but not before seeing a frown flash across Pete's brow. He would expect an explanation.

She washed her face and stalled as long as she dared. The question itself and her reaction would suggest that a man was involved and that the relationship didn't end well. She'd have to tell the truth.

"Are you alright, dear?" Cathy asked as she returned to the table.

Jenny nodded and took a moment. "Dad, I met a guy, a teacher. I fell in love with him." Tears flowed again. She whispered, "I'm pregnant."

Pete's face paled. After a brief moment of silence, he asked, "Won't the guy do the right thing and stand by you?"

"Dad, he's a good guy."

"The hell he is if he won't stand by you." Pete came to his feet. "The son-of-a-bitch, I'd like to—"

"Pete, please, this is about Jenny. She needs us now," Cathy said.

Pete looked at his wife and muttered, "Of course it is." He slowly settled back onto the chair. Jenny wanted to cry. The disappointment in his face showed the depth of his hurt. She would die if they suggested she give up her baby. She stated firmly, "I'm keeping my baby."

"Good for you," Cathy said. "We'll help, won't we Pete?"

"Yeah, of course we'll help. Do you love the guy?"

"Yes."

"But he never loved you back?"

"Not enough to marry me. Please believe me, he's a good guy."

"Baby Girl, I can't accept that. You loved him and he took advantage of you. A good guy knows when he's expected to stand up and be a man."

Jenny knew it was useless to try and change his mind. "You might as well know, Mom wants nothing to do with the baby or with me unless I agree to put my baby up for adoption."

"Oh, no, honey," Cathy said.

"Damn that woman," Pete shouted as he fisted the table and knocked over a wine glass.

"We have an extra room here, don't we, Pete?" Cathy grabbed a towel and dabbed the spilt wine while waiting for Pete to speak.

"We'll move you in here tomorrow," Pete said. "It's going to be okay, Baby Girl."

28

Nick took the L train across town to Eddie's old address. He was told to take his time in gathering Eddie's belongings by a buxom landlady. She pointed to narrow steps and told Nick that it led up to Eddie's attic room. "You can't help but find it. It's the only door up there."

The small room was crammed among the rafters like an afterthought. Faded blue linoleum covered the floor. Minimal light from a round peephole window failed to rid the room of dreariness and the space appeared crowded even with the sparse furnishings.

Nick felt like a trespasser, a feeling enhanced by the stillness of the room. Eddie had performed so many final acts here before leaving for his death at the hands of a killer. He'd pulled the coverlet tight on the cot and had placed his shirt on the back of a chair. A book was left open on the desk, perhaps at the page where he intended to resume reading.

Nick squinted in the dim light to look at a faded photograph taped on the slanted wall above the bed. In it Ducky and Mae smiled with Jane and Old Nellie standing behind them. It had to have been the first thing Eddie saw when he awoke each morning.

Two books were stacked on an old veneer-covered chest by the door. Nick leafed through them. One was Alain Locke's anthology *The New Negro*, the other James W. Johnson's *Autobiography of an Ex-Coloured Man*. Both reflected Eddie's intellect and hunger for knowledge, something Nick had already sensed from their brief exchanges.

A tug on the desk drawer brought no results. A hard jerk on the third try sent the empty drawer crashing at his feet. In an attempt to replace it, he discovered the track was blocked by a small zippered leather pouch. It contained a key, railroad ticket stubs, and a half-dozen or so scribbled notes on torn scraps of paper. The notes contained what appeared to be codes beside a column of figures. Vale's name was scrawled across the bottom followed by a question mark. Nick shuffled through the papers and noted that initials were used instead of names when referring to a person. One said, "V may suspect, be cautious." That must be Vale. But who was C.V.? Those initials were used a number of times.

Nick slipped the pouch into his coat pocket and gathered Eddie's personal items into a box, and then looked around the room one last time. He'd gotten everything except Eddie's clothes that hung behind the door. Mae had requested that Nick arrange for them to be donated to someone in need. He reached for the door and then stopped. People sometimes left items in coat pockets, especially notes and scraps of paper.

He worked his way through several garments and found nothing until he came to a heavy blue wool coat. His hand went all the way down into the lining and came out with a bulging brown envelope secured by a rubber band. Dozens of crisp twenty dollar bills were stuffed inside. Puzzled, he stared for a moment, disappointed that it could mean that Eddie was into something illegal. He was saving to move his parents to Chicago, but no way could he accumulate that much money, legally, not during his short time in Chicago.

"Are you doing all right up there?" the landlady hollered from downstairs.

"Just finishing up," Nick answered. He slipped the envelope into an inside pocket. Mae and Ducky could use the money.

The landlady waited at the bottom of the stairs. Her dark eyes took note of the box under his arm.

"I see you found his things," she said.

"Yes, thank you." He handed her Eddie's room key. "I left his clothes. His mother wanted them given to someone in need."

"I'll take care of it. Eddie was a good kid. When I got the letter from a woman named Loretta saying he had passed and you would get his things on your next trip to Chicago, I locked the room." She chuckled and showed a gold tooth that dominated her smile. "I've been telling the man that owns this house that nobody wanted to rent the room."

"I know Eddie's parents appreciate what you've done," Nick said.

"The other white man got mad when I wouldn't let him see the room."

"What white man?"

Her laughter shook her large gold earrings. "Can't recall his name, but since it wasn't Nick I sent him on his way. He was a little spindly guy that looked up to no good with his polished shoes and fancy suit. The speakeasy type, if you know what I mean. He was nothing like the friendly fat man who gave Eddie money."

"Wait a minute. Were there two men?"

"Yes, but they weren't together. A big heavy man had the money."

"Was he also white?"

"Sure was."

"Do you recall his name?"

"No, but he come to see Eddie often."

"You actually witnessed Eddie receiving money?"

"It happened once right here in this hallway. I was coming down the hall and the man handed Eddie something. He dropped it. I didn't know it was a wad of cash until both men went down on hands and knees grabbing for it."

"What did he look like?

She pointed. "He was a fat white man with a bald spot on top."

"Could it have been Eddie's boss?" Nick asked.

"Eddie didn't work."

"You mean he never had a job?"

"Not while living here. He paid his rent on time. His girl could tell you more about personal stuff."

"Where does she live?"

"Two doors down. The two had something going, if you know what I mean. She was the one who told him about the room here being for rent."

"What's her name?"

"Retha."

Nick knocked a second time before he heard footsteps. A slim, thin-lipped woman cracked the door. Her eyes scanned Nick up and down. "If you're selling something, I've got no money."

"I'm looking for Retha."

"What do you want with her?"

"It's about Eddie."

The woman's eyes questioned briefly. "I'll get her."

Moments later the door opened a little wider and a beautiful mulatto girl stood clutching her robe together. She stayed well back with a hand on the door, ready to slam it shut. "I know nothing about Eddie," she snapped. The tremor in her voice said she lied.

"I understand you and Eddie were a couple."

"No! That's not true. I met him at the club where I dance. He was looking for a place and I did him a favor. That's all."

"His landlady said you two were involved."

"I don't know what Eddie was into. He traveled a lot to Kentucky or somewhere down there. He talked about making big money. Always had a lot of cash and talked about knowing the whiskey operation. That's all I know. Besides, I haven't seen him in a few weeks."

"What kind of work did he do?"

"That's all I know." She started to close the door and stopped. "Oh, Eddie bragged about knowing some government people." She closed the door and the lock clicked.

While taking the train back across town, Nick examined the contents from the leather pouch. All the ticket stubs were trips back and forth to Paducah. Most were issued about two weeks apart, going back to the time Eddie first moved to Chicago. He'd traveled within a few miles of his parents every two weeks and never visited them. He would only keep a secret from them if his activities were illegal. What was going on with him?

Nick felt more puzzled than ever about Eddie's activities. He'd apparently had a double life, one unknown to his parents. Maybe he was the baby's father, but nothing Nick had learned suggested who killed him, though the coded messages seemed to prove he had a relationship with Vale.

Nick had another surprise when he stepped inside the kitchen door and saw Kincaid sitting at the table. It was midafternoon on a work day. The man had never missed a day of work in his life, except when his parents died.

"What's wrong?" Nick asked, feeling an immediate concern. "Where's Mom?"

"Don't know. Probably down at the market. Get some coffee and sit down. We need to talk."

How many times had Nick been told they needed to talk? It'd been the opening line to what always became a verbal confrontation. He didn't want that today with him leaving tomorrow. "What are you doing home?"

"Took a half day off."

Nick slipped into the chair across from him without the coffee. It had to be serious for Kincaid to take even an hour off. "Are you sure there's nothing wrong?"

Kincaid dropped his head. "Yeah, I guess there is something wrong. It's between you and me, boy."

"What do you mean?"

"If my old man had called your mom a knocked up bimbo, I'd have kicked his ass or got mine kicked. I feel real bad about that."

"Why did you say it?"

"I don't know. That's why I took off and come home."

"You must have some idea."

"I know that I've treated you different than I did your brothers."

"I noticed." Nick could have added how much it had hurt, but decided against it.

"But I liked you just as much."

"Liked me? You liked me just as much? Are you afraid to say you loved me?"

Kincaid's eyes glistened and turned red. "I've always loved you, boy." He whispered, "Still do."

"What's going on with you, Kincaid? What are you trying to say?"

"You nearly died as a baby. Always sick for those first few years of your life. Last night your mom reminded me that I've never stopped being afraid of losing you. I think she was right. I never stopped pushing you to grow, be as big and strong as your brothers. I never stopped seeing you as that baby fighting for each breath. You never seemed strong like your brothers. She also reminded me that you're a man now, that you're in love and want to get married. I remember how it was to feel like that."

"Her name's Jenny. I'm happiest when I'm with her. That says it all for me."

"She sounds like a nice girl."

"I think I feel about her exactly like you feel about Mom. It's an emotion strong enough to make me want to cry, but we men aren't allowed to cry, are we?"

Kincaid glanced away.

Nick smiled. He couldn't expect a miracle overnight. He'd finally heard his dad say he loved him and that was good enough for now.

29

Nick felt a surge of excitement as the train rolled to a stop in Eddyville. Even the stark landscape or the trouble over Eddie's death couldn't dampen the warmth he felt for this place. It felt like home in spite of an injustice yet to be resolved.

The afternoon sun dipped behind the tree line and cast a golden glow over Main Street. It was deserted except for Cleve Underwood who sat on the boarding house porch, puffing a pipe. According to Fanny, he often sat there to view arrivals and departures at the depot.

The drafty train left Nick chilled. He welcomed warmth from a potbelly stove as he stepped inside the depot. Henry Walker sat bent over a ledger behind the ticket counter. He pushed a green visor up on his forehead and stared briefly, then pulled it down and resumed shuffling papers.

A small Christmas tree crammed in the corner near the stove had shed its needles, leaving red ribbons dangling from bare branches. While the heat warmed Nick's backside, his gaze moved across the back wall where shelves were filled with every size and color suitcase. He blinked twice when he saw one on the top shelf with a belt around it. It was Eddie's case, proof that he reached the depot before being taken by his killers. "Whose case is the large black one tied with the belt?"

Henry glanced toward the shelf. "Don't know. All of 'em was left here and never claimed." He returned to the papers in the stack, but the question had caused a slight tightening of his jaw.

"That case belonged to Eddie," Nick said.

Henry pouted his lips. "Eddie? Don't recall ever knowin' no Eddie."

"Sure you did. The Eddie that was killed and left on Buzzard Hill."

"Oh, that Eddie." He shook his head. "Don't know why it would be his."

"May I look at it?" Nick asked.

"Sorry, regulations won't allow."

"Why not?"

"It's railroad property until claimed."

"Maybe John Frank should examine it."

Henry removed his visor with a look of disgust and snarled, "Course John Frank can see the case, he's the law. But I don't see John Frank here, do I?"

"I can change that."

It took only minutes to reach John Frank's house on the hill above the jail. A light knock brought Anna Louise to the door. John Frank was out, but expected back soon. Nick left word that it was urgent and he would wait for him at the boarding house.

Cleve Underwood fanned a spiral of smoke away from his eyes as Nick approached. "Hello, Mr. Kincaid. How were things in Chicago?"

"Good, if you like snow," he answered. Nick was surprised that Cleve knew he went to Chicago. But here everyone seemed to know everyone's business except where a still was located or when a colored was hanged.

Cleve tapped his pipe against a porch post, dislodging burnt sediment. "It's getting nippy out here. Time to go inside, I suppose."

Nick held the door as Cleve trudged through. "Heard any more about who hung that colored man?" Cleve asked.

"Nothing new," Nick said. "We may never know."

"Be guided by patience, young fellow. All good things come to those who wait." Cleve turned back to Nick. "Maybe the colored baby had nothing to do with Eddie being killed. Ever think of that?"

Nick hadn't considered that possibility. The new information found in Eddie's room made such a theory more plausible. "Do you know something you want to tell me?" he asked.

"No more than you, it would appear."

"You had a reason for asking. Was Eddie involved in something illegal that you know about?"

Cleve chuckled, his jowls rolling against his shirt collar. "Don't let your imagination get away from you. When an inexperienced hunter goes bird hunting, he will hit more by shooting at the covey rather than at one single bird." He stared for a brief moment. "Just something to consider," he said, turning away.

Cleve climbed up the stairs, gulping air with each step. He left Nick with scrambled thoughts that made no sense. Cleve had told him to look at other possibilities for Eddie's killer. Or had he? Nick's imagination was doing backflips. No, no, bigotry and hate over a little colored baby had caused Eddie's death. That was the most logical reason.

John Frank appeared at the boarding house within the hour. His wrinkled brow forecast concern when he entered. "What's this about Eddie's suitcase?" he asked from the doorway.

Nick sprang to his feet. He didn't remember telling Anna Louise why he wanted to see the sheriff but he must have. "Eddie's suitcase is on a shelf at the depot. It places Eddie there before being killed."

"I just walked by there and Henry told me you was seein' things. Let's go see what's goin' on."

Nick led the way with John Frank hurrying alongside. Henry rolled his eyes and moaned when they entered. "Well, well, it looks like the teacher is all worked up and wastin' your time, Sheriff, just like I told you he'd do five minutes ago."

"We'll see, Henry." John Frank adjusted his baggy pants upward with a quick tug. "Kincaid has some concerns about a piece of luggage. He thinks the boy's suitcase is on your shelf."

"Don't know how that could be." Henry twisted around to look. "Which one?"

"The one with the belt." Nick pointed and then let his hand drop. He stared in disbelief. A smaller black suitcase sat on the shelf with a brown belt around it. "That's not the same case," Nick challenged. His eyes focused on Henry.

"Only one I see with a belt around it," Henry said. He pulled the case down and placed it on the counter.

Anger welled up in Nick's throat. "This is not the same case. The one I saw was larger."

"This is the only one that's got a belt around it," John Frank offered. "Maybe you're mistaken about the size, it bein' high up on the shelf."

"I'm not mistaken." Nick's eyes narrowed as he took a step toward Henry. "You changed cases."

Henry slipped off the stool. "Who are you accusin'?"

"We ain't havin' no trouble," John Frank placed himself between the two men.

Henry eased back upon the stool. "Sorry, Sheriff, I don't take to bein' falsely accused of stuff. I've got no reason to change nothin'."

"Let's see what's inside the case," John Frank said.

Henry loosened the belt and opened the case. He baited Nick with a puckish smile. "Ain't the nigger boy's case unless he took to wearin' women's things."

John Frank's eyes confirmed that Nick had lost this round. "Kincaid, I don't want to rub you wrong, but maybe you're overanxious to catch Eddie's killers and let your imagination get the best of you. Ain't it possible this is the same bag?"

"No, it's not and here's why." Nick closed the case and flipped the latches. "Why use a belt when the latches work?"

John Frank nodded. "I'll agree with that unless it's so full it won't close, but where's the proof that Henry changed the cases?"

"Sheriff, I'd swear on it," Nick said.

"It's your word against his, and you have to admit you're hell bent to find a killer for Eddie. Under the circumstances, ain't it possible you might of seen it wrong?"

Nick expelled a rush of air, knowing he'd been outfoxed. He also knew he'd tied the suitcase to Henry, but with no way to prove it.

John Frank shrugged. "Sorry, Kincaid. Got a man and his wife fightin' to check on." He stared for a second and walked out the door.

Henry turned toward Nick and smiled, showing his tobacco stained teeth.

A Woodson neighbor gave Nick a ride back to the mill. Darkness had closed in by the time he arrived. Dog raced down the hill and jumped, taking Nick to his knees while the dog kissed and whimpered his excitement.

The store stood dark, except for an upstairs window. Nick went to his room and built a fire before crawling into bed. His mind remained focused on the fiasco at the depot. Henry had changed the cases and that could mean he knew about Eddie's murder. Maybe it was Henry and fellow members of the Nightriders who'd killed Eddie.

Nick didn't know how long he'd been asleep before being awakened by a low rumbling growl from Dog. Moonlight spilled through the small window and filled the room with an eerie glare. He quieted the animal with a pat on the head. The faint sound of male voices came from the mill room below. He dropped to his knees and pressed his ear to the floor. Boyd was in a heated exchange with a group of men. Nick heard mostly mumbled sounds, but enough to know his name was being tossed around.

30

"Let's all calm down and talk about things that could spell trouble for us all," Boyd said in a raised voice. He stood in a small perimeter of light cast by a lantern hanging in the center of the millhouse. In the circle of darkness cigarettes pulsated with the regularity of fireflies. He scanned the room and didn't speak until the room fell silent. "The Feds have a warrant out for Vale. They destroyed your whiskey shipment and his still. He'll be livin' in the woods for a while and lookin' to us for some grub, so help him out. The timin' of the raid seems a bit suspicious. What you ain't heard is that the teacher knew the cave's location. Vale thinks Kincaid turned him in to the Feds."

A low murmur grew into angry curses and shouts until Boyd held up his hand for silence again.

"Vale thinks the boy turned him in over something personal that Vale knew about."

Brady's voice rose above the clamor. "I guess we know what to do about that."

"Like what was done in the old days by takin' care of the son-of-a-bitch," another echoed.

Boyd raised his hand for quiet again. Voices dwindled. His dark Cherokee eyes demanded order as he stared at the group until silence returned.

"Let's think this through and not go off half-cocked. The teacher gets back tomorrow. We gotta decide where we stand and what we do. I, for one, don't believe the teacher did it." Boyd peered into the shadows and waited.

A man with a raspy voice spoke. "Vale's solid with his friends. He must have his reasons for thinkin' the teacher turned him in."

A tall thin man bellowed, "You can damn well bet your boots he had his reasons. Vale ain't no fool. He knows what's goin' on. Think how much more money we've made after he took over shippin' for us."

Another voice added, "Maybe the teacher is really a government man."

"Some people said he worked for the Feds from day one," Brady said.

"Whoever heard of a man teacher?" another man barked.

"Yeah, he's a spy," Brady shouted.

A chorus of angry opinions melted together until Boyd shouted, "Hold it." He pointed at Brady. "You're hollerin' loudest for the teacher's skin because you and Vale had a fight with the kid. My understandin', according to him, is that you and Vale started it."

"This thing ain't personal," Brady said. "Makin' a livin' for our families is at stake. I could hide behind a tree with my squirrel rifle. It'd all be over."

"I know what's at stake, but we can't act like some fools did by killin' Eddie."

"You're lookin' my way, Boyd. You accusin' me of killin' that colored boy?" Brady shouted.

Boyd bristled. "Damn you, Brady, you know better. I don't know the killers. We gotta assume somebody in the room killed him or knows who did. They don't have the guts to stand up and ask forgiveness for breakin' the group's code. The code says we share secrets with all members and we don't act alone outside the group." Boyd's gaze moved around the room. "Somebody broke the code and now we're in a mess of trouble."

"When you get down to it, somebody did us a favor by hangin' that nigger. We can't have them and whites mixin'," Jed snarled.

"That's why I'd like to put a bullet in the kid," Brady said.

"Listen and remember this," Boyd shouted. "Anythin' that pulls the law into this area ain't doin' us a favor. Somethin' is goin' on and I don't know what or who, but we'd better find out what it is damn soon. No wild ass statement or renegade actions like what happened with Eddie will help. So we'd better be together on this teacher matter."

"What do you think is goin' on, Boyd?" a gentler voice asked.

"I'm not sure, but if we don't find out, I won't be sellin' sugar and some of you won't be makin' whiskey. Vale was gettin' shipments through to Chicago for all of you, but that's over for now. I suggest everybody stop brewin' for a bit and let things cool off. Get a handle on what's goin' on."

"That still don't answer the question about the teacher," Brady said. "What about him?"

"Do nothin'," Boyd snapped. "I'm askin' you to go along with me on this. I feel strong about it."

"But what if he was to turn one of us in next? With me in prison, my wife couldn't make it."

"Trust me," Boyd said. "The teacher didn't do it. If you all can't be with me on this, I need to step aside and let you get a new advisor. That's how much I believe in the boy."

"We don't want that to happen," a choir of voices echoed. Nods and shouts of approval followed.

"In my gut, I feel right about Kincaid," Boyd said. "We don't want no innocent man killed. Let's break and everybody go home. It's dangerous us meetin' here. Just wanted to keep somebody from doin' somethin' foolish with Vale talkin' against the teacher."

Mingled goodbyes and boots trudging across the millhouse floor signaled an end to the meeting. Nick climbed into pants and slipped out onto the deck, leaving Dog inside, whining to follow. He crept down the stairs to watch from the shadows near the corner of the building. He hoped to identify some of those attending, but a cloud moved in front of the moon and the men became moving silhouettes in the darkness. Their walk indicated mostly older men, a generation where hatred and bigotry thrived even more. He only recognized a couple of them.

The cloud moved past the moon and Nick sank further back against the millhouse wall. His heart pounded. Brady had stayed behind and Nick heard raised voices. The argument was about him, but he couldn't hear well enough to follow what was said.

Nick remained pressed against the building and watched Brady leave. He decided to wait for another cloud to provide darkness before going back upstairs for fear Boyd might emerge and see him on the stairs.

Boyd came out and stopped to fill his pipe less than ten feet from Nick. A quick swipe across his pant leg ignited a match. He extinguished it just as fast when Dog barked. Crouching low, he pulled a handgun from inside his coat.

Another round of barks came from Nick's room. Nick held his breath. Boyd took a few steps toward the stairs, paused, and stared toward the sound. He'd been caring for Dog and must be wondering how the animal got into the room.

Nick flattened against the building even more, scared to breathe. A muscle spasm danced across his back. The pain became intense. He made a slight move to adjust his weight and caused gravel to crunch beneath his feet. Boyd whirled in Nick's direction and pointed the gun. "You're a dead man if I don't see hands, now."

"It's me, Nick." He stepped out into the moonlight with his hands raised.

"Kincaid? What in the hell?"

"I came back a day early."

Boyd grabbed Nick by the shirt collar and shoved him down onto the steps. Anger flashed across Boyd's face. "You was spyin'?"

"No, no—"

"You're lyin'."

"Listen to me, Boyd. I heard what was said. Vale is wrong. I never told anyone about the cave or anything else to do with whiskey running."

Boyd leaned close with the weapon inches from Nick's head. Time seemed to stop before Boyd stepped back. "Damn it, I want to believe you, Kincaid, but I can't be sure you ain't in with the Feds."

"I'm not." Nick pulled himself up from the steps and adjusted his shirt. "I swear on all that's sacred."

"You said you heard us talkin'?"

"I did."

"I told Vale that you didn't snitch, but somebody damn shore did. It weren't by accident that three cars loaded down with revenue men took hours to come up from Nashville and avoid the ferry. They did it to bypass the fox horn signal."

"Fox horn signal? What's that?"

"You must of heard it. It lets people know a stranger has crossed the river."

Nick had heard a series of fox horns, but never dreamed it was a signal to moonshiners. The operation was more sophisticated than he'd imagined. "Shoot straight with me, Boyd. If I'm in real danger I need to know."

"The less you know the better."

"No, I deserve to know. Some of the men here tonight were ready to take me out just because Vale thinks I ratted when I'm innocent. All they needed was a word from you. Brady can't wait to put his gun sight on me."

Boyd hesitated.

"Come on, tell me. How much danger am I in?"

Nick waited.

"Aw, hell. You ain't give me reason not to trust you. I'll tell you this much. By overhearin' us, you already know that Vale is a shipper."

"What do you mean by shipper?"

"Vale transports the whiskey that others make as well as his own. He got the idea from readin' about a coal miner's union in West

Virginia. He deals with the Chicago buyers and keeps the prices fair by controlling the deliveries. Vale was carryin' a bundle of cash the night you come here. He suspected somebody of tippin' off the Feds and decided to use your suitcase to get the cash back here. The Feds wanted it for evidence."

"So it was money he put in my case. How did he know where I was coming?"

"From me. I told him you was comin' one of two days. He hung around the train station and paid the ticket agent to let him know if somebody got a ticket to Eddyville."

"And how was Eddie involved?"

Boyd gave Nick a quizzical look. "Don't reckon he was. Why'd you ask that?"

Nick shrugged. "I heard he was connected."

"Not for a long time. Eddie had a rough edge and Vale let him go."

"What do you mean by rough edge?"

"Stealin'. The Feds never suspected a young colored boy drivin' a wagon and team with booze fillin' the special built under belly of the wagon. Vale found out he was siphonin' a little from every jug and fillin' fruit jars to sell to coloreds in Paducah."

Boyd was either lying now or unaware that Eddie and Vale may have been partners when Eddie was killed. The coded notes and train stubs in Eddie's room suggested as much. "Did stealing whisky have anything to do with the lynching?"

"No, but it could of been the reason he moved to Chicago. That colored baby is what got him killed."

"Be honest. Do you know who killed Eddie?"

"I should, but I don't. It could be most anybody. Nobody likes niggers and whites mixin'. Vale says he didn't do it."

After a slight pause, Nick asked, "Wouldn't you expect him to deny murdering Eddie?"

"He'd lie to you, but not me."

"Apparently, I've made enemies by wanting to follow the law."

"You're doin' fine, except talkin' too much. You get high marks for teachin' the kids. You pushin' for Eddie's killers to be jailed makes some people suspicious."

"Thanks for going to bat for me tonight."

"I try to be fair-minded, but you still gotta be careful. Keep that little handgun in your pocket at all times. Remember how I said to hold the gun? Practice some more. Keep it a secret that you have it."

Nick frowned. He thought about the previous lessons from Boyd, remembering that at first he'd almost needed a stick to knock the jar off the fence post. Boyd had showed patience and finally gave him passing marks. He still knew zero about guns and was unsure if he could shoot another person.

Boyd added, "If I was a sound sleeper, I'd push some furniture against the door."

Nick didn't volunteer to tell him that he'd been doing that. "I got the impression you have those men under control."

"I think so, but there's no guarantee. I'm supposed to know who killed Eddie, but I don't. And there's the note you found on the schoolhouse door. So it's better not to take chances."

Nick nodded and felt a chill invade the warmth of his back.

Sleep returned slowly. Mice making their nightly runs caused Nick to think a key turned in the door dozens of times. When daybreak came, he dressed after seeing a light flickering in Ducky and Mae's cabin. With the bundle of money inside his coat and the box of Eddie's things tucked under an arm, he headed up the hill to their cabin. Though frost lay thick alongside the path, the clear blue sky suggested a warmer day, perfect for Jenny's homecoming. The excitement of her returning overshadowed concerns about Vale being out to get him. He was anxious to surprise her with a proposal and news about purchasing the cabin. Nick's grandmother had left him sufficient funds after the sale of her Wisconsin farm to pay a good bit on the cabin.

Mae answered the door with a generous smile and motioned him in. Ducky sat at the table with a half-eaten plate of grits and eggs in front of him. "Good mornin', Mr. Nick." He rose and pointed toward a chair. Mae scurried to the stove and returned with a cup of coffee and placed it in front of Nick.

He set the box on the table and spoke quietly. "Here are Eddie's things."

Mae reached for the box but then withdrew her hand, not ready to go through them or else she wanted to do so in private.

"Thanks fer bringin' 'em," Ducky said. Sadness hung heavy in his eyes as he stared at the box.

Nick was unsure about how to explain the large sum of money. Nothing would be gained for them to think that Eddie was involved in some crooked scheme. "I remember you told me that Eddie was saving money to move you to Chicago." Nick placed the money in front of Ducky. "This is yours. I found it in his room. Eddie must have been saving it for you."

Ducky thumbed through the bills. "Where did Eddie work?" he asked.

"I'm not sure."

"Did he have a job?"

Nick hesitated a moment too long. Ducky raked the money off the table with the quickness of a cat. "It ain't honest money."

Mae gasped as bills floated to the floor.. "Have you lost your mind, old man?" She began picking up the money. "You know he was savin' to move us to Chicago just like Mr. Nick said."

"The money's got a bad smell to it," Ducky said.

A scowl rested on Mae's face. "What does you mean?"

"He ain't had time to save up that much money and stay honest."

"Are you sayin' my baby was breakin' the law?"

Ducky dropped his head and didn't answer. She turned her gaze on Nick. "Was he, Mr. Nick?"

Her large dark eyes begged for the right answer. He cleared his throat and knew he was ready to tell a little white lie if she refused to accept his explanation. "There's no proof that he broke the law. He'd want you to have the money."

Ducky pounded the table. "No! It could be blood money."

"It ain't blood money," Mae cried. "My baby would never do anything bad. He was a good boy. Old man, are you tryin' to ruin the rest of my days by talkin' bad about my baby? I won't stand it, do you hear me?" Mae clutched the bottom of her apron with both hands and pressed it against her mouth. She smothered a sob and hurried out of the room. The silence she left behind was overwhelming. Nick had nothing more to say. He'd already said too much and upset an old couple that didn't need memories of their son shattered.

Ducky spoke without looking at Nick. "Eddie weren't perfect, but I loved the boy. How do you tell yo' boy there ain't no justice with black skin. Him bein' young and foolish, he tries to make his own justice by breakin' the law."

"There's no proof that he did anything illegal."

"You ain't tellin' me that he didn't."

"No, but give your son the benefit of the doubt now that he can't speak for himself."

Ducky nodded without looking up.

Nick picked up the remaining scattered bills and placed them on the table. He turned at the door. Ducky had his face buried in his hands.

31

Claude peeked from behind the stove and waved at Nick with a gangly arm. Scars were still visible from the burn weeks earlier. "I was wantin' you to get back. Had somethin' to ask you, but now it's gone clear out of my head."

"Maybe you'll think of it later. How are you feeling?"

"Wantin' spring to come."

"It'll be here soon."

"Did I tell you that fool bird attacked me?"

"No, sir, you didn't."

Claude pulled open his shirt. Nick stared at deep scab-covered scratches that crisscrossed the old man's chest. He had mutilated himself, again. First the stove burns and now this. "How did this happen?" Nick asked.

"While I was swimmin'."

"You can't swim now. Spring is still a few weeks off."

Confusion twisted Claude's face. Nick repeated, "It's winter and cold outside."

"I reckon, if you say so," he muttered, and then continued. "I was standin' on the rock above the spring, ready to jump in. The Bird come at me with fire bouncin' off its wings. Its claws dug into my chest and I screamed to God Almighty for help. We fell into the water and thrashed about. I finally got my hands around its neck and squeezed, askin' God to give me more strength. The Bird's face changed into my wife's with the same look she had the day I choked the last breath out of her ugly old face."

Nick was speechless. Had the old man confessed to murdering his wife? No wonder he was haunted by memories. Fearing the answer, he asked, "Claude, are you saying you choked your wife?"

Anger flashed across Claude's face and settled in his eyes. "Did she say I choked her?"

"No."

"Then I must of not done it."

Nick hoped that what he'd heard was just confusion in the old man's head, but he would never be sure.

Loretta shouted down the stairs. "Poppa, who are you talkin' to down there?"

Claude whispered, "Not a word about my daddy's gold." He leaned back, closed his eyes, and let his mouth fall open.

Loretta hurried down the stairs. "Oh, Mr. Kincaid, I didn't know it was you." She giggled. "Here I am hollerin' like a fool to Poppa and him deaf. I'm sure you had a nice time in Chicago, but I had the worst Christmas ever. Ella saw fit to bring that colored baby to the church's Christmas service, after me tellin' everybody that my poor sister was violated. She sat there and refused to admit that some colored forced hisself on her against her will. That's more believable than sayin' she found a baby in the woodbin. I still tell everybody it was rape, but I can see doubt in their eyes. Can you imagine how that makes me feel?"

"No, ma'am, I guess not."

Claude snorted.

"Oh, Lord, Poppa, if you only knew how you sound." She rolled her eyes. "I'm sure you've noticed that Poppa is losin' his mind a little more every day. I found him bleedin' with cuts across his chest. Said the bird did it, but I think the cuts come from a parin' knife he used to peel an apple."

Nick whispered. "He showed me the wounds."

"I don't know what I'm gonna do, with havin' to watch him every second."

Claude opened his eyes. "I see your mouth is workin', Loretta. I suspect about me."

"I was just tellin' Mr. Kincaid that I needed to get you all some breakfast and I'm gonna do it now."

She headed up the stairs. Claude chuckled. Nick shook his head. "Why do you pretend to be deaf to your daughter?"

"I learn stuff. That woman moved me in here wantin' to find my gold, just like her mama."

"Do you really have gold?"

"You'll know more when it's time."

"I didn't mean to be inquisitive."

"If that means nosey, the Bird said to trust you."

"The bird?" Nick chuckled, but stopped when he saw the hurt that crawled across the old man's face. "What did the bird tell you about my future?"

"Didn't tell me nothin' good. Somethin' bad is gonna happen. I asked what and the bird just laughed."

"If you find out, will you let me know?"

Claude nodded and smiled like a child.

Before Nick could say more, Boyd's truck horn sounded. "I'm riding into Eddyville with Boyd."

Upon arriving in Eddyville, Nick went directly to the tax office to inquire about ownership of the cabin. Unpaid taxes had the property tied up until John Frank used his connections. Arrangements were made at the bank and the purchase was completed by noon. Nick slipped the deed inside his jacket pocket and walked with a lighter step toward the boarding house. His excitement soared at the thought of seeing Jenny. Not only was she coming back on the noon train, he was a property owner and wanted to marry her. He pictured her jumping into his arms after hearing about the cabin. Tonight, he'd take her there and ask her to marry him just as he'd planned to do before the holidays.

Muted conversation mixed with clinging flatware met Nick at the boarding house door. Smoke hovered above the tables where men were enjoying a cigarette after their meal. Fanny came hurrying across the room and pulled a letter from her apron pocket.

"Mattie said to give you this letter. It's from Jenny. You know Mattie's gotta visit her casket once a week." She glanced around the half-filled room. "Excuse me, dear, I've got customers waitin' to be fed. Find yourself a seat and I'll be with you shortly."

Had Jenny delayed her return for some reason? But why send the letter to Mattie? He smelled a faint scent of lilac when he ripped the seal.

Nick— I sent this letter to Mattie for fear it might fail to reach you before the date I was to return.

Nick felt confused. Why would she change her return date?

I've spent most of the holidays thinking about us, actually about my impulsive nature. To say I'm a romantic is an understatement. To your credit, you're more of a realist. I pressured you for a commitment about us that you weren't prepared to make. I realized once I was away, it was only an infatuation on my part and so unfair of me. Remember that day at the spring when you kissed me, I told you it was just a kiss. That's all it was until I turned it into my personal fantasy. I've moved home to stay.

He felt the wind go out of him. The last line echoed in his head. Nick stomped out the door, brushing past two ladies who gasped at his rudeness. His head reeled with random thoughts, dredging his memory for a reason, only to come up dry. He headed alongside the river, walking aimlessly. It didn't make sense. He stopped and forced himself to continue reading.

Thanks to you, Nick, I've made peace with my dad, though my mother is not pleased. I simply repeated with you the same mistake I made in a previous relationship. I saw the man a few days ago. Seeing him made me re-evaluate my mistakes in that relationship also.

He punched the air with both fists and screamed. "I love you, damn it." He felt physically ill for a moment and then began shaking his head. No, he didn't believe it. She loved him. He couldn't be

231

wrong. He blinked watery eyes back into focus and continued to read.

> *Nick, I will always treasure our friendship. You may think I'm a coward for not coming back and facing you. Perhaps I am. I know you believe we were good together, and we were for a summer, but not for a lifetime. Had we been meant for each other, we both would have felt it by the time I left. I cannot trust myself from being caught up in a romantic storybook fantasy. It's my nature. I wish you the best always.*
>
> *Jenny*

Claude's warning that something bad would happen came to mind. He crumpled the letter and threw it into the river. It floated away to finally disappear in the whirling eddies.

32

Misery became Nick's partner without Jenny as one day melted into the next. His mood mirrored the dark clouds that hovered low in the sky, typical for Kentucky winters according to Claude. He completed another letter to Jenny, the second one in three days. He'd sent a dozen or two without receiving a response, yet he refused to accept that she was gone forever.

The schoolhouse shuddered against the wind as Nick went outside to bring in dry logs in case the overcast sky brought rain before morning.

He felt something tear through his sweater before he heard the sound of the shot. The impact knocked the firewood from his arms. Instinct took over. He plunged headfirst through the doorway and kicked it closed. Rolling to his feet, he quickly pushed a heavy table against the door as a second bullet exploded just above his head and sent splinters flying.

Fear sent him crawling across the floor to his desk where he kept the handgun locked in a drawer during school hours. Cocking the weapon, he snaked his way into the corner behind the stove. The shooter wouldn't know about the gun.

A slight burning sensation made him reach inside his shirt. He withdrew his hand and found it covered with blood. His mind raced. He wanted to pull his shirt open and look, but he dared not take his eyes off the door or the windows. Perspiration dotted his forehead and his shirt was becoming saturated as his eyes fanned the room. Pains began shooting through his shoulder. He'd read that people could be seriously wounded and not feel the pain until later. Could that be the case?

Minutes passed. Nick had both arms extended with the gun pointed at the door when the doorknob slowly turned. Adrenaline shot from his head to his toes. He rested his arms against the warm stovepipe to hold the weapon steady.

The door opened and bumped against the table. Tension molded Nick in place. He gripped the gun with both hands, squeezing it tighter and tighter. The door strained against the table. Suddenly the gun exploded with a deafening sound that echoed around the room.

A man screamed.

Silence followed. Nick stood frozen. Had he killed the man? He listened and heard nothing.

"Oh, my God," he muttered. The gun going off had been an accident, but he'd been prepared to kill. He heard Father O'Brien's voice in his head. "Kincaid, don't you know what the Bible says about taking a life?" Had he killed a man?

The thought made him retch. His legs felt weak and perspiration seeped from every pore. The room was out of focus. Something was happening to him. "Help me, dear God, please."

He heard someone shout, "Kincaid, are you okay?"

The door burst open and sent the table sliding across the floor. Boyd waved a handgun around while his eyes searched the room.

Nick stepped out from behind the stove. "Is the man dead?"

"Ain't nobody out there."

"But I heard a scream." Nick stepped forward and staggered slightly.

"You're white as a ghost." Boyd moved toward him. "You've been hit. Get yo' head down before you pass out."

Nick's legs gave way and Boyd grabbed him by the shoulders and let him down easy. Buttons flew as Boyd ripped open Nick's shirt. "Son-of-a-bitch." Boyd quickly removed his own shirt, folded it into a pad, and placed it against Nick's shoulder.

"Is it bad?" Nick asked.

"You're gonna be fine." Boyd slipped his belt around Nick's chest and buckled it tight to hold the makeshift bandage. Nick opened his eyes and moaned.

"Stay with me," Boyd urged as he lifted Nick up in his arms. "We're gonna get you patched up."

Nick sniffed a second time. The smell was antiseptic. He opened his eyes and rose up on an elbow, sending a pain through his side.

Boyd smiled down at him. "You're finally awake."

Nick blinked and looked around the strange room. "Where am I?"

"At Fanny's place. Doc said you needed rest, so I put you here instead of takin' you back to the mill. He took the bullet out and gave you a little pain pill that knocked you out like a baby. A good bit of blood loss, so you'll be a little weak for a couple of days. You'll be fine."

"I don't remember much about coming here. The man . . . did I shoot him?"

"Yeah, and it's a shame you didn't kill him."

"Thank God for that," Nick said. "The gun went off accidentally."

"Hell, man, he was tryin' to kill you. You had a right to shoot his ass off on purpose. I tried to rein Brady in, but it didn't work."

"It was Brady?"

"Yeah. Doc patched him up and sent him on to the hospital in Paducah for surgery."

"Was he hurt badly?"

"We can hope." Boyd chuckled. "Funny thing, you kept sayin' something about wantin' to see Jenny and the Ten Commandments."

"I remember nothing after you picked me up off the floor. How did you know about the shooting?" Nick asked.

"I heard the shots and got over to the schoolhouse fast. You needed some sewin' up, so I brought you here."

"Thanks, I appreciate it."

"Think nothin' of it."

After a light tap on the door, Fanny came in carrying a tray. "Hey, sleepyhead, you decided to wake up." She smiled. "I made you some more liver soup. Liver builds the blood back according to Doc." She placed the tray on a stand beside the bed. "Want me to feed you?"

"No, I'll get up." The thought of liver soup gagged him until he pulled himself up and realized how weak he felt. He cringed from the soreness in his side.

"Don't get too close to him, Fanny," Boyd cautioned. "He'll pinch your butt again."

Nick blushed.

Boyd laughed. "Look, his color is comin' back. See how he's turnin' red."

"Don't let him get to you, Nick," Fanny said, "It's been a spell since my butt's been pinched. Honey, it was the pill that made you do it."

Nick blushed even more. Had he actually pinched Fanny's botton, a woman old enough to be his mother, even his grandmother?

Fanny reached down beside the bed and came up with a chamber pot. "I'll take this as I go."

Nick didn't recall using the pot. When the door closed, he turned to Boyd. "Did I . . . I mean, did she?"

"Yep, she held the pot and you yanked your business out and let go."

"You've got to be teasing." He'd never be able to look that woman in the eyes again.

Boyd laughed. "I'm jokin'. I helped you with the pot."

"Thanks." Nick smiled. "You saved my life too."

Boyd shrugged. "Doc said for you to stay here tonight. I'll be back for you tomorrow afternoon. You'll be good to go except for the sore shoulder. The bullet sliced it open like a knife, but doc sewed it up real good."

Nick nodded and watched him go, thinking he'd been a true friend. Jenny had been right when she said there were a lot of good people living at Woodson Chapel. Boyd was one of them.

Nick could hardly believe it was morning when the knock on the door awoke him. Doc had given him another pill and he'd slept through the night and most of the morning.

John Frank stepped inside. "I'd say somebody is out to get us. They don't want Eddie's killer caught."

"It seems that way," Nick said.

"I'm goin' to pass the word along to the Feds to see if they can sniff out any information. Since Brady shot you, I'm concerned that Vale could be behind it with them two workin' together. Word is, Vale thinks you told the Feds about his still."

"Yeah, I know."

"Either way, you won't have to worry about Brady any more. He died on the operatin' table."

Nick felt as if his heart had stopped. He could hardly breathe and gulped for air.

"You mean I killed him?"

"Self-defense. Just popped in to let you know there won't be charges. Gotta go, but I'll tell Boyd you're awake."

Nick closed his eyes. He could see Father O'Riley's chubby finger pointing at him and his booming voice demanding to know which of the Ten Commandments was the greatest sin.

Each time Boyd's truck hit a rut in the road it awoke the soreness in Nick's side. His strength was returning, but guilt from shooting Brady had enveloped him like a river fog. His dad had been right. He didn't belong here. He should have stayed in Chicago.

Boyd glanced over at him. "You said it was an accident. Get over it, Nick."

"How do you get over killing a man?"

"I'm not very religious, but even I believe God can fix anythin' if he's a mind to."

"If I'd stayed in Chicago it never would have happened."

Boyd glanced at Nick and frowned. "If a frog had wings, it wouldn't bump its ass every time it jumped. Nobody can live life on ifs. Get past it."

"I can't do it. I'm thinking about going home."

"I'd hoped you was home," Boyd snapped.

They continued on in silence until reaching the mill. Women and children bundled in coats and headscarves poured out of the store onto the porch. "Look, there's a bunch of people waitin' to see you," Boyd said.

"Drive on down to the mill. I don't want to see anyone right now."

"Them people are standin' out there freezin' their asses off just to see you. You need to stop."

"No, drive past. I don't feel like talking."

Boyd continued on down to the mill. He didn't say a word until Nick got out of the truck and started toward the steps. "Damn you, Kincaid, you're actin' like a pussy. So you shot a man that wanted to kill you. That's called self-defense. Ever hear of it?"

Nick jerked around so fast a pain tore through his side. "It's not that simple, Boyd."

"It's what you decide to make it," Boyd shot back. "Everythin' in life is what you make it." He shifted into gear and stomped on the gas. The truck spun around and shot up the hill.

Soreness made the climb up the steps a slow process. Out of the corner of his eye, Nick saw Boyd talking to those gathered on the end of the porch. Once inside, Nick peeked past the curtain and saw the group leaving. He eased down into the rocker. Dog came over and reared up on him. He hugged the animal and began to cry.

The knock on the door seemed too timid for Boyd. Nick ignored it. After a brief silence pounding started and didn't stop. Nick wiped away tears with his shirt and jerked the door open. Stan Kramer stood in the doorway. Nick's first impulse was to tell the boy to go home. "What do you want?"

"To talk."

"Maybe you should take your daddy's advice and have nothing to do with me."

"No, Mr. Kincaid. It was a mistake for me to walk out of school like I did that day."

"When did you decide that?"

The kid shrugged.

"What changed your mind?" Nick said.

"You. You talked about me goin' off to college, maybe gettin' a scholarship. If you leave what will I do, Mr. Kincaid? Do I make 'shine' like my daddy?"

"No, no, you can still go to college and do the things we talked about."

"If you're leavin', tell me how, Mr. Kincaid, 'cause I trust you."

Would the kid ever stop? Exasperated, Nick said, "I'm just thinking about leaving. That doesn't mean I've decided." He paused. "Don't you understand that I killed a man?"

"I know. Ain't you glad it wasn't you that got killed? I am."

How could he answer that? Stan had hit him with the truth and Nick felt pissed for some reason. "Maybe it would have been better had it been me," Nick snapped.

"You ain't bein truthful, Mr. Kincaid. Even animals want to live."

"Jesus," Nick muttered as he threw up his hands. "Please go home, Stan."

"I ain't done talkin' yet. You said if people want somethin', they have to risk somethin'. Don't that mean me and you too? You said the framers of the Constitution risked everythin' for the freedom we're promised."

"I guess I said that."

"You said it, Mr. Kincaid. You said you wanted to be a teacher more than anythin'."

"You've made your point, Stan. Listen to me. I haven't decided to leave."

"Well, then me and the other kids are goin' to be at school in the mornin'. I'll go early and start the fire so you can sleep late after bein' shot."

Stan walked out without a goodbye. Nick was glad to see him go. Did the boy expect Nick to be responsible for him? He hadn't adopted the kid. Nick eased down into the rocker again.

Boyd came in the door and set a tray on the desk without a word. As he left, he turned back in the doorway. "If you're the man I always thought you was, you'd stay until school closes for the summer. If you leave without sayin' goodbye to them kids, I'll beat yo' ass before you board the train." Boyd slammed the door closed behind him.

What was it with these people? In the beginning they wouldn't have cared if he'd been dying and now they were . . . Damn it to hell, why were they being so nice?

He knew there was no way he could leave until the end of the term four months away. He sank into the chair at the desk and uncovered the tray. Liver and onions. They were trying to starve him.

33

Claude predicted an early spring when March lilies peeked through the winter mulch in mid-February. The approaching change of season had little effect on Nick. He was still haunted by the school-house shooting and lonelier than ever without Jenny. Time spent at school was a distraction, though minimal at best. He spent most of his time alone in his room reading or walking in the woods with Buddy, the name he finally bestowed on Dog.

Nick often visited the cabin where memories of Jenny were most alive. He couldn't accept that their relationship was just a summer romance, and her failure to reply to his letters was a mystery that dogged him all the time. He was determined to see her and get an answer while school was in recess for spring planting.

Claude's mental lapses occurred more frequently and reminded Nick of his grandfather's final days. Battling with his own loneliness and depression, Nick avoided Claude by eating in his room. Why share his misery with him or anyone else?

Boyd usually brought Nick his evening meal. His arrival and departure was done with a monk's vow of silence. He arrived earlier than usual one evening and placed the food tray on the desk, and then faced Nick who was slumped in the rocker.

"You're pissin' me off actin' like a dead man. As soon as your side gets well, I'm gonna kick your ass for bein' the way you are."

Nick rose. "I don't want to fight you, Boyd, but I don't like threats, so don't push me. I appreciate you saving my life, but—"

"You ain't got a life. It's good that Jenny ain't here to see the real Nick Kincaid."

Nick dropped back down into the rocker. "Come on, Boyd, I know what you're trying to do. Just leave me alone. I'm fine. And for your information, Jenny could care shit about what happens to me."

Boyd frowned. "You're talkin' out of your ass. That girl is crazy about you."

"Yeah . . . she won't even answer my letters."

"What did you do to her?"

"I did nothing to her."

"You had to do somethin'."

"Damn it, I did nothing. I wanted to marry her."

Boyd shrugged. "Don't make sense. You did *somethin'* to cause her to say no."

"Oh, hell, Boyd, will you stop? I've never had a chance to ask her. She never came back from Christmas break."

Boyd took a moment. "Ain't you lucky she didn't? You wouldn't want her to see you like this, would you?"

Nick glanced away.

"I didn't think so. If I was you, you know what I'd do? I'd go to Paducah for a couple of days and get fucked, or I'd fix up that cabin and bring my girl back and marry her. I wouldn't act like a dried up piece of shit." He pointed at Nick. "And I don't want to kick your ass unless I have to, either." Boyd sailed out the door and left Nick shaking his head.

Buddy came over and reared up on Nick's leg and whined.

"Do you agree with Boyd or do you just need to pee?"

The dog ran to the door, whining to get out.

"I thought so."

He opened the door and walked out on the landing to wait. Boyd was right. He'd been in the pits ever since Jenny failed to return. And Brady's death had added to it. He had to get his head straight. Repairing the cabin might be a good thing to get him centered again. That had crossed his mind a few times.

Ducky showed up on Saturday morning with a wagon loaded with lumber and announced that Boyd had sent him to help repair the cabin.

A wave of anger came at first. Knowing that Boyd had good intentions, it made no sense to get pissed off when someone was displaying real friendship. "I don't think so today," Nick said in a reasonable tone.

"Mr. Boyd, he say today."

"Not today, Ducky. Maybe another time."

"Mr. Boyd, he say I's to do it by myself if you won't go help me."

"Did he say that?" Nick asked.

"No, sir, not exactly. He say for me not to go without you. I wants you to go."

245

Nick sighed. The old man looked like he was holding his breath waiting for an answer. "Why not?" He'd toyed with the idea of fixing up the cabin even before Boyd suggested it. After all, repairs on the cabin would increase the value of the property, if nothing else. "Let me get my pants on."

Repairs got under way on weekends and after school. The cabin came to life and stirred memories of Jenny, along with dreams of what could have been. Nick vacillated between being hurt and feeling angry until frustration drove him to see Mattie. She received mail from Jenny on a regular basis, though she'd showed him a cold shoulder and might tell him nothing.

Mattie answered the knock. Her mouth flattened into a look of disgust and her eyes squinted as if looking down a gun barrel with him in the cross hairs.

"Mr. Kincaid, I take kindly to you stayin' on to teach the children until school is out. I prayed when you got shot, but I don't like you much anymore."

Nick couldn't imagine what he had done to the woman and felt somewhat surprised that it mattered to him.

"I'm sorry you don't like me," he said, "I'm here about Jenny. Have you heard from her?"

"Yes, of course."

He waited. Mattie stared.

"Is she okay?"

"Yes, she's fine." She placed a hand on the doorknob, an obvious gesture to dismiss him.

"Look, it's cold out here. I'm not leaving until I know something. May I come in?"

She rolled her eyes and stood with the stiffness of a sentry as he stepped inside. Mousey came from the front room and stood in the doorway holding a broom.

"You must know why Jenny decided not to come back," Nick said.

"I'm told she made plain her reason in a letter to you. I'm not one to interfere in other people's business."

"When did you hear from her last?"

"Ain't missed a week since she left." She took a handful of letters from a shoebox on the table. "Of course I answer her each week. She wants to know how we're all doin'."

"Does she ever mention me? What did she have to say about the shooting?"

Mattie crossed her arms and spoke with a pious tilt of the head. "Mr. Kincaid, I didn't write her about Brady. That's no interest to her. I've thought about you and Jenny, me bein' your matchmaker. The Lord has allowed me to have a special feel for matchin' up people. Your Yankee ways don't match up with Jenny's sweetness."

Nick threw up his hands in disbelief. "Mattie, she's from Cleveland, a Yankee too."

Taken aback, she snapped, "Well, she's certainly not your kind."

"What is my kind?"

"It wouldn't be Christian of me to speak my mind. I promised Jenny."

"What did you promise her?"

"It's just between me and her."

247

Nick couldn't take any more of her self-righteous posturing without exploding. "Coming here was a mistake." He excused himself, but stopped and turned back in the doorway. "You've treated me as if I forced her to go. It was her decision, hers alone. If she ever asks about me tell her that I love her and I don't know how to stop."

Nick only heard "Mr. Kincaid" before he jerked the door closed with a bang.

He'd seen the letters. They had to have some answers and he was determined to read them.

On the following Saturday morning Nick went to the cabin as usual. He stopped and stared as he approached. If only Jenny could see all the improvement. He and Ducky had added a room, cut away all the underbrush, and chinked the logs with fresh clay. The roof was patched with raw wood shingles that stood out among the dark weathered ones, but the sun would soon bleach them to match, according to Ducky. A climbing vine that Jenny had identified as a Trumpet Creeper thrived at the end of the building.

Smoke floated from one of the chimneys that sandwiched the building. He'd heard foxhounds running last night. Hunters probably used the place to escape the night chill and listen to the chase. Scent left by the hunters unnerved Buddy. He sniffed around the room, making his concern known with low, rumbling growls. Nick failed to reassure him that everything was fine and shuffled him outside to chase rabbits.

A board squeaked behind Nick as he closed the door. He turned to find a straggly bearded man standing on the attic stairway with a rifle, pointed. With rumpled clothing and uncut hair, the man no longer looked like a riverboat gambler or a movie hero.

Vale chuckled. "I hear Brady is takin' a dirt nap, so I suspect you're carryin' a gun. I didn't know you had the balls to shoot a man."

Nick could feel the veins in his temples pulsate. "The shooting was an accident."

"Yeah, like it was an accident that the Feds raided my still and that you've got a handgun in your inside coat pocket. Turn around and put your hands behind your head with your fingers locked together." After taking the gun, Vale motioned toward a chair.

Nick sat at a rickety table abandoned with the cabin. He felt nauseated. Never had he thought himself capable of taking a life, especially a second time. Now he knew he could when his own life was at stake.

Vale stood across from him and kept the weapon pointed. Even with a beard and long hair, his face looked thinner. Fear crawled around in Nick's stomach. His mind searched for options. "Believe me, killing Brady was an accident, and I kept my part of our agreement. I never revealed the still's location."

"I could care less about Brady, but I'm still pissed that somebody ruined my business. The only reason you ain't dead already is 'cause Boyd says you didn't do it. Make me believe you." The rifle pointed at Nick's head. The weapon was cocked.

Nick licked his lips. Honesty was his only option. He sucked in air to steady his voice and looked directly at Vale. The man's dark eyes squinted as if waiting to catch Nick in a lie. "I never hit it off with you. I'm the private type, like you, and believe in tending to my own business."

Vale chuckled at the answer for some reason. He leaned toward Nick with a twisted smile. "Little Partner, we're alike 'cause we both killed a man. I did it on purpose and might do it again."

Nick's heart skipped, but he never blinked.

"And I don't mean Eddie if that's what you're thinkin'." Vale stroked his beard. "Both of us is claimin' to be innocent. You for turnin' me in. Me for killin' Eddie. I know about me, but you're still a question. You've got to give me an answer that satisfies. I could plant your ass up here on a hillside. If you was ever found, it'd be a little at a time after animals dug you up and scattered your bones from the Cumberland to the Tennessee. You're wrong about thinkin' me or any of my friends took care of Eddie. None of us did it. I've checked it out. Now am I wrong in thinkin' you ratted on me?"

Vale respected strength. Nick took a deep breath. "You're wrong. I kept the code. Am I wrong by saying Eddie worked for you?"

Vale raked stringy hair away from his furrowed brow and smiled. "You're way behind, Little Partner. I let Eddie go more than a year ago. That little fucker stole from me."

"Is that why he came here to see you twice a month all last year?"

"To see me? No, not me. You're pissin' in the wind with that story."

"I've got ticket stubs that prove he took the train to Paducah to see somebody every other week. If not you, who?"

Vale looked thoughtful for a moment. "What else do you know?"

"I've got other stuff. I cleaned out Eddie's Chicago room and talked to some people. He worked with a mystery man. I thought that was you."

250

Vale lowered the gun. Though subtle, his eyes had showed surprise. "Little Partner, you may of just saved your ass. If what you say is true, you may have confirmed somethin' I've suspected. Eddie didn't meet with me." Vale's dark eyes narrowed. "You've given me reason to think somebody else put the Feds on me. You'd better be tellin' the truth, 'cause I really did kill a man once for crossin' me. Keep that in mind if you ever think about talkin' too much." He paused and looked Nick in the eyes. "I'm gonna walk out now and you'd better forget I was here."

The tension drained from Nick as Vale crossed to the door. He turned back toward Nick. "You right-handed or left-handed?"

Frowning, Nick answered, "Right."

"Then that handgun should of been in your coat pocket on the other side." He laughed and reached for the door, but slammed it shut when met by a ferocious growl. "Your bad ass dog don't like me neither. I can walk out the door and shoot him, or you can hold him until I'm gone. Which will it be?"

"You know the answer."

Vale laughed. "Course I do, Little Partner. I always try to know the answer before I ask the question."

Nick relaxed. He wouldn't have to look behind every tree now that Vale had offered a temporary truce. If Vale and his cohorts didn't kill Eddie for racial reasons, then Cleve might be right. With Chicago mobsters involved, the killing had become more of a mystery.

Nick left the cabin at noon and began the half-mile trek through the woods to Mattie's house. He had to see the letters. The weather was nice, and she would be in Eddyville to visit her casket like she did every Saturday. He hated to break into her house but knowing about Jenny was worth the chance.

He approached the house with caution and confirmed that neither the horse nor buggy was in the barn. There was no need for a key. Neighbors never locked their doors, which seemed strange after growing up in Chicago.

The shoebox remained in the center of the kitchen table. Guilt hovered as if a thousand eyes were watching and they all belonged to Mattie. He shuffled through envelopes, comparing dates until finding the first letter. Jenny wrote about the problem of adjusting to her mother's demands and complaints. Toward the end she stated that her leaving had been the right decision without question. The next letter was about chatty things, along with her father's plans to come down to get the car in the spring. Upon finishing the fourth letter, Jenny had revealed nothing out of the ordinary, except in every letter she referred to having made the right choice by leaving.

If it's so right, why does she keep repeating it in every letter? Who is she trying to convince? That means she's still not sure.

With a crumb of hope, he opened the next to the last letter.

Dearest Mattie. I was happy to receive your letter, though I've been rather puzzled by it. I think you might have heard Nick incorrectly about being in love with me, but I do agree that he is a great guy. I couldn't live with myself if I forced him into something he didn't want. I haven't received one letter from him, which validates my decision not to return. It makes me think you misunderstood what Nick said. Thank you for keeping my secret. The doctor said I'm doing fine and the baby will be here in early summer.

Adrenaline took Nick's breath. He stared at the letter and read the line again. Jenny was having his baby. "Damn it," he yelled. "Why didn't she tell me?" He dropped down into a chair. He kissed the letter and inhaled the sweet scent of lilac while reading it a second time. What had he put her through?

"I love you Jenny, I love you," he muttered. His eyes teared as he kissed the letter.

In the excitement of the moment, he failed to hear the buggy arrive, but there was no mistaking the shrill voice approaching the door. He was trapped with no way to escape. Better to face embarrassment than be seen running away like a thief. He would face them and confess. The information about the baby would be worth whatever punishment.

Mattie pushed open the door and froze for a moment. "What are you doin' here?" she demanded. Her face flushed.

Nick tried a smile but Mattie's expression remained unchanged. "The letters." Nick held them up. "I came here just to read Jenny's letters."

"Them letters ain't none of your business." Mattie dashed across the room and reached for them. Nick jerked them away.

"No. They are my business. I read about the baby."

Mousey made an audible gasp. Mattie's mouth went slack and her eyes bulged. "You gettin' Jenny in trouble, you don't deserve to know nothin'."

"I do deserve to know. That's my baby and I love Jenny. You can damn well bet I'm going to bring her back here the first chance I get."

Mattie's brow softened. "The baby don't make no difference?"

253

"Of course it makes a difference. The baby makes me love Jenny even more. I'm going to marry her if she'll have me."

Mattie giggled and clasped her hand beneath her chin. "Oh, Mr. Kincaid, I knew you two were right for each other the first time we met. There's no matchmakers around better than me. I forgot my pocketbook today and had to come back for it. The Lord meant for me to find you here in my kitchen."

"I apologize for coming into your home. I'd never steal from you."

"Oh, my Lord, course you wouldn't. We've got nothin' worth stealin'."

"I'm going to bring Jenny back during spring break. I've written her dozens of times, but she apparently never received them. I think it was because of her mother. Don't let her know I'm aware of the baby. I suspect her mother would make her life more miserable. Say nothing until I make plans."

"Mr. Kincaid, this is like a movin' picture show. You two in love." Mattie giggled. "We won't say a word. "I'll give Jenny a weddin' shower and a baby shower, even though it will cost me a good much."

Nick smiled. "She'll appreciate your kindness."

"I'll bring Jenny's letters for you to read each week."

"That would be nice."

"'Member last summer I said there might be a spring weddin', and now it'll be a baby shower too. Praise the Lord. I'm so happy."

Nick swore them to silence and left. He could hardly contain his excitement. He wanted to leave for Cleveland immediately, but he'd have to wait a few weeks. School was dismissed for two weeks in

May to allow children to help parents with spring planting. It would be his first opportunity to bring Jenny back.

He arrived back at the mill at dusk and hurried up the steps, but stopped abruptly when Buddy growled at the door. Someone had been in the room. Things were strewn out of place enough that Nick could tell. Buddy ran around the room sniffing and voicing his objection.

Eddie's ticket stubs and notes were gone. This was Vale's way of letting Nick know his room had been searched. He now knew Nick was telling the truth. If Vale could really be trusted, Nick had gained some needed credibility with him.

34

The weather had teased with a promise of spring during the last two weeks of March. Nick welcomed the changing season. Even a few birds voiced their approval as he hurried up the hill toward the schoolhouse. He'd be bringing Jenny back in a couple of weeks. Thoughts of Brady sometimes interrupted his day, but less frequently as time passed. He prayed for himself and Brady each night and that brought some comfort.

Boyd saved Nick's life by getting him to the hospital, then he was relentless in pressuring Nick to move past the shooting and get on with his life.

The schoolhouse door stood open. He remembered giving it an extra tug to make sure the latch caught when he left yesterday. Paranoia stopped him for a moment until his rational side took over. If someone wanted to shoot him, they would wait behind a tree or shoot him as he opened the door. Thinking a child must have arrived early satisfied his concern as he stepped inside.

Meglena sat in front of the stove with her face smeared with soot. She held the doll against an exposed breast. For fear of frightening her, he stood frozen in the doorway, unsure about what to do. She saw him and smiled. She kissed the doll. "Ma Baa."

Nick nodded. He decided to say nothing.

She began rocking back and forth, babbling about a boy . . . a bad man . . . doctor. Was she saying a doctor was a bad man? Nick caught her eye and shaped each word. "Meglena, what . . . bad . . . man?"

She threw the doll against the floor and began wiping soot off its face with the bottom of her dress. When soot remained, she became agitated and pawed at its face with both hands. Her whimpering became louder. Nick hoped to break her focus by moving toward her. She whirled around and faced him.

"It's okay," he repeated, hoping she could read his lips as he backed away to give her room to escape. She rose and crossed to the door, but stopped and smiled before running into the woods.

Could she be the baby's mother? The attitude displayed toward the doll suggested as much. In spite of what Mae said, Eddie could be the father. He had other secrets. Even Ducky suspected his son of illegal activities, yet both parents were certain about Eddie not being the father. Nick's meeting with Vale had nearly convinced him that Eddie's death had nothing to do with the baby.

The sound of a motor drew him to the door. He stepped outside as the sheriff's car came over the hill. John Frank waved and braked to a stop. He climbed out and waddled toward Nick with excitement dancing in his eyes. He grabbed Nick's hand with a politician's grip. "I come to see you this mornin' 'cause this is to be private, just 'tween us. I'm tellin' you this to keep you from gettin' yo'self killed. I have proof of who killed Eddie."

"Who?" Nick heard himself ask in a hushed tone.

"I ain't ready to go public yet, but for your own safety, I think you should know." He paused. "It turned out to be Vale, just like I said all along."

"Vale?"

"Yeah. I wish the hell it was somebody else. He's gonna be hard to catch 'cause a lot of people protect him. They ain't gonna want him arrested. Could affect votes."

The news challenged all the conclusions Nick had reached favoring Vale's innocence. "Are you sure about Vale?" Nick asked.

"Yep, 'cause I've got witnesses. Vale and two other men from up river was involved. The two men was picked up by the Feds. To keep their own asses out of jail, they cut a deal by agreein' to testify against him. I've gotta find him. I figured you might know where he hides out."

"Why me?"

"You live with his family, maybe hear talk."

"I'm aware he moves around. That's all I know."

"You can bet your sweet ass Boyd knows, if you could get him to talk. You want justice and I want everythin' wrapped up, all shipshape before the election. If I knowed Vale's routine this case would be over. Will you help me?"

"Boyd doesn't think Vale or any of his cohorts killed Eddie."

"Well, I guess not. Them two is tied in together business wise, not to mention family. You gonna help or not?"

Nick paused. "There's something I should tell you."

John Frank tilted his head and looked down his nose. "Like what?"

"I ran into Vale. We talked and I have my doubts that he killed Eddie."

"Based on what, son?"

"He thinks someone wants his operation. If Eddie wasn't murdered because of Ella's claim that she gave birth, it might have been because of whiskey running."

John Frank smiled. "Both of the things you just mentioned are possible. The whiskey business ain't no game. Somebody is always tryin' to take over an operation. Chicago mobsters and people who work with 'em play for keeps."

"I tend to believe Vale. I found some items in Eddie's room that suggested he was into whiskey running with a partner. I thought it was Vale, but apparently a mystery man was involved."

"Did you know Eddie worked for Vale?"

"Yes, but Vale said that stopped over a year ago."

"Vale said? And you believe him?" John Frank smiled and shook his head. "Listen, son, unless you take Vale at his word that Eddie no longer worked for him, he had two reasons to kill him. Either 'cause of whiskey runnin' or 'cause he thought his sister was violated. All I know is that I've got two men who will testify he shot the boy. Him and Brady strung Eddie up in a tree. He wanted to let the Woodson community think the killin' was because of his sister when it was really about business."

Nick knew everything the sheriff said was possible. He also remembered Boyd admitting that Vale would lie about murdering Eddie. "Who were the two men that helped Vale?"

"Two Klansmen from up river. You don't know 'em. That's all I can tell you. Only telling you this now to keep you from bein' shot. When I catch Vale, you'll know."

"How did you learn about the two men?"

"Don't guess it hurts for you to know that now. Like I told you before Christmas, the Feds have been on the case. I don't help revenue men find whiskey stills, but I do work with them to a degree. With you and me bein' shot, I asked 'em to keep an eye out. A government man passed the information on to me. The two men were sent out of the county to protect them from Vale or some of his friends until I need 'em to testify."

"Could that government man be Cleve Underwood?"

"I can't reveal names of revenue men, and I've said all I'm gonna say, except you've got to believe people will kill yo' ass without givin' a second thought. Be careful. You know that by experience."

"I'll keep my eyes open."

"Good. You still carryin' a gun?"

Nick nodded.

"Don't be afraid to use it if you have to. Vale's killed before. The man who shoots first will be the one left alive." He tapped Nick on the arm. "Take care, and watch your back. A dead teacher would shore as hell affect votes."

35

Witnesses to testify against Eddie's killer short-circuited Nick's concentration all day, though it was still difficult to accept Vale as the killer. He hurried back to the store as soon as school was dismissed and found Claude asleep in his chair. Boyd sat on a stool reading the paper as Nick entered. He looked up and smiled. "Did you send them kids home smarter than when they got there this morning?" Boyd teased.

"I wouldn't bet on it today."

Boyd pitched the paper aside and pointed to the stove. "Some fresh coffee there. You look like your ass is draggin'. Them kids that hard on you?"

"No, it's not the kids."

Boyd chuckled. "You've been without a woman for a long while. Maybe that's the problem."

"No, that's not it. I need to ask you something, Boyd. You seem certain that Vale wasn't Eddie's killer."

"I am. Vale knowed the truth about Ella before the killin'. Besides, he would of told me if he'd done it. We're that close."

"You told me once he'd lie if he did it."

"I told you he'd lie to you, not to me."

"I'd like to talk to Ella and Frank."

"If Frank will talk, it'll surprise me, but go to it. You're invitin' a punch in the nose by mentionin' anythin' about the baby."

Nick smiled. "That's been done before. I'm going over that way now."

"Good luck," Boyd called as Nick went out the door.

Ella came out the door with a shawl draping her shoulders and sat on the steps beside Frank. He glanced at her and took a long drag and then stamped the cigarette butt into the ground. She brushed sawdust off the back of his coat.

"You all right, baby?" she asked. "I didn't know you was home until seein' you sittin' here lookin' like you don't have a friend in the world."

"Maybe I don't."

"Course you do. Everybody likes you." She smoothed stringy wisps of hair back away from her eyes. "I'm worried, Frank. That girl was here again today."

"Who?"

"You know, I told you about seein' the Ireland girl circlin' the house for over a week. She always stayed out in the woods until today. I caught her peekin' in the window."

"That girl ain't right in the head."

"I think she was tryin' to see the baby. She run when she saw me."

Frank sighed. "We're gonna have to move away from here."

"Because of the girl?"

"No. Because the baby won't have no chance here. She'll always be half of nothin' here 'tween the rivers. People are never gonna stop thinkin' you laid with a colored. That girl baby will always be colored no matter how white she looks."

Ella leaned her face against his shoulder. A tear escaped. "I got us into all of this. What are we gonna do, Frank?"

"We gotta save our money and move up North."

Ella's eyes filled. "I ain't never lived anywhere but here."

"Me neither, but we gotta do it for the baby's sake."

She took a moment. "I'll move anywhere as long as I'm with you and the baby."

He put his arms around her and snuggled close, and then pulled away. "Somebody's comin' up by the garden."

Ella straightened up to look. "It's the school teacher."

Frank rose. "What would he be doin' here?"

"Frank, please sit down. Don't start nothin'. Be nice."

Nick saw them sitting on the back porch stoop as he came down the hill beside the garden. He'd never met Frank and was unsure about how to approach him or how he might react to questions about the baby. As he drew near, he smiled and called out. "Hey there, I don't know if you know me. I'm Nick, the schoolteacher." He extended his hand to shake.

"I know who you are," Frank answered, but made no effort to shake. Nick saw suspicion in the man's eyes and withdrew his hand.

"Ma'am," Nick said with a slight nod. He brushed away the awkwardness of the moment by clearing his throat. He pointed up the hill. "I cross up by the garden going to my cabin."

"I've seen you before," Frank said.

Nick decided to state his reason for being there and talk or take a punch in the nose. He inhaled and asked, "May we talk?"

"What about?"

"Eddie."

The muscles in Frank's face tightened. Nick hoped they would hear the sympathy he felt as he spoke. "You two have had your share of trouble, and you're to be admired. Caring for the baby is a wonderful thing. I just wanted to ask if you knew who might have put the child in your woodbin?"

Ella hugged Frank's arm. "Honey, Mr. Kincaid believes the truth."

Frank's shoulders relaxed slightly. "We only know we found her there."

"Has anyone asked about the baby, maybe wanted to see her?"

"Every gossiper here 'tween the rivers wanted to see her," Ella said. "That little Ireland girl was lookin' in my window today with black stuff smeared all over her face."

The news silenced Nick for a moment. "Have you seen her here before?"

"Yeah, she's been watchin' the house from the woods from the beginning. Makes me nervous," Ella said.

"She's not right in the head anyhow," Frank added.

"It's sad about that girl. I need to ask you another question," Nick said.

Suspicion returned to Frank's eyes.

"Did Vale learn the truth about the baby before or after Eddie was killed?"

"I know nothin' about Vale's business," Frank snapped. "We ain't been close in years."

Frank held his gaze until Nick looked away. "I've kept you long enough," Nick said. "Thanks for talking to me." He extended his hand. "Good luck with the baby." Frank slowly took his hand. As he walked away, Nick heard Ella whisper, "He seems real nice, Frank."

Frank never replied.

36

Nick tossed the book aside and jerked the window curtain open after hearing what sounded like a shotgun, followed by Loretta's scream. He saw nothing. It must have come from inside the store.

Nick charged up the hill at full speed and popped in the door. Loretta came forward with bony fingers clutching her housecoat together. "The old fool nearly kilt me," she cried, pointing at Claude who sat in the corner chair and stared into space.

Boyd came forward and pointed toward Claude. "The old man gave us a scare for sure." With a nervous chuckle, he broke down a double-barreled shotgun and removed the spent casings.

"Where am I?" Claude shouted. His gaze traveled around the room.

"You're all right, old man," Boyd said. "Just take it easy." He pointed toward two gaping holes in the ceiling.

"He did that?" Nick asked.

Boyd nodded.

Loretta whined. "Poppa claims he was shootin' at the bird he talks to." Her voice melted into more nervous whimpering. "My own Poppa nearly kilt me."

"Take it easy, Loretta," Boyd urged. "Go upstairs and take some nerve medicine. A nap will make you feel better."

"What about Poppa? He might shoot me in my sleep."

"Don't worry. I'll watch him."

Loretta left and Boyd turned to Nick. "The old man just about shot her right through the floor." He glanced at Claude who had leaned back and closed his eyes. "When I got down here, he was staggerin' around tryin' to reload and screamin' at a bird that nobody sees but him. We may have to tie him in the chair. I don't know what else to do. I've got to run my business and Loretta can't babysit him all the time."

"Let's hope it doesn't come to that," Nick said. The idea of tying the old man in a chair repulsed him.

"Loretta was fixin' your breakfast when it happened. If you'll watch him a few minutes, I'll bring it down."

He gave thumbs up and Boyd disappeared up the stairs. Nick poured coffee from the pot brewing on the stove and turned as Claude opened his eyes. He sat up and stared at Nick. "I didn't know you was here. I'm glad you're takin' yo' meals here again instead of stayin' in your room."

"Me too, Claude. How are you?"

"Don't know. Had a bad dream or else it was The Bird here to take me away."

"What happened?"

"I saw my wife's face in a dream or it was The Bird in disguise. I tried to kill it." He stared up at the holes in the ceiling and laughed.

"I shot the tail feathers out of that bird's ass. Now Loretta's got to believe me 'cause them holes is proof there's a bird."

"What happened to the bird?"

He frowned. "I don't know. Guess it flew away."

The door swung open and Mattie came charging in with drama in her eyes. "Where's Boyd?" she asked. Her breath came in gasps.

"Upstairs," Nick pointed. "Something wrong?"

"Boyd, come down here," she hollered and then turned back to Nick. "Somebody stole that colored baby out of its bed while Ella and Frank was asleep."

Nick immediately thought of Meglena.

"Poor Ella, she's carryin' on like it's her natural child."

Boyd and Loretta came rushing down the stairs. Her nerve powder was taking effect by the way she clung to Boyd's arm to walk.

"What is all the hollerin' about?" Boyd asked.

"Somebody stole Ella's baby."

Loretta rolled her eyes. "Who would steal a colored baby, for heaven's sake?"

"Now, Loretta, coloreds are God's creatures too," Mattie said.

"Boyd, I may know where to find the baby," Nick said.

"Where?"

"Let me check it out first. I assume you'll organize a search party."

"Of course. We'll start a search as soon as you get back if one is needed."

"Boyd, don't go," Loretta whined. "What if Poppa tries to shoot me again?"

"Nick, take the truck. Meanwhile, I'll use the dinner bell and fox horn to get people here should they be needed."

Mattie's eyes danced with anticipation. "Mr. Claude tried to shoot you?"

Loretta pointed at the ceiling. "Scared me to death."

"You do get next to people bein' high strung and the nervous type, but what did you do to make your own daddy want to shoot you?"

"I ain't high strung and I ain't nervous," she snapped. "How dare you say such things about me."

"But, Loretta—"

"Don't but me. I'm always calm."

Nick left before the argument had time to escalate. He hoped he'd figured right about Meglena.

37

Nick descended the hill above the farmhouse and saw Alfia Ireland down by the henhouse feeding a flock of chickens from her gathered apron. The old lady stared until Nick stopped the truck near the front porch. Her son emerged from the house. He hooked a bib overall strap and pushed tousled hair away from dark, distrusting eyes. Gray-stubble beard camouflaged a disappearing chin.

"Good morning, Mr. Ireland," Nick called.

"What's yo' business with us?" Hubert asked.

"I'd like to speak with your daughter."

"Ain't seen her this mornin'."

"It's important that I talk with her," Nick said.

"You ain't hearin' so good. I just said she ain't here."

"A baby was taken from—"

"Ain't no concern of mine."

Alfia approached with the chickens scurrying after her. She focused on her son. "What's goin' on, Hubert?"

"He's lookin' for Meglena," Hubert said.

Alfia caressed the large crucifix that hung from her neck and faced Nick. "What are you wantin' with Meglena this time?"

"I believe she might know something about the baby taken from Frank and Ella's house."

Hubert bristled. "If you're sayin' she took a colored baby, you're wantin' trouble."

"I believe Meglena may know who gave birth to the child."

Alfia's face paled. Her hand tightened around the crucifix enough to turn her knuckles white. Rage spilled from Hubert's eyes. "You accusin' my girl?"

"Hush, Hubert, I'll handle this," Alfia said.

Hubert advanced toward Nick until his mother stepped in front of him. Her eyes remained on Nick. "Hubert, them goats ain't been fed."

He didn't move and continued to stare at Nick.

She spoke without looking at Hubert. "Son, them goats ain't been fed, didn't you hear?"

Hubert turned and walked toward the barn. He glanced back with a scowl.

Alfia fumbled with the crucifix. She wet her lips. "She ain't been herself since going to Saint Louis to see that ear doctor. Somethin' happened."

"What?"

"I've never asked."

"But you know something?"

She pressed her lips but failed to hide a flicker of fear in her eyes. "I never asked," she repeated, louder.

My God, Nick thought. She knew the child was pregnant and did nothing. This was the first time she's been forced to face the truth. "Where do you think Meglena might be now?"

She brought her hand up and covered the quiver in the corner of her mouth. "She goes up to the spring a lot. I don't know."

"If she should show up with the baby, please let me know."

Alfia gave a defiant thrust of her chin. "If Meglena shows up with a colored baby, you can take both of 'em. That's all I have to say." She turned and walked away.

Nick felt certain that Meglena had given birth to the child. As he climbed into the truck, a scream for help came from the barn. Hubert staggered out the door and dropped to his knees. Both Nick and Alfia raced toward him.

"Mama, it's Meglena," he sobbed.

Nick stepped inside the barn. The girl hung from a rafter. Her face was covered in soot and her body was as limp as the ragdoll that lay on the ground at her feet. He checked for a pulse. Sadness swept over Nick, then anger. There had been no one to rescue Meglena.

Alfia stood in the doorway clutching the crucifix in both hands. She stared up at the lifeless girl. Her mouth trembled, betraying her calm exterior.

"Oh, God, our baby is gone. She's gone, Mama," Hubert moaned from behind his mother.

Alfia's eyes flashed as she whirled and faced him. "Stop carryin' on." She turned back to Nick. "I'll go fix a place to lay her out. My son could use some help gettin' her inside. Then you can leave." She disappeared out the door.

Nick picked up the doll and wondered about the real baby. The possibilities frightened him. He turned to Hubert cowering in the doorway. "You hold her up and I'll loosen the rope."

"No, no, you hold her and I'll cut the rope."

Hubert was afraid to touch his own child. He was as worthless as the cow dung under his feet. Nick managed to lift the girl and cut the rope, allowing her body to ease down upon his shoulder. A lump settled in his throat as he cradled her in his arms.

Hubert followed as Nick started toward the house. A flock of black birds passed overhead and settled in a tree near the barn. Hubert rushed past Nick, his eyes wild with fear. "Them birds tried to eat my eyes out once."

Nick didn't comment. He took the girl's body inside and placed her on a sofa draped with a white sheet. Hubert dropped down beside his kneeling mother who clutched the crucifix with both hands.

The two mumbled prayers. Nick needed to get back to alert neighbors and organize a search party to find the baby. Dark clouds had moved in from the south. After an awkward moment, he stammered his condolences and volunteered to make neighbors aware of Meglena's death.

"No pryin' eyes needed," Alfia said. "It be best you don't tell what happened."

38

Aging coffee steamed on the stove. Its warmth offset the bitter taste as Nick and Boyd sipped in silence, heartsick over the lack of success in finding the baby. Neighbors had searched until growing darkness and a driving rain made conditions impossible to continue until morning. Everyone had gone home with the promise to resume at first light.

The eerie silence was shattered when the storage room door suddenly popped open and Claude appeared in a baggy union suit. He tottered over to the stove and looked around the room as if in a strange place. "Where's the baby?"

"We haven't found her," Nick answered.

"The Bird come to see me," Claude bellowed.

Boyd rolled his eyes and shook his head. "Go back to bed, old man. That's where I'm goin'. See you at daybreak, Kincaid." He made his way up the stairs.

"Has Ella done come and got the baby while I was sleepin'?" Claude asked.

"No, we didn't find her."

"Did you look where I told you?"

"You didn't tell me where to look."

"I didn't? Maybe it was Boyd I told."

"No, you didn't tell either of us." Nick was too weary to have much patience dealing with Claude tonight. He waved goodnight and started toward the door.

"Vale said to tell somebody that he was keepin' the baby at the schoolhouse."

Nick stopped and turned, unsure if he'd heard correctly. "What did you say?"

Claude frowned and rubbed his chin. "I, uh. The Bird told me—"

"No, that's not what you said. Think. You said Vale told you to tell somebody that the baby was at the schoolhouse."

"Did I?"

"Yes, you said Vale."

"He was here, all wet from the rain." Claude looked confused and shook his head. "But The Bird was here too."

The truth might be found somewhere in the old man's confusion, but Nick didn't take time to wait. He grabbed the lantern and charged out into the night. Alerting Boyd came as an afterthought. He kept running. If Vale thought the law was involved in the search, he had reason not to show himself. Under those circumstances it was possible he left the baby at the schoolhouse. The chance of finding the child couldn't be ignored, even if the message came from a fading old man.

Rain beat against Nick's face. He raked wet hair out of his eyes and kept running. His breath came in gasps by the time he topped the hill and saw a lantern flickering inside the schoolhouse window.

He burst through the door and stopped. Vale jumped up from behind the desk and pointed a rifle. Wet curls framed his face and the long black coat was covered in mud. Some was even on the side of his face as if he'd rolled in a mud puddle.

Nick made an easy target in the doorway. He'd left the handgun in his room. Now that John Frank had identified Vale as Eddie's killer, thoughts of never seeing his own child ran through his head. That was reason enough for Nick to fear.

"What in the hell are you doin' bustin' in a door like that?" Vale asked. "You're liable to get your ass shot off scarin' people." Vale lowered the rifle. "I told Poppa to send Boyd. Why'd he send you?"

Nick took a breath, the first one he remembered taking since entering the room. "I guess Claude got mixed up."

Nick took comfort in seeing Vale place the rifle down on the desk.

"The old man's mind is about gone. I know nothin' about babies. You've gotta deal with the kid." He nodded toward a cardboard box hidden in the shadows.

"You found her?" Nick crossed to the sleeping child. "Is she okay?" he whispered.

"I guess so."

"She's got to be hungry, maybe even wet. Did you change her?"

"Hell no, she's on her own in that department. She's a girl baby."

"Shouldn't that make her cry or something if she's hungry or wet?"

"She ain't hungry."

"You fed her?"

"Yeah," he muttered.

"Where did you get milk?"

"Stole it from a goat. Had to chase the damn thing and got all muddy."

No wonder Vale looked so wet and grimy. He'd been rolling in the mud to get milk. Then it dawned on Nick. Vale had saved the baby's life. If he'd killed her father, why would he save the baby? "Where did you find her?"

"Heard her cryin' in a cave. I thought it was a wild puppy lost from the litter."

Nick wondered why Vale didn't take the baby with him to the store. The answer came when Vale blurted, "I ain't havin' my name connected to savin' some nigger kid." He leaned back in the chair and crossed his arms. "You ain't plannin' on tellin' nobody, I hope?"

"No, no, I won't tell," Nick said. "May I ask you a question without getting shot?"

Vale chuckled and then nodded.

"Why didn't you leave the baby in the cave?"

He frowned and shifted in the chair. "That's a damn fool question."

"Why? I know we cleared up a lot of stuff between us at the cabin that day, but some people still think you were somehow involved in what happened to her father."

Suspicion darkened Vale's eyes. "Partner, I thought we had things straight between us. You done gone past bein' funny if you're still listenin' to lies about me. I had nothin' to do with Eddie's killin'. I've told you that before."

"I know you have. Your sister didn't give birth to the baby."

"I've done learned that a long time ago, before the lynchin'."

Nick knew he was treading deep water and tried to phrase the next question to avoid an explosion. "When we talked at the cabin you thought someone was trying to take over your business. Would that someone attempt to provide proof that you killed Eddie?" Nick held his breath but not for long. Vale came up out of the chair.

"What's goin' on here? Has Cleve Underwood been fillin' your head with lies?"

Nick could hardly suppress his surprise to hear Cleve's name tossed into the mix. His thoughts flashed back to Eddie's landlady who said a fat man with a bald spot visited Eddie.

"Some son-of-a-bitch is tryin' to set me up," Vale shouted. "Did Cleve say I killed Eddie?" He took a step toward Nick. "He must be the one tryin' to take over my operation."

Nick's hands went up. "Hey, hold on, I'm just repeating rumors. I don't know the truth."

Vale circled the room and turned back to Nick. "Okay, Partner, I'm gonna tell you the truth as I know it and what I suspect. I broke into your room and took some notes and things that belonged to Eddie."

"Yeah, I know."

"They made me start thinkin' you could be trusted. It saved your ass, if you remember. Them notes had to do with gettin' deliveries up to Chicago. They was codes used when Eddie worked for me. They only made sense to me and certain drivers. I went to Chicago and paid Eddie's girlfriend a visit. She said there was a fat man named Cleve who come to see Eddie. I figure Cleve and Eddie was working together to take over my business. They wanted me out of the way. It was perfect. Blame me. Put my ass in prison and I'm out of business. Don't forget, one of the notes was signed *CU*, Cleve Underwood."

"I thought the initials were *CV*."

"No. That was a *U*, not a V."

"You're telling me that Eddie's death was related to whiskey."

"Yeah, 'cause it was. If I'd wanted Eddie killed, I would of taken care of it in Chicago. Think about it. People I do business with would of done it in a cat's meow."

Nick was stunned. It made sense. John Frank had named Vale, and he'd got the proof from a Fed. That Fed would have been Cleve.

"Cleve is the only one I can figure," Vale said. "Tell me who else. If you've got a better name, give it to me."

It sounded logical for Cleve to feed John Frank false information and point the investigation in the direction he wanted.

Vale tilted his head and looked down his nose. "Look, Kincaid, I'm the best friend in the world to a man who shoots straight with me. May not be many things good about me, but by damn, I'm loyal. I need somebody to fuckin' believe me for once."

"Then you believe I'm being straight with you?" Nick asked.

"Yeah." He pondered for a moment and cleared his throat. "I'm honest in my own way, but not like you."

"I'm far from perfect," Nick said.

"If it's Brady you're thinkin' about, Boyd said you did a right good bit of grievin' over killin' that fat son-of-a-bitch. It was him or you. The word is that you're givin' more by teachin' kids than he was worth."

Silence followed. Nick hoped that was true. At least it might be some kind of penance. Vale rose abruptly and crossed toward the door. "Sounds like the rain's let up." He pulled the door open. "Yep, it has." He turned back to Nick. "It looks like Cleve has put me out of business, but he'll get his. Then I'm leavin'. I've been thinkin' about movin' to California so I can look ahead instead of back at what I've done. You ought to do the same for yourself. I mean to look ahead and not back."

Nick nodded.

"And don't ever mention me findin' that kid, you hear?" He disappeared out the door.

Nick stared after him. Not only had he connected with the man, maybe Vale had also given Nick some good advice.

The baby whimpered. He had no clue about what to do should she start crying. He held his breath and slipped the child inside his coat against his shoulder, and then buttoned it around her for the walk back to the store.

39

Boyd stood on the porch and blew the fox horn at midnight. Mattie and Mousey arrived first. As usual, Mattie led the way in the door and wanted to know who found the baby.

Boyd pointed to Nick. "He found her at the schoolhouse."

"You mean that baby was right under our noses all the time? Who put her there?" She directed the question to Nick, who pretended not to hear by peeking at the baby asleep in an apple crate on the counter.

"Don't know," Boyd said.

"Thank the Lord, anyway," Mattie said. "Guess one blessin' offset another tragedy. Did you hear about little Meglena Ireland gettin' killed this mornin'? A terrible accident, terrible."

"An accident?" Nick asked. He faced Mattie.

"Poor little thing, a cow got her tangled in a rope. Choked her to death, accordin' to Alfia. I dropped by to pay respects and didn't get inside the door."

Nick shook his head in disbelief. That saintly acting old woman had lied. When would she get her comeuppance? She'd committed child abuse by the way she neglected her granddaughter. He hoped there was such a thing as Karma, but it was just as well to say nothing about Meglena's suicide. It wouldn't change things for her.

Mattie gushed, "How does it feel to be a hero, Mr. Kincaid?"

"I'm no hero. I only brought the baby from the schoolhouse." He wanted to defuse all talk about the rescue before he had to tell a little white lie. There was no way he'd break his promise to Vale even if he had to do just that. Before Mattie could say more, Ella and Frank rushed in the door. She grabbed the baby, cuddling her and crying softly. Everyone watched in silence until Claude's booming voice interrupted.

"I want to see the baby."

Claude stood in the storage room doorway draped in a blanket. He came forward and was met by Ella, who held the baby out for him to see. He leaned close and squinted. "A right pretty grandbaby I've got."

Loretta snorted. "Poppa, it's not really your grandchild. Your eyes is gettin' as bad as your hearin'. Don't forget it has a colored daddy."

The room fell silent for a moment. Then Ella handed the baby to Frank. No one made a sound as she moved toward Loretta. The tremor in her voice underscored her anger as she said, "You're a sorry excuse for a sister and a human bein'."

Loretta opened her mouth to speak, but Ella snapped, "Don't say a word or you'll eat my fist. I've seen your whinin' and jealousy at work. You're mean, Loretta. Poppa, she's begged me for years to get you to talk about the gold. That's why she moved you in here." She pointed her finger. "You say you're Christian. Well, Loretta, you ain't."

"That's a bald-faced lie," Loretta cried. "I moved Poppa here 'cause I love him. Ella, how dare you. I've always been nice to you."

"No you haven't. You're not a nice person and everybody knows it. I'll soon no longer have to look at your face. Me and Frank are movin' north as soon as we sell our place."

"Boyd, listen to her attackin' me. You gonna let her talk to me like that?"

"I ain't in your family fights, Loretta. Never have been."

Loretta whined, "Why does everybody mistreat me all the time?"

Mattie spoke up, "I treat everybody good, Loretta, includin' you."

"Shut your big mouth, Mattie," Loretta barked.

Mattie's face turned crimson. She pursed her lips as if to block a flood of fiery words.

"I can't stand here and be attacked any longer." Loretta erupted into tears and bolted toward the stairs.

Ella followed her to the steps and called after her. "You can't sing worth a flip, either."

Boyd broke the silence that followed. "I'll check on her." He took the steps two at a time.

Mattie looked around the room. "I'm one of the nicest people you'll ever meet, but Loretta come within an eyelash of makin' me lose my good nature." She turned to Ella. "Honey, everybody except Loretta knows she can't sing worth a hoot. I want you to know, even though the baby's colored, I'm happy she's safe. That's just bein' Christian, I say." She checked the wall clock. "Milkin' time is gonna come soon. It's best we get home. Come, Mousey. Good night, all. "

After the door closed behind them, Claude shuffled across the room. "I want to see the baby again."

Frank held the sleeping child out toward him. Claude ran his hand gently across the child's forehead. "Frank, The Bird said for you to leave here."

Nick spoke up. "I believe Claude sees the bird."

Ella questioned with a frown. The old man turned toward her and smiled. Nick winked, unseen by Claude.

"This young fellow is the only friend The Bird allows me to have." Claude reached to pat Nick on the shoulder and lost his balance. Nick grabbed Claude's arm and eased him into a chair.

"The Bird shoved me," Claude shouted.

Ella smiled and smoothed his ruffled hair. "You stay there and let the bird leave before you get up."

The old man leaned back and smiled at his daughter. "I want you and Frank to have my gold. It ain't made me happy."

"Poppa, you don't really have gold."

"Yeah, there's gold. Gold coins in a pouch under a white stone at the base of the spring." Claude chuckled. "My old pappy stole it from the Union army. Frank, dig it out and take that baby away from here."

"The gold is for real?" Ella asked.

"It's for real."

Ella hesitated, and then she kissed Claude on the forehead. "Daddy, I ain't ever told you before, but I've always loved you." She motioned to Frank and hurried toward the door. Frank followed with the baby.

Claude laid his head back and tears flowed down his cheeks. He'd grown paler during the last few months.

Nick sat in a chair next to him. He was drawn to the old fellow for some unexplained reason. Perhaps because Claude would die soon and no one would care. He had been a mean man by his own admission, maybe even killed his wife. But tonight in the sunset of his life, he gave his gold to a colored child. There was no way to discern the old man's motive.

The excitement in Frank's eyes had confirmed that he would be at the spring moving rocks by daybreak. Nick hoped there was gold and Frank would find it for the child's sake.

Claude opened his eyes and cut them toward Nick. "Helpin' that colored baby leave is the only good thing I've ever done in my whole life."

"Why did you do it, Claude?"

The clock chimed before he spoke. "The things you think and do seem right at the time, but don't make no sense later in life."

Letting Jenny get away came to mind. It wasn't too late for Nick to correct that, but Claude was nearing the end of his journey. Birds had about stopped singing for Claude.

40

The doctor thumbed back through a wall calendar as Nick watched. "Oh, here it is," A long, skinny finger tapped the date. "That's when I took Meglena to see the hearing specialist." Sliding wire-rimmed glasses down on the end of his thin nose, he peered over them as he spoke. "You're correct, Mr. Kincaid. From the date of Meglena's trip to Saint Louis until Ella found the baby allowed for a full-term birth." Anguish furrowed the doctor's brow. He raked unruly gray hair away from his face and shook his head. "In thinking back, it's likely the poor child was raped while there. I feel responsible, though she was under the care of her strange acting grandmother."

"What makes you think she was raped?" Nick asked.

"One afternoon the old woman left the child alone in the hotel and went to a church down the street. She was gone for hours from all accounts. Praying for the girl's hearing to be restored, so she said. The hotel housekeeper found Meglena crying and curled up in a knot. A good bit of blood was found on the bed. The old woman said the girl was getting her first period." The doctor stared at Nick for an instant, bowed his head, and muttered, "Regrettable tragedy."

Neither man spoke for a long moment. Nick rose and thanked the doctor and left. Sadness slowed his steps as he headed up the hill to John Frank's office. An unknown person had raped Meglena. If Eddie's death was about whisky running as Vale suggested, who had a motive? The mystery man had to be Cleve. Nick decided to offer such a possibility to John Frank before he left to bring Jenny back.

The sheriff's office was locked with a note on the door that stated he would not return until late afternoon. Nick planned to be in Cleveland by then. Cleve must be the one trying to take over the whiskey operation but Nick had decided not to delay his trip. He could alert the sheriff about Cleve as soon as he returned.

Nick took a deep breath and exhaled. He would put Eddie's killing and whiskey making aside for a few days. His time and thoughts would belong to Jenny.

It was a beautiful day. Clouds had moved out after the rain and left the bluest of skies. Hints of spring appeared everywhere as opening buds tinted the hillsides green. The changing season would make a perfect homecoming for Jenny.

Nick dozed while the train moved north. He awoke to find that winter had left its bite on the northern Indiana and Ohio landscapes. But the thought of being with Jenny made the world right, regardless of the season or the weather. He closed his eyes and images of her floated through his head.

"Well, Mr. Kincaid. What a surprise to see you."

The voice confirmed the speaker's identity. Nick opened his eyes and looked up into Cleve Underwood's face. His jowls hung heavy against the folded layers of his neck. Nick's drowsiness evaporated in a flash. He sat up, glad to see the coach filled with people. His heart pounded, but he forced a smile and attempted to appear relaxed. "How are you, sir?"

"Fine, thank you." Cleve pointed at the seat next to Nick. "May I?" He lowered his large bulk into it without waiting for permission. "I was stretching my legs a bit when I saw you sitting here."

"I didn't see you come aboard."

"I boarded in Paducah. I took a seat back in the last coach, away from that disgusting coal smell. Where are you headed?"

"Cleveland." As an afterthought, Nick added, "And you?"

"Same place. It's my home, but I'm in the process of moving to Chicago."

Cleve's answer sent adrenaline pumping even more. Nick hoped his expression gave no hint that he knew the man beside him was a killer. Chicago would be the perfect location to control the whiskey running business. "Why Chicago?" Nick asked. "Isn't your company headquartered in Toledo?"

"It is, but I'm changing positions. Taking on a new project."

"A new line of work?" Nick asked, thinking Cleve would elaborate. He only nodded. What a setup. The man would have inside knowledge of government operations against whiskey running.

"We finally know why the colored boy was hanged, thank goodness," Cleve said.

Nick made no comment. He was being led into deep water with that subject and he wasn't about to acknowledge knowing anything.

Cleve added, "And then there's Vale, an expert in evading the law. His success speaks for itself."

"I guess so," Nick answered.

"Rumor is that he has a small fortune hidden away in a California bank." Cleve chuckled enough to make his belly shake. "Let's assume Vale was big in whiskey running. That'd be his only reason to kill that young man since his sister didn't give birth."

"Unless he killed Eddie before he learned that," Nick said. He didn't want to eliminate Vale as a suspect and make Cleve suspicious.

"A perfectly acceptable assumption based upon Vale's threats and the climate of the community," Cleve added. "But it's only an assumption."

"You once suggested someone killed Eddie because of whiskey running. What made you change your mind?"

Cleve's brow wrinkled as a look of surprise spread across his face. "I haven't."

Perspiration came alive across Nick's back. Cleve was not John Frank's source. While Nick tried to decipher where the truth lay, what he heard next made his brain go dead for a moment. He asked Cleve to repeat himself.

"I said Vale made me a surprise visit last night."

"What did he want?" Nick asked. His mind was unable to compute what he was hearing.

"I guess he wanted me to feel the end of a gun barrel against my temple to start, but later we had a nice talk, put two and two together, so to speak. We became convinced that Vale had no reason to kill Eddie. In fact, we came to an understanding that Vale would leave the county and I would refuse to believe he was in the whiskey business."

"But then who?" Nick's voice trailed off. The annoying hot perspiration suddenly turned cold. John Frank.

Cleve twisted his short neck around and looked directly at Nick, who imagined himself chalk white.

"I thought you had this figured out, Kincaid."

Nick muttered, "I thought so too, but no, I never suspected John Frank."

"It's simple. He wanted more power and money. His personality type suggests that power was more important to him than money."

Doubts tugged at the confusion Nick felt. Cleve might be lying. "How do I know you're telling the truth about meeting with Vale?" Nick asked.

"My young friend, you don't. I mentioned this only because I thought you had concluded it was John Frank. He'll be arrested in a couple of days. Should his arrest be delayed, for your own safety you should know that John Frank has a Chicago partner, a revenue man that once worked the area and got to know the sheriff. He's talking like a parrot. The investigation is ongoing. If you get back from Cleveland before he's arrested, keep a low profile and don't talk to anyone other than Vale."

It all fit together except for one thing. Who shot John Frank? Nick proposed the question and watched for any little telltale sign in Cleve's expression as he answered.

Cleve jerked a large handkerchief from inside his coat pocket in time to catch a sneeze. "The smell of coal makes my asthma kick in." He wiped his mouth and replaced the handkerchief. "I talked with the doctor in Paducah who took care of the sheriff. It was a minor wound. We've concluded it was self-inflicted, substantiated by the fact that John Frank insisted on being hospitalized, clearly unnecessary according to the doctor. It eliminated him as a suspect to have people believe he'd been shot. Who would believe he was involved after being shot?"

Cleve failed to smother the next sneeze, and it echoed throughout the coach. "I got to get out of this smell." He rose. "Kincaid, reject everything I've told you if you must, but not the part about keeping a low profile. Go talk to Vale, but stay clear of the sheriff. Things are lining up for an arrest. Hopefully, before you return."

41

The woman crouched beside the hedgerow that lined the front porch of the small white clapboard house. Her long arm withdrew a fistful of leaves from the shrub and stuffed them into a paper bag. The yard's neatness reflected the need for order, a trait that applied to Jenny's description of her mother. Nick pulled an envelope from his pocket. The address matched the house. His heart beat faster at the thought of seeing Jenny.

Jenny looked nothing like her mother. Dorothy was tall and willowy. She mumbled while reaching to capture a stray leaf and failed to hear Nick call to her. He called again, louder.

She rose and faced him. Her gaze moved down to his feet. "You're on my property."

Nick's shoe extended off the street onto the grass a few inches. He pulled it back, wondering what happened in her life to make her tightly drawn lips forget how to smile.

Hoping to avoid confrontation, Nick kept his voice level. "I'm here to see Jenny."

A flicker of surprise raced across her face and disappeared behind a scowl. She drew herself up to her full height and spoke with venom. "I know you, you sorry bastard. Leave now."

"I'm here to see Jenny," he repeated.

"She doesn't want to see you," Dorothy shouted.

"Let Jenny decide that."

"She's not here."

"Then I'll wait."

She advanced with clenched fists and screamed, "I should kill you, you sorry son-of-a-bitch."

Nick held his ground. He thought she might attack him, but she stopped a few feet away. Her body shuddered. "Leave. You got what you wanted."

"It wasn't like that."

"Go home. She's getting married now."

The words silenced him. Before he could find his voice, she turned and ran up the steps.

"Just a minute," Nick shouted.

In the doorway, she whirled and screamed, "I'm calling the law." The door closed with a bang.

He dropped down on the steps to wait. Her saying that Jenny was getting married spun around in his head. Jenny was in love with him. Dorothy had lied or Jenny was marrying to give the baby a name. Her sweetness would allow that. The baby was his and would have his name and so would Jenny.

The older model Ford rolled up in front of the house and stopped. Printing on the door indicated official business. A policeman crawled out and adjusted the nightstick attached to a belt hidden under a balloon belly. "Hey, young fella, are you trespassing?"

WHEN THE BIRDS STOP SINGING

"Yes, sir," Nick answered as he rose.

"Well, at least you're honest." He smiled. "You got a name, fella?"

"Nick Kincaid."

McCloud was printed across the scarred surface of his badge. "You got business here?"

"I came up from Kentucky to marry my girl and her mother objects. "

"Oh, it's about love. Why did the mother take a disliking to you?"

"She had good reason, but I'm here now. She says Jenny's not here."

"Don't you think that could be true? If the girl was here and really loved you, she'd be out here with you."

"Yeah, that makes sense."

"Let's find you a place to stay. What does her father have to say?"

"I've never met him. He doesn't live here."

"Well then, you've got to ask the old man for his daughter. Do you know where he stays?"

"I only know a last name and that he works for the city."

"So do I. Let's go down to the station. If he works for the city, we'll find him."

Night had closed in when Nick left the hotel to meet with Jenny's dad at a small café a few blocks away. He felt nervous after having failed completely with the mother. He needed to win over the father for Jenny's sake.

The café was a ten-minute walk. Nick paced himself to be on time. It stood on a corner and looked to be the kind that survived on lunch business. Daily specials were hand-painted on the window.

A couple at the counter looked up as Nick entered, and then resumed chatting with the waitress. The only other person in the room sat at a table in the far corner. Light danced off his balding head as he leaned back with arms folded. His eyes were the color of Jenny's, except lacking the same warmth.

"I'm Nick." He hoped his voice didn't betray his nervousness.

"So I gathered." The man snapped with the coldness of an icehouse. His name was Pete, according to what the policeman had learned. He nodded toward a chair across the table. Nick settled into it with nerves doing a dance in his stomach.

He glared at Nick. "I've kicked your ass in my head hundreds of times. I'd be doing it for real now, except McCloud convinced me I should at least listen first since you traveled such a distance."

Nick smiled, hoping the man was joking, but it didn't sound like a joke and he never smiled back. The guy sure knew how to tap Nick's sweat glands. He swallowed to find his voice. If it meant getting an ass kicking, he'd take it. He wasn't leaving without Jenny if she'd have him, and that was what her daddy was going to hear. "I've come to take Jenny back home with me if she'll still have me."

"And if I say no?"

"I'll take her anyway, if she'll go."

Pete's eyes bored into Nick's, but he met the man's gaze.

"I can keep her here if I want." He emphasized each word.

"No, sir, you can't, if she wants to go."

The man stared for a moment. His expression revealed nothing. Nick prepared for a punch in the nose, but then came a little softening of the man's eyes. "Look, sir, I love Jenny and want to marry her. You might as well know I'll do anything next to kidnapping her."

"She said you didn't want to marry her."

"At first, I didn't. It's not that I didn't care for her, but the idea of marriage took some getting used to. After she left, I knew I wanted to marry her. I even purchased some land and fixed up a place for us to live. It was to be a surprise, but she never came back. I wrote her every day for weeks. She never answered. I believe her mother might have intercepted the mail."

A relaxing of Pete's shoulders followed. His eyes filled with sadness. "Her mother's sick." He glanced away.

Silence followed.

"Dorothy said Jenny was gonna marry some guy." Nick held his breath and waited for an answer.

"What?" Pete shook his head. "No, Dorothy lied. Jenny can't get over you."

The words were what Nick wanted to hear.

"My friends call me Pete." He smiled for the first time.

"Glad to meet you, Pete." Nick felt all the tension of the moment dissolve and stuck his hand across the table.

Pete took it with a firm grip. "You'd better take good care of her or I'll still kick your ass." A smile followed the threat. "I won't lobby for you. You'll have to make your own case with Jenny. She's staying with us now. Here's my address." He pushed a business card across the table. "She'll be home in the morning. I leave for work before seven. My wife, Cathy, will be gone by eight. Jenny will be there all alone.

"Thank you, sir."

"If she goes with you, I'll be making a trip down to Kentucky more often than you will want."

"No, sir, you'll always be welcome anytime."

Patchy sleep came between dreams in which Nick searched for Jenny. He saw daybreak and left the hotel early, positioning himself down the street among a grove of trees to wait for Pete and his wife to leave. Jenny came out and retrieved the morning paper. He wanted to shout at her, but waited.

Half an hour passed before both Pete and his wife were gone. He hurried to the house and knocked.

"What did you forget?" Jenny asked as the door opened. She turned pale and stepped back, clutching the folds of her housecoat over her stomach.

"Hi," Nick said.

Panic swept across her face for an instant. She glanced behind her as if cornered and needed to escape. "I thought you were my dad."

"Are you okay?" he asked.

"Of course, why wouldn't I be?" A nervous chuckle smothered a flicker of warmth and excitement in her eyes. Nick could tell she was glad to see him, but how to get past the awkward role-playing? She fidgeted with her robe again and tried to coax an unruly sprig of hair into place. "Why are you here?"

"To see you."

She looked away and then moved into the kitchen. "I have fresh coffee."

Nick followed and stood in the doorway. With her back toward him, she began taking cups from the cabinet.

"Jenny, I've come to take you back with me."

She froze for a moment, and then faced him, careful not to catch his eye. The corner of her mouth quivered. "Why would you want to do that?"

"Because I love you and I want to marry you."

Her body stiffened and her eyes filled with anger. She started to speak, but caught herself. Her body relaxed and she laughed, one that Nick pegged as fake. "We had fun, a summer romance," she said, careful to avoid his eyes by turning away and taking more unneeded cups from the cabinet.

"You're a lousy actress, but you'll make a great wife and mother."

Her hand quickly muffled an audible gasp. She faced him. "Mattie told you?"

"No, no, she didn't tell me."

"You're lying." Anger spilled forth as tears flooded her cheeks. "I don't want to marry you, so you can just go back and leave me alone."

"You don't mean that."

"Yes, I mean it. And you don't want to marry me either."

"I do, more than anything in the world."

"Stop being so damn noble," she shouted as she charged and slapped him hard across the face. He never flinched. "Oh, my God," she gasped and backed away. "I'm sorry, I didn't mean to do that," she cried.

He pulled her to him and held her close.

After a moment, she pulled away and wiped her eyes with a dishtowel. "I'm sorry, Nick, but I can't marry you."

"I'm willing to get down on my knees and beg."

She gave a faint smile. "A good try, but no, thanks. I'll make it just fine. My dad and Cathy will help."

"That night at the pie supper, do you remember me telling you we would be good together? Deep down I knew it even then. We're meant to be together. I know it and so do you."

"Stop it, Nick. If you'd wanted to marry me, I would have heard from you before now."

"I've purchased the cabin and have my grandmother's ring to give you. I even waited at the train with the ring."

Her face paled. "I don't believe you," she said in words barely audible. "Why didn't you write?"

"I wrote you every day for weeks and begged you to marry me. When you didn't answer, I broke into Mattie's house and read your letters to her. That's how I found out about the baby."

"Your letters must have gone to my mother," she muttered.

"I'm sure. That was the address I had."

"You're not upset about the baby?"

"No, I love the baby. I love you. I want to marry you today, tomorrow, whenever you say. Then I want to take you home. I want us to gaze down at the old Cumberland and watch the sun disappear behind the hill. I love you, Jenny. I can never be happy without you. Please marry me."

She moved into his arms, crying softly.

42

Buddy reared up on the side of the bed and woke Nick before the knock came. He removed his arm from under Jenny's head and eased out of the narrow bed. After slipping into pants, he groped his way into the front room and ran his hand along the shelf above the desk until locating the handgun. Jenny insisted he take it every time he left the room while John Frank was still free. "Who's there?" he called.

"It's me, Vale."

He stuck the gun in the back of his pants and squeezed out the door, leaving Buddy behind. Vale stood leaning against the landing rail with arms crossed. His beard and long hair were gone. Except for being thinner, he looked as he did the day Nick met him on the train.

"This had better be important to wake me at this hour."

"I was told you got married in Ohio. If everythin' is workin' right, a new bridegroom should be in a better mood." He chuckled.

"You just woke me from a sound sleep. It's not my best time."

Seconds ticked by. Vale coughed. "It's hard to figure why I'm sayin' this to you. I shouldn't of poked at you and started a fight over Eddie that time. Just felt like sayin' I shouldn't of done it, and bein' drunk don't excuse it."

The man had struggled through an apology, though he would never consider it one. He might be able to salvage something of himself after all. "Thanks," Nick said. "I haven't always been at my best with you either. Are you going to California like you mentioned at the schoolhouse?"

"Yep. Gonna buy me a hillside, stick a few grapevines in the ground, and who knows, I might find me a lady to keep me company."

"Hope you can. I wish you the best," Nick said.

"I come to tell you, I made a deal with Underwood. I'm goin' by way of Chicago to tell the Feds about the Chicago part of my operation. Doin' it to stay out of jail. The Feds get nothin' from me about what goes on here 'tween the rivers. I'm dependin' on you to get the word out to them that's makin' corn liquor. They ain't got to worry about me spillin' my guts. They'll believe you."

They'll believe you were words sweet to Nick's ears. "Sticking to the code, huh?"

"Yeah. There's honor in it."

Nick nodded, though he thought it could be debated. Even a bad law like Prohibition was still the law until people voted to change it. That was why the Republic worked and pure democracy never would.

"I guess you heard that Frank and Ella took that baby and moved to Gary, Indiana," Vale said. "He's workin' in a steel mill there."

"Yeah, Boyd told me last night." Nick paused for a moment. "May I ask you a question?"

"Shoot."

"There are few coloreds in California, but there are lots of Mexicans. Will you feel about them the way you feel about coloreds?"

"Don't know. Depends on how they treat me."

"Then I take it coloreds have mistreated you sometime in your life."

"Not really. My old man didn't like 'em and neither did his."

"And you want to be like Claude?"

"Hell, no, that's the last thing I want. I just never thought about them people in that light. I didn't come here to talk about likin' niggers, but I get your point and I'll think on it."

"It was an act of kindness for Ella and Frank to leave for the sake of the baby," Nick said.

"Maybe so. I just can't figure where they got the money, 'cause nobody's got money to buy them out."

Nick smiled. What would Vale think if he knew Claude gave the gold coins to a colored baby?

"You know John Frank killed Eddie," Vale said.

Nick nodded. "Yeah, Cleve told me."

"Here's somethin' you may not of heard. Earlier tonight the sheriff arrested Henry Walker for the killin'."

"What? I knew Henry was a low life, but I never thought he had the balls to kill."

"Henry didn't. Everythin' that happened was because of whisky runnin' and not about niggers and whites. John Frank used the baby thing, hopin' to get rid of me."

"The sheriff had Chicago connections," Nick said.

"Yeah, an agent by the name of Arnold Ashcraft was a partner. The two planned to boot me out and take over."

"How did Eddie fit into their scheme?"

"He didn't. Eddie wasn't workin' with 'em. Underwood was sent down here from Washington, DC. They knowed somebody in the Chicago office was leakin' information. Eddie no longer worked for me, but he knew my operation. Underwood hired Eddie and give him cash to be seen in clubs, follow people around, and buy information. Him and Cleve usually met in Paducah. That's why Eddie had all them ticket stubs."

It was good to know Eddie wasn't involved in something illegal for Ducky and Mae's sakes. "Did they kill him because they knew he worked for Cleve?"

"No. His killin' was bad timin' accordin' to Ashcraft. He said Eddie got to the depot before daylight. Fog was all over, rollin' in and out every few minutes. Cleve thinks Eddie hid in the shadows because of all the talk about Ella and him, or just stayed back like a nigger who knows his place. Ashcraft was meetin' with John Frank. They stood on the boardin' platform in the fog talkin' about gettin' you to shoot me."

"So that's what John Frank was doing. He advised me not to be timid about shooting you, while he wanted you to shoot me. It didn't matter which happened. If you shot me you'd go to prison. If I shot you, you'd be out of the way. Either way, he'd have control of whiskey running."

"You got it. Did you think about killin' my ass?" Vale asked.

"No, just protecting my own."

Vale chuckled. "Anyway, the fog lifted or somethin'. They spotted Eddie standin' in the shadows, not ten feet away. He tried to run. They caught him, dragged him inside, and beat him. John Frank gagged him and took him away in cuffs."

"They didn't have to hang him," Nick said.

"They did that to blame me and some of my friends. Ashcraft will testify to it. I 'spect Henry will also when the Feds talk to him. That's the only reason John Frank ain't been arrested by the Feds. They need two witnesses to have a solid case against him."

"When will they talk to Henry?"

"Don't know now that he's been arrested. It may delay John Frank's arrest a few days."

"How did this Arnold Ashcraft know the sheriff?"

"The greedy son-of-a-bitch worked these parts before Cleve, and I was payin' him wads of money to stay off my ass."

"What was the extent of Henry's involvement?"

"He knew John Frank took Eddie away in cuffs. He saw the boy get roughed up and thought it was all because Ella had a nigger baby with Eddie."

"But I still don't understand why John Frank arrested Henry Walker."

"'Cause John Frank is runnin' scared. He don't know the Feds have Ashcraft locked up. He tried to contact Ashcraft, but couldn't. He's gotta be worried that somethin' is wrong. So Henry is the fall guy. John Frank's spreadin' the word he has a witness who saw Eddie's suitcase at the depot. The case and blood stains on the floor will go against Henry."

"I saw the case myself."

"Yeah. You're the witness."

"What?"

"He says you reported the suitcase, but when he investigated it was gone."

"That's true. You mean they can't arrest John Frank?"

"It's Henry's word against the sheriff's. You'd testify the truth about seein' the case at the depot, wouldn't you?"

"Of course, I'd have to."

"Your testimony would make Henry look guilty. They need both Ashcraft and Henry to testify they saw the sheriff take Eddie away. That would lock up a murder case against him. John Frank ain't broke the law unless we can prove murder."

"So what am I supposed to do?" Nick asked.

"Nothin'. Just let the lid stay on things. The Feds are gonna come swarmin' in like bees in a clover field any day now and this county will have to elect a new sheriff."

The sound of crunching gravel sent both men scrambling into the thin shadow in the doorway. "What was that?" Nick whispered.

"Somebody's climbin' the bank by the garden."

"Is someone there?" Nick called.

"It's me," Ducky answered. "Been checkin' my trout lines."

"Where's his lantern?" Nick whispered.

"Maybe he can see in the dark."

The clouds opened again and washed the hillside with light. Ducky trudged up the hill toward the cabin.

"He's carryin' no gear and didn't have no luck catchin' anythin'," Vale said.

"Do you think he heard us talking?" Nick asked.

Vale shrugged. "Who knows? He's up in age, so his hearin' is not the best, I'd say."

43

Light snoring came from Mae as Ducky lay beside her and listened to the clock ticking. He hadn't slept much. His mind wanted to dwell on his daddy and Eddie. They were in every dream that awoke him during the night. His daddy had been the same kind of man he'd tried to be as an example for Eddie. He was glad that his son wasn't mixed up in the devil's work up in Chicago.

Thank the Good Lord for letting him keep his good hearing and dimming his eyes a little instead. The Lord sent Ducky past the mill at the right time to hear Mr. Nick and Mr. Vale naming the man who killed his boy.

Now that the money Mr. Nick brought down from Chicago wasn't blood money, he felt better about letting Mae spend some of it. It'd been stuffed between two logs over the door ever since the morning Mr. Nick brought it to them. Mae should buy herself a ready-made dress from the catalog. Miss Loretta would help her order it. She never in her whole life had a store-bought dress.

He heard the clock chime. It was time to go. This was the third morning he'd gone to the river to kill what needed to be killed. He had a taste for fresh meat. Maybe he'd get a rabbit or even a deer. Yep, stewed rabbit and dumplings would fill his belly tonight. Rabbit would be good this time of year before ticks and fever got to them. He'd have rabbit for sure or maybe even deer steak if luck was his partner this morning.

Ducky eased both feet onto the floor and then slipped into shirt and overalls. He picked up the rifle beside the door and started to leave. Mae's snoring stopped. "Old man, what you gettin' up fer? You been up and down all night. Has yo' kidneys done wore out?"

"Lookin' fer a rabbit fer some stew. Gonna find me one this mornin' fer sure."

"Dats what you be sayin' three days. It be dark. You ain't gonna see no rabbit 'fore daylight."

"Gonna start early so as I can see da tracks 'fore da dew dries dem off."

"Well, don't shoot yo'self."

Ducky chuckled. He'd never gone hunting without Mae telling him not to shoot himself.

He started up the hill toward Eddie's grave. He needed to talk to the boy a little this morning. Tell him he was sorry about doubting him and thinking he was mixed up in no good.

He walked with the rifle pointed toward the heavens. His daddy had said, "You hold it pointed down, boy, to keep from accidentally shootin' somebody. Killin' a man is the worst sin in the world." This would be the first time he ever went against his daddy.

When he was younger, he'd wondered why his daddy never wanted to kill a man, him being a slave and working over in the Birmingham foundries, a place hot like the devil's house. As years passed, he learned that the hot blood in a man cools down to reason.

Dawn began to chase shadows away as Ducky knelt beside the grave. Egg-shaped rocks covered the mound, each lined up as perfectly as the bricks in a wall. Fresh flowers in a mason jar indicated that Mae was up here yesterday.

Ducky sat on his knees, rocking back and forth, talking to Eddie and praying for extra strength today.

The sun silhouetted the treetops on the highest hills when he rose and said goodbye to his son. A blanket of fog covered the river bottom. It'd be an hour or more before the sun burned it away. Maybe a breeze near the river would move the fog about enough so he could make his kill. He'd been trying three days and couldn't get a clear shot. He needed to be home before noon to pick up furniture in Eddyville for Mr. Nick. A new bed and dresser were being sent up from Paducah by train.

Ducky climbed up on a flat rock at a bend in the river. His knee joints hurt from the long walk and he needed to rest for a spell. He and Eddie used to fish from the rock. Up by the sandbar was where he'd taught Eddie how to swim. The boy had been seven or eight.

A slight noise drew his attention. Three deer appeared briefly, but the fog swallowed them up. He'd be patient.

Birds in the trees along the river announced the day with a chorus of sounds. Ducky sat as still as death. He heard the sound of oars cutting through the water. The fog opened and his target came into view. His heart pounded. He raised the long rifle and held his breath. The shot echoed up and down the river. "Thank you, Lord," he muttered. "You has lifted my burden."

44

With a mug in each hand, Fanny hurried across the dining room toward Nick and Jenny. Her smile grew as she approached the table and placed the coffee in front of them.

"Nobody is hardly stirring this mornin' 'cause the fog's so thick. But somebody is huntin' up river 'cause I heard a shot. Didn't you two come in on the mornin' train?"

"Yes, we've been in Paducah furniture shopping. Spent the night," Jenny said. "A bed and dresser are being sent up on the freight train later this morning."

"Then you ain't heard about Henry Walker?"

"We heard about his arrest before we left yesterday," Nick said.

"No, not that. He hung himself last night."

Jenny gasped. Nick tried to appear calm as he weighed the effect it might have on John Frank's impending arrest. Their safety was the question in his mind.

"Why would Henry kill himself?" Nick asked.

"Don't really know. John Frank found him hangin' in the cell. Seems he used his belt."

"When did it happen?" Nick asked. Dozens of questions jammed his head. Should he get Jenny away to a safe place until all this played out, or just act natural and run a bluff?

"Nobody knows exactly," Fanny said. "John Frank found him when he took breakfast." She frowned. "Now that's odd."

"What?" Nick asked.

"It just dawned on me. The county pays me to furnish breakfast for them in jail. John Frank didn't order no breakfast for Henry last night."

Jenny gripped Nick's hand tighter. He returned an understanding glance. John Frank must have been feeling desperate to kill Henry. "Where's the sheriff this morning?"

"Said he was goin' fishin'."

"In this fog?" Jenny asked.

"That's what he said. He looked like he ought to be sleepin' instead of fishin'. Had bags under the eyes and acted nervous, like something was botherin' him."

The door opening startled everyone. Fanny laughed. "Lordy me, look who walked in the door."

Vale smiled and came toward them. Once again he had the persona of a riverboat gambler. Fanny crossed to meet him. "You finally come out of hidin'? Good thing the sheriff is up the river fishin'."

"You notice I only show myself when it's foggy." He wrapped his arms around Fanny. "I come to get a hug before I leave."

"Where you goin'?" she asked as he released her.

"California."

"My Lord, what's out there?"

"Sunshine and oranges, so I'm told. Thought I'd have some of your ham and eggs 'fore the train gets here."

"I'd better get to fixin' 'em, then. Train will be here 'fore long." She hurried toward the kitchen.

Nick watched Fanny disappear and then turned to Vale. "There's still one thing I don't understand. How did Brady fit in?"

"He was greedy for more money and left me. Him shootin' you was his own idea as far as I know." He glanced at his watch. "Better get in the kitchen and eat 'fore that train leaves me." He looked from Nick to Jenny and smiled. "You two have a good life and a lot of babies. That's somethin' folks do real good 'tween the rivers. That and makin' whisky." He laughed and headed into the kitchen.

Jenny leaned toward Nick and whispered, "Vale didn't mention anything about Henry. Why didn't you tell him?"

"Maybe he hasn't heard if he crossed the river this morning. Besides, why involve him when he's leaving to start a new life?"

"I'm scared," she whispered. "What if John Frank comes after you?"

"He won't. John Frank has no reason to think I know anything." Nick hoped he'd sounded more convincing than he felt.

"Let's go to the cabin when we get back until after he's arrested," Jenny said.

Nick checked his watch. "The train should be here within the hour with the furniture. We'll go as soon as we sign for it. Until then, we'll go about our business. While you shop, I'll sneak up and talk to the doc."

"Why him?"

"He'd be the one to examine Henry's body and sign off on the cause of death."

Jenny went into the general store with a list of things for the cabin, and Nick continued up the street past the jail toward the doctor's office. He found the doctor hunched over a desk covered in papers. Peering over his glasses, he smiled and motioned Nick inside. "The word around town is that you're no longer a free man."

Nick grinned. "Yes, sir, that's correct."

The doctor added, "It's good to be young and in love. Can't stay young forever, but you can stay in love. What can I do for you?"

"Did you examine Henry's body?"

He leaned back in the chair and frowned. "Yeah," he said slowly.

"Were there any unusual markings or anything?"

The doctor crossed his arms. "What are you after?"

Nick paused. "I understand that Henry hanged himself. Is there anything that might cause you to think he would have needed help?"

The doctor nodded. "It's funny you asked that. I questioned some bruises and markings on his wrists. John Frank said they were made by handcuffs at the time of his arrest."

"Does that seem plausible?"

He stroked his chin thoughtfully. "Not really. Not with the depth of the lacerations."

"Meaning?"

"They were severe enough to be made by a man in a life and death struggle. May I ask you what's going on?"

"I wish I could tell you, but I really can't say yet. It'll be clarified soon. And please keep this conversation confidential. I suggest you write up a report about Henry. It will be needed in a few days."

"I've done that already."

Nick thanked the doctor and left, convinced that John Frank had caused not only Eddie's death, but Henry's also.

He met Jenny in front of the general store. She had purchased cooking utensils and bolts of fabric for window curtains and bed covers. Her excitement ignited enthusiastic chatter about color and kinds of spreads and curtains. Nick was smart enough to smile and nod approval on faith. He had no idea what she was talking about. At least her mind was diverted from John Frank for the moment.

They'd left the car on the far side of the river. The boat horn announced the ferry open, though the fog allowed minimal visibility. Nick and Jenny were the only passengers. As the ferry reached mid-stream a small fishing boat appeared but was quickly swallowed up by the fog. Nick squinted. "There's no one in that boat."

Jenny shaded her eyes with both hands. "It didn't look like it."

Nick hollered up to the Captain who stood at the wheel. "What's with the fishing boat?"

"Can't see to tell. Fog's too thick," he replied.

The river was lazy due to lack of rain and the fishing boat seemed to stand still. The three strained to see, each time catching a hazy glimpse before a curtain of fog thickened.

"There's nobody in it," said the Captain. "It's strange a boat would get loose in such calm water. We'll pull it in. Somebody will come looking for it." The Captain tied off the boat's wheel, shifted the throttle back, and climbed down to the lower deck.

The fishing boat inched forward and faded from fuzzy to nothing, like a mirage. It bumped the side of the ferry and a wave of fog moved out. "Oh, my God," Jenny cried.

John Frank lay sprawled on his back with a bullet hole in his forehead.

45

Claude dozed in the porch chair while Nick sipped a second glass of iced tea. The sound of Mattie's horse and buggy moving at a fast trot drew Nick's attention. After tying the horse beside the store, she hurried up the steps, gulping for air. "Been rushin' too much." She patted her chest. "Hard to breathe." From her cleavage, she unfurled a pink handkerchief and began wiping her neck and face. "Where's Loretta and Jenny?"

"They're inside," Nick said. "Are you okay?"

"I'm fine, just spring ragweed stoppin' me up." She tugged on each side of the loose fitting pink floral dress. "Do have a little problem. Excuse me for adjustin' myself. Stretchin' and decoratin' the church got my underclothes all twisted."

Nick felt a blush and glanced away.

"There, that's better." She gave the dress a final tug. "How you, Mr. Claude?" she shouted.

He didn't respond. She turned to Nick. "He doin' okay?"

321

"He's not feeling well today," Nick said. Claude had eaten little lunch and had acted confused. Nick was keeping an eye on him while the women attended the shower.

"He looks poorly." Mattie shook her head and pursed her lip. "He ain't been baptized." She snapped her fingers. "One of these days he gonna go like that, and then you know where he'll be?"

"What time is the shower?" Nick asked. The question might remind her that Jenny and Loretta were ready and waiting inside.

"Gonna be soon," she said. "What time are you goin'?"

He chuckled. "It's for ladies, right?"

"Here 'tween the rivers the groom and daddy-to-be is expected to drop by. You gonna have to make two speeches to all the women, one for thankin' everybody for weddin' gifts and the other for baby things." She giggled.

Nick smiled, thankful that she was teasing.

"It'll surprise me if Loretta is ready." Mattie rolled her eyes. "Knowin' her, she's still fussin' with her hair." She lowered her voice. "Just 'tween you and me, it's always stringy lookin'. I wanna get Jenny over to the church 'fore the crowd gets there." She started toward the door and turned. "Why didn't you go to John Frank's funeral?"

"Funerals are to honor the dead. I couldn't honor that man."

"I love funerals. Did I tell you about goin'?"

"No, ma'am."

"John Frank didn't look that good, but then I don't expect he would, bein' such a crook. Weren't even a hint of a smile on his face. Sam did real good coverin' the hole in his head. He said he used putty. Did you know they use putty, Mr. Kincaid?"

"No, ma'am."

"But we'll never know who shot him."

Not as long as the code of silence exists, Nick thought.

The screen door opened and Loretta hurried out followed by Jenny. "You're late, Mattie."

"I'm not late."

"Course you are."

"I'm waitin' on you, Loretta."

"Nobody ever waits on me 'cause I'm never late." She started toward the steps and abruptly turned, colliding with Mattie. Loretta's disapproving frown spoke for her. "Mr. Kincaid, Ducky is out back turnin' the freezer. He's hummin' and actin' happy. He ain't been that way since Eddie died. I think he's been drinkin' and the cream ain't even hard yet. Would you bring it over to the church when you come to thank everybody for the gifts? Use Boyd's truck. The key is in it."

Mattie wasn't teasing. Nick was expected to make an appearance at the shower. He nodded that he would.

Loretta turned and nearly collided with Mattie again. She snorted, "Mattie, for God's sake, get out of the way. We're goin' in Jenny's car. I ain't ridin' in no buggy."

Mattie started to respond, but before she could speak Loretta brushed past and hurried down the steps. "Help me, Jesus," Mattie muttered as she followed. Nick winked at Jenny, who puckered her lips and formed a kiss.

The three women climbed into the car. Mattie had difficulty squeezing into the back seat and voiced her complaints about being rushed, while Loretta insisted she must ride up front to avoid motion sickness, though the ride would take no more than three minutes.

Claude jerked awake when the engine caught. He appeared frightened and thrashed the air with both hands.

Nick rose and took a step toward him. "Are you okay, Claude?"

"Where am I?" He looked at Nick. "The Bird was chasin' me." He squinted at Nick and a faint smile followed. "Oh, I thought you'd gone for good. Been a year or more since I've seen you."

"I've been back from my trip for a few days. You just forgot. "

"Did I forget?" He frowned. "I can't keep things in my head. The bird is about to drive me crazy." He cupped both ears to listen. "The squawkin' is killin' me. Hear 'em?"

Nick heard nothing. He humored the old man and pretended to listen, and then nodded that he'd heard. Claude smiled and settled back in the chair. His hand trembled as he smoothed fuzzy hair into place. "I'm glad you heard 'em too. My mama used to say, when the birds stop singin'. . ." His voice trailed off. "I heard birds singin' real pretty once when my mama come back from bein' dead and hugged me at the spring. She put her arms around me and they was soft as feathers. I want to go back to the spring." Excitement filled his eyes. "Maybe she's waitin' there for me. Can you take me there now?"

"She's not there today, but I'll take you back real soon."

Ducky came around the corner of the building. "Da cream be hard, Mr. Nick. I's packed ice around it and put it in da truck."

"Thanks, Ducky. You doing alright today?"

"I's happy as the Good Lord allows." He smiled.

Nick hadn't seen Ducky in such good spirits since Eddie died. The sadness that had claimed him seemed to be gone. Maybe he was finally moving on. A thought flashed through Nick's head. When Ducky heard that John Frank had been shot, he didn't seem surprised. "An eye for an eye," he'd muttered. The thought hit like a punch in the belly. Ducky may have told him something with that quote.

Nick left Claude napping and took the ice cream to the church. After a thank you speech before the ladies, and after using up every blush in his body because of their teasing, he hurried back to the store.

Claude's chair was empty. Nick went to the screen door and called him. He then circled the building and outside grounds, calling for Claude. He even checked the outhouse. An uneasy feeling crept over him.

Nick climbed into the truck to report Claude missing, and then remembered he'd wanted to go to the spring. His first impulse was to alert people at the church, but that would waste time if the old fella had fallen beside the path and couldn't get up. He took off running, hoping Claude had just left minutes before Nick returned. He wished he'd taken the old man to the spring.

Nick ignored the stepping-stones and splashed through the knee-deep water down by the gristmill. Perspiration soon soaked his shirt. Without slowing, he pulled his shirttail out, ripped open the buttons, and kept running.

He was starved for oxygen by the time he reached the spring. He clutched his chest, gasping, as his eyes searched the area. Where was Claude?

Birds chirping pulled his gaze to a tree standing on the far side of the spring. It had been stripped bare of all its foliage, now in a heap at the tree's base. Birds lined the naked branches.

A muffled call for help broke the stillness.

It came from the far side of the pool. Nick jumped into the waist-deep water and pushed his way across. The groan must have come from the pile of leaves beneath the tree. He shouted and watched for any movement. The moan came again. Nick dropped to his knees and pawed leaves aside, digging until finding the old man. He pulled him onto his lap and wiped his face with his shirttail. Claude's bony hands clutched the dried leather pouch that Frank left after taking the gold coins.

"Somebody took my gold," Claude gasped.

"You gave it to Ella for the baby, remember?"

He struggled as if trying to rise. "That's Mama callin' me." His body began to quiver. "Mama, help me," he cried, gulping for each breath. His parched lips formed broken sounds, and then Nick realized Claude was asking to be taken to the water. He lifted the old man and waded out into the pool. He sank to his knees and eased all but Claude's head down into the cool spring.

"Hold me tighter, Mama, I'm afraid," Claude cried.

Nick cradled him closer to his chest. He recognized the raspy death rattle from watching his grandfather die.

Claude opened his eyes. "I give my gold . . . will God give me points?"

"I'm sure he will."

"I hope so, 'cause I've . . . done bad things."

"Did you ever think about asking forgiveness?" Nick asked.

"What if . . . nobody . . . is listenin'?"

"Someone is always listening."

Claude closed his eyes.

"Did you hear me, Claude? He's always listening."

Claude didn't respond and Nick repeated a prayer he remembered as a boy. He didn't stop until he no longer heard Claude's labored breathing. The only sound was water bubbling over rocks.

Fluttering wings reminded him of the birds overhead. Moments later the tree stood empty. He lifted Claude's body from the water and placed it beside the spring.

The birds never sang much for Claude and that was sadder than dying.

46

Shadows crept across the field of ox-eye daisies that covered the hillside. The sinking sun colored the Cumberland a golden yellow. A whippoorwill called to its mate as Nick stood on the cabin porch and stared toward the river.

It seemed a lifetime ago when he'd stepped off the train in Eddyville to search for the romantic paradise that Gramps had described. Instead, he'd been embraced and challenged by both sides of man's nature. The experience had taught him that Gramps was describing what he felt and not what he saw. He experienced Gramps's paradise by looking at a sunset, in hearing a child's laughter, and most of all by feeling Jenny's touch and seeing her smile.

His most challenging resolve had been to sustain his voice against injustice and to come to terms with Brady's death, a moral dilemma that still haunted him, though less often as time passed.

The measure of a man must be about leaving a moral footprint. Brady had died while trying to take a life. Claude had ended his journey unloved by his children and haunted by past sins. His only

329

redeeming quality seemed to have been giving a bag of gold coins to a colored baby, an act that may have been an attempt to bargain with God.

But Nick had kept his *voice*. He imagined Father O'Riley would say, "Good job, Kincaid."

The community's outpouring of gifts at the shower included baby clothes, jars of fruits and vegetables, cooking utensils, a side of bacon, and five hens accompanied by a rooster. Even Jed Harris sent a wagonload of slabs for firewood. The gifts were heartfelt and received with humility. Nick finally belonged.

His heart was full, except for the sadness caused by Claude's death. The old man's life had been an enigma. Nick would remember him because of it. His eighty years had been a fleeting moment in the whole scheme of things. Claude's funeral was held earlier in the afternoon. There had been a small turnout, according to Mattie's standards. Of his children, only Loretta attended. Vale was on his way to northern California. Sadly, he probably wouldn't have given a second thought to the old man's passing even if he could have been reached. Ella had settled in Gary, Indiana. Her letter contained only a postmark, and no one knew if omitting a street address had been an oversight.

Loretta spewed bitterness when the leather pouch was found empty beside the spring. She had developed a list of people suspected of finding the gold. Her sister's name was not on it.

The preacher had read from Ecclesiastes. Nick was so taken by one piece of scripture, he'd pulled out the Bible his mother had slipped into his luggage and reviewed the passage. "To everything there is a season, and a time to every purpose under the heaven. A time to be born, and a time to die; a time to plant, and a time to

330

pluck up that which is planted; a time to kill, and a time to heal; a time to break down and a time to build up."

Nick let his gaze travel as far as his eyes could see. He loved the gentle green hills, the winding river, and the magnificence of the sunset. People between the rivers were like the daisies in the field, all the same, yet each different.

Jenny came out and stood beside him. "Have you ever seen anything more beautiful?"

"Only when I look at you." He slipped his arms around her waist and she laid her head back against his shoulder. "Do you remember the first time I kissed you at the spring?"

"Please don't remember that."

"Why? I can't forget it. I somehow knew we would be good together. We have something special."

She turned her face up toward his and smiled. He gave her a quick peck.

"Listen," she said.

"What?"

"Whippoorwills."

"The fellow's been calling to his mate and now she's answering back." He pressed his cheek against Jenny's.

"Your beard is rough." She giggled.

"That's 'cause I done got tough livin' here 'tween the rivers, but I ain't got no taller," he teased.

She giggled again. "You're the tallest man I know. Oh! Did you feel that?"

"Yeah, what was it?"

"That flutter was a kick."

"The baby?" Nick moved both hands around her abdomen. She began to laugh. "That tickles." She took his hand and placed it. He held his breath.

"I felt it." A surge of happiness welled up inside, a feeling that made him think he would explode. Today he had seen death and felt new life. He looked into Jenny's upturned face. It was their season to hear the birds sing.

About the Author

Dwain L. Herndon grew up in western Kentucky, earning his undergraduate degree at Murray State University and a graduate degree in drama from Southern Illinois University. He taught at colleges and universities before joining the corporate world for several years before he and his wife started their own art business. They live in Grayson, Georgia and have three children, Kim, Myles, and Devin, as well as three grandchildren, Amanda, Maya, and Mason.

Dwain became a writer after retiring. His first novel, *Beyond the Next Hill*, was published in 2013. He writes most every day and finds pleasure in pulling characters from the rural South, hardworking, patriotic, and fun-loving Americans who are the heartbeat of this nation in bad times and good times.

Dwain would love to hear from you. Let him know if you like his stories at herndondwain@yahoo.com.

Made in the USA
Columbia, SC
06 September 2017